A bronze-br... ...y sun, was darting tow... ...east, moving along the beach, outpacing running dogs with ease. Fisherfolk fell back as if in fear as the bright dot passed. In a few moments I was sure that the figure was that of Talus, coming at a run along the coast to overtake us. Perhaps someone had seen us rising on wings from the palace; perhaps the Bull still lived, to give his metallic servant orders, or perhaps the Bronze Man was capable upon his own initiative of taking revenge.

Though it seemed we must be safe from him at the distance we had attained, I did not in the least like the sight of that purposeful onrush, whatever authority had ordained it. "Higher, son. And we had better turn more out to sea."

Scarcely had we altered course in that direction when something, a missile of some kind flying too fast for me to see it, sang past us through the air.

"Faster, Icarus! Out to sea. And higher!"

Glancing back I saw the bronze arm, almost invisible with distance, draw back and then flash in a twinkling movement. A breath later, something, another invisible projectile, came whining straight between our airborne bodies.

"Hurry, Icarus! Twist and turn in flight!"

"Father—I—"

Then it was as if the Sun himself had stabbed us.

FRED SABERHAGEN

THE WHITE BULL

BAEN BOOKS

THE WHITE BULL

Copyright © 1988 by Fred Saberhagen

A portion of this book appeared in substantially different form in *Fantastic*, Copyright © 1976 by Ultimate Publishing Co. Inc.

A Baen Books Original

Baen Publishing Enterprises
260 Fifth Avenue
New York, N.Y. 10001

First printing, December 1988

ISBN: 0-671-69794-3

Cover art by Gary Ruddell

Printed in the United States of America

Distributed by
SIMON & SCHUSTER
1230 Avenue of the Americas
New York, N.Y. 10020

MATRICULATION

I, Daedalus the artisan, having learned late in life the Egyptian way of writing, take up my reed pen (one day perhaps I will design a better writing instrument) and my papyrus to try to recapture something of the truth of my own history. It is high time that the truth about me, and about the strange beings with whom I have dealt, was known.

Scarcely a month passes that I, Daedalus, once the famed maker of wings and currently the manufacturer of terra cotta plumbing, do not encounter some version of the blasphemous rumors about myself: they say that I have somehow become a god, or that in some incomprehensible way I have always been one. Nothing could be farther from the truth. And the truth in itself is quite strange enough. I have been the shipmate and the counselor of kings, and once I was the comrade of heroes and of gods.

3

Let me not begin this testimony, as do so many writers of memoirs, with a tedious recounting of the sweet memories of my childhood and the mistakes of my callow youth; it will be enough to say here that that epoch of my life was fully as human as your own—and I should add that to the best of my knowledge neither of my parents had any trace of deity about them.

Let me also pass over in silence the early years of my manhood and increasing fame, ending with the time I spent in the court of King Aegeus of Athens; if it is true that I built marvels there—and perhaps it is—those marvels were not so great as the rumors of the present time would have them. And they were as nothing to the prodigies that I later beheld, and those I was later able to create—having in those later days the help of the gods, for which there is always a price to pay.

Let me begin my story instead with my arrival upon the island of Crete—then and now a most beautiful and accursed place. Looking back to that day from this, I can see my earlier self almost as a stranger, connected only by the thread of memory to the old man I have become. He was an ignorant stranger in the world, that younger Daedalus, though he counted himself knowledgeable—or perhaps he had already begun to suspect that he was not really wise.

Let us observe him, then, this rather self-satisfied fellow, in the middle—so he thought—of a successful life. Though as he approached the island of Crete he was coping with an episode of turmoil, he was indeed managing to cope, as he thought, rather well.

See him, I say, this tough-looking man, of medium size with already graying hair who stands on the raised stern of the small ship. He is dressed in the fashion of an Athenian gentleman: tunic, trousers, and sandals. Standing close beside him is a young woman, and between them is a child, a small boy of about six. The child is almost invisible, because all three people are wrapped together in a wool blanket, tightly-woven in some highland village of mainland Greece.

The man stands with his left hand holding a taut rope for balance. It is a strong, callused hand, as practical as one of the tools that it so often held—the hand of a workman or a soldier, despite the gentlemanly clothes of its owner. His right arm is holding the upper edge of the blanket around the woman's shoulders, while the boy peers out from between its edges in front.

All three people are peering silently forward between the two ranks of rowers, six or seven men on a side, and past the raised, fish-headed prow of the Phoenician trader in which they ride.

The sun was almost down now, muffled and dim behind fog-banks off to starboard; the captain had pushed his luck, but the gods had favored him this time. Landfall, though partially obscured by autumnal mists, lay close ahead. Torches outlined the still-distant shapes of quays and docks, and the last rays of direct sun played

on the snow-touched mountain peaks not far
inland.

The man's right hand squeezed tightly on the
woman's shoulder, working the blanket a little
more snugly into place. Just beside her the
ship's captain was keeping his own balance by
holding another rope, while he called sharp orders to his rowers.

"So huge a place," the woman murmured,
pushing strands of wet hair away from her eyes
so they could rove unhindered over the mountains, the harbor, and the dusky shoreline. She
was some fifteen years younger than the man
beside her. Her voice, always soft, was almost
lost beneath the captain's bellowing. "You told
me that Crete is an island," she said uncertainly.

"And so it is." The voice of her companion,
that clever fellow, Daedalus, was—and still is—
deep and harsh. "A very big island. So big that
the only way to demonstrate the fact would be
by sailing around it. Shall I ask the captain to do
so for you?" I teased her gently. Despite its
natural harshness my voice was really gentle,
like my strong grip, aimed at protection. At
least I like to think so.

What with the spray on my woman's face, and
the deepening dusk, it was hard for me to tell
whether she was reassured or not. She asked:
"And what are all those lights halfway up the
hillside?" More bright little torch-specks, considerably more distant than those along the waterfront, were irregularly clustered there.

I did my best to sound completely confident.
"That'll be King Minos's palace, I suppose. The
famous House of the Double Axe. I've heard

that it sits not far inland above the port. One of
his palaces, actually; they say he has others
scattered up and down the island."

"I fear to see him."

"Well, you who have served the royal family
of Athens should not fear that." I suppose that
the confidence in my voice took on stern under-
tones. "Minos has told a number of people that
he's anxious to see me, that he would like me to
live here and work for him. And what if he is a
greater king than Aegeus of Athens? You and I
have both seen kings before, haven't we? At
close range, too. They're only men, when it
comes right down to it. They need to eat and
sleep, like any other men, and to have their
backs rubbed sometimes, I suppose."

That last small effort at humor drew a wan
smile. I went on: "Here, Kalliste, do you want
to sit down? There'll be a little time yet before
we dock, though we've got safe in the harbor
now."

The young woman nodded in agreement.
When she moved to sit down on the edge of the
raised planking that made the small deck at the
stern, the blanket fell away from the front of her
body. Under a plain slave's tunic her belly bulged
with six months' pregnancy. The child who was
already born tried to squirm into her lap when
she sat down, while I, crouching beside my
family, readjusted the warm covering round my
woman's back and shoulders.

The oars stroked and stroked. The oarsmen
mumbled prayers and curses. Now and then the
captain cried out a sharp command, while dark
water gurgled musically beneath the hull. Other

traffic in the harbor glided past our ship, the steersmen on all vessels doing their jobs well. And now docking was imminent. Out of the dimness of mists and twilight just ahead the docks and the nearby buildings were taking firm shape, as were the masts and hulls of fully a score of moored ships. Even Piraeus, the chief port of Athens, was small compared to this.

The ship's captain, who had been friendly and helpful toward his passengers all the way from mainland Greece, was now smiling at us more broadly than ever. In an interval between his shouting orders he turned to me. "When we dock, sir, just wait on board if you will. I'll be back in a moment with someone to see that you're welcomed properly."

Now that land had appeared in easy swimming distance, I, the distinguished passenger, grew somewhat bold. "We'll wait on shore, captain, if it's all the same to you. I'd prefer to have solid ground under my feet."

"Of course. But—"

"Don't worry, we aren't going to wander away. You'll get the credit for bringing me here, if there is to be any credit."

Almost immediately after I said that there came the gentle bump of docking, the terse exchange of command and acknowledgment as the ship tied up. Then the captain was gone, leaping away into the twilight dimness along the quay. One or two curious onlookers strolling there stopped to stare at the new arrivals, but at this hour of the evening there were few people on the waterfront; who would be mad enough to begin a voyage at night?

The distinguished passenger carefully helped his beloved slave and their child ashore, and saw the weary young woman seated there again, upon a baulk of timber someone had misplaced. Meanwhile the crew of the ship, working under shouted orders from the mate, were unloading their vessel's small cargo from the small cabin in which it had been sheltered. The few idle on-lookers on the dock were already drifting away —in the port of Heraklion, the arrival of one more ship from anywhere was hardly noteworthy.

Looking around, I thought that even at mid-night this waterfront would probably never be completely deserted. There would always be someone—and here came a pair of women, ele-gantly dressed but walking freely, unaccompa-nied, bare breasts showing under winter capes.

"Are they prostitutes?" Kalliste asked me in a whisper when they had passed.

"I don't know. Quite possibly not. I have heard many times that customs here are not what we are used to on the mainland, though the language is almost the same. But wait: here comes our noble captain. He's bringing some-one with him."

As soon as he was back aboard the captain busied himself in some discussion with the mate, while the well-dressed newcomer proceeded to where I stood with my family.

Bowing slightly, he said, "I am Hecateus, harbormaster of Heraklion. And you are—?"

I returned his greeting in kind. "Daedalus, artist and artisan formerly in the employ of Aegeus, king of Athens."

"It is a pleasure to welcome you. What stroke of fortune brings you here, sir?"

"I have heard that King Minos of Crete is generous to artists, and appreciative of cleverness and skill. I am here to offer him my services."

The harbormaster bowed again—actually it was more like a thoughtful nod—and considered this. "And the lady?" he asked.

I turned to look at her, an immigrant trying to see her through a stranger's eyes. Yes, she might well have been a lady, seated and resting, wrapped in fine wool for warmth. I said: "I am sorry. This is my slave, named Kalliste; my well-loved concubine. And this is Icarus, our freeborn child."

What might have developed into quite an awkward social moment on the mainland was passed over as a trivial error by this Cretan harbormaster. "I see . . . by the way, do you come here direct from Athens?"

"From Piraeus; yes."

"And did you by any chance sail near Thera?"

I was not surprised at the question. There had been stories about strange happenings on Thera since the days of my childhood, and I supposed that there were new stories now. "No, our course lay well to the west of that island."

"I see. Thank you. Well, welcome to Crete, eminent Daedalus. You'll be wanting to go up to the palace right away I suppose, to the House of the Double Axe." He eyed Kalliste's pregnancy; she was standing now. "If you wish to spare yourself and the woman a long walk, you

could ride—either on donkeys or in a wagon.
The road is good."

"The wagon, then," I said with gratitude. "And
my thanks for your assistance, worthy Hecateus."

The other shrugged. "It is little, but you are
welcome. Remember me when someday you
are influential in the House."

In less than half an hour the arrangements for
our ascent to the palace had been completed.
The ship's captain and I rode ahead on horse-
back, escorted by a few of the soldiers who had
appeared from somewhere at the harbormaster's
bidding, while Kalliste and Icarus and some
miscellaneous baggage followed in a creaking
wagon, escorted by a few more soldiers.

My first real surprise in Crete, a pleasant
one, had been the harbormaster's casual cour-
tesy. The second surprise that I experienced
was neither pleasant nor unpleasant. It had to do
with the House of the Double Axe, and came when
I obtained my first look at the great palace at
close range, in the light of the nearly full and
newly risen moon. It was not the vast size of the
House that was startling; I had expected that.
Rather what astonished me was the builders'
obvious indifference to defense. There were outer
walls, and in places those walls were high enough
to make them difficult to climb, but they were
certainly not of sufficient height or thickness to
offer a serious impediment to an attacking army.
There was a town here too, but it was hard to
tell where the town ended and the sprawling
complex of the palace began.

It took that younger self of mine a moment to

understand: the sea, and his navy upon it, were all the walls that Minos needed.

The town adjoining the House was easy enough to enter, but the sentries stationed there were efficient enough when at last our little procession came to the gate in the palace wall. In a few moments the horses we had borrowed had been led away, and I, along with the ship's captain and one escorting military officer, were entering an anteroom, where we were told to wait.

So far all the walls that I had seen inside the House were red with horizontal stripes, and a carefree pattern of symbolic fronds, added in cream color. Never before had this Athenian artisan seen art that looked like this, and I was interested. Either the decorations were more familiar to my companions, who ignored them completely, or else such matters did not interest them.

After a little while a small and inconspicuous door opened softly, and a pair of well-dressed little ladies silently appeared, evidently come to satisfy their curiosity about visitors. The two men with me stood at attention, and I took my cue from them. The Princess Phaedra—though I did not then know her name—was about ten years of age; her sister Ariadne, taller and fairer, was a little older, perhaps thirteen. These children inspected us solemnly for a moment or two, and then were gone, without having spoken to us. The military officer then explained to me in a whisper who they were.

Presently a pair of anonymous officials, also given to whispering, came in through another door to lead the distinguished newcomer away alone. They led him deeper and deeper into the House, past row after row of black, downward-tapering columns supporting a roof of gleaming tile. The visitor noted with approval the economical construction of the arches.

The palace was nowhere more than two stories high—but from the outside I had not been able to appreciate its full size. It seemed to go on forever. The floor level was forever rising or falling by means of stairs or ramps, and so probably staying in rough congruence with the level of the hilly ground upon which it had been built, while a prodigality of oil lamps, torches, and even candles testified that this imperial domicile was occupied by no stingy monarch.

My escort, certain of their route, proceeded, and I followed. Now, somewhere not far ahead though still unseen, a celebration was in progress. As we approached, voices raised in song broke off at frequent intervals to indulge in laughter. And there was music, made by two pounding drums, not always in consonance, along with wind instruments and strings that I could not at once identify.

Another door was opened before me now, and I was ushered into a hall, vast even for this building. It was by far the biggest room that I had ever seen; King Aegeus had nothing in his palace that could match it. Here the lighting was different. Oil lamps were clustered near the middle of the vast space, abandoning the outer precincts to the night. Above, a high-arched ceiling vanished into shadow.

There were nearly a score of people gathered in the center of the enormous room, most of them performers of one kind and another: musicians, dancers, acrobats. Meanwhile, seated on plain, hard-looking couches were the high-born celebrants, men and women together, enjoying their wine and entertainment. One of these, a weighty, masculine figure, surged to his feet so promptly as we entered that he might have been watching for the door to open. Having arisen, this man set down a golden cup upon an inlaid table, and strode toward me with the unmistakable confidence of majesty.

As my escort stepped back, I began to make obeisance; but this was cut short by the rumble of King Minos's voice, for King Minos it was, urging me to stand up straight and have a drink. A youthful cupbearer and wine-pourer, looking like twins, were standing beside me almost instantly.

The king's voice rumbled. "You must be Daedalus."

"Yes, sire. I had heard that you wanted—"

The hair on the king's head, glossy with oil, was raven black, as was the matted growth on his bare chest and arms, the latter adorned by circlets of heavy gold. He squinted at me closely; we were very much of a height, neither of us more than ordinarily tall. "It's really you. Yes, yes indeed, I've heard your description several times." Minos reached out to pinch my shoulder with a large, strong hand, adorned with many rings. To me it felt like a hand accustomed to assessing horses and draft animals as well as humans for their potential value to the throne. "Come to work for me, have you?"

"Yes sir, that is, I hope so, sir. That's what I want to do."

"Good, good!" The king stood back a step, his fists on hips. "What made you finally decide to leave Athens?"

Certainly the king was going to hear the full story from someone, sooner or later. Almost certainly he would also hear exaggerated and distorted versions. During the voyage, in consultation with Kalliste, I had made up my mind to simply tell the truth when this moment came.

I said: "What with one thing and another, sire, I had been falling more and more out of favor with King Aegeus. Things came to a head a few nights past. My nephew Talus—I suppose you will have heard of him—paid me a visit when I was working alone in my workshop, late at night."

Minos rumbled: "Talus—yes, I've heard of him—some say that his skill as an artisan rivals yours." He watched me carefully for my reaction.

"I think, sire, that it never really did. But however that may be, Talus is now dead." Becoming suddenly aware of thirst, and of the full cup in my hand, I gulped wine, then let the emptied vessel hang at my side. "We quarreled that night, my nephew and I. Then we fought. When he entered my studio that night I had no intention of killing him; but when I left it, he was dead."

"I see. And Aegeus—?"

"Talus was related by marriage to the king of Athens, Your Majesty. I thought that if I stayed to try the king's reaction, I would be lucky to escape execution."

"I see," said Minos again. He gestured, and both our wine cups were refilled. There was a burst of noise, laughter and music, from the happy group still gathered in the center of the hall, who were determinedly going on with their revel. Glancing in that direction, I caught a glimpse of a woman I supposed must be Queen Pasiphaë. She was a large, dark, still-beautiful woman of about the same age as her husband, who I supposed to be a few years younger than myself. She was wearing a great amount of jewelry, and a blond wig.

It was at about this moment that her royal husband clamped his hand upon my neck, rather like a farmer about to lead a young bull-calf to be gelded, so that for a moment I feared a fit of royal jealousy. But the king was not jealous— not then. He only wanted to lead me with him, into another and much smaller room where we would be able to talk in greater privacy.

The small room held a table with a lamp already lighted on it, and two chairs. Minos did not carry his friendly and informal approach so far as to invite me to sit down at table with him. Instead Minos sat, while I was beckoned to stand close across the inlaid board. An open window high in one wall let in some of the misty night.

The king started to say something, was struck by a second thought, and voiced that instead: "Your ship came here direct from Piraeus?"

"Yes, sire."

"Pass anywhere near Thera, did you?"

I remembered the harbormaster's asking the same question. "No, sire."

"The strange stories, the rumors, keep coming out of that island, Daedalus. Some of the original population must still be living there, because people seem to keep fleeing the place in small boats, and some of them end up here. Each refugee brings with him wilder tales than the last. None of my captains will go ashore on Thera, and I don't suppose I blame them. I don't even ask them to land, only to sail near the place and reconnoiter. When they do that, or say they do, they come back with more wild tales of their own. Reports of gods flying over the cliffs of Thera, and monsters waddling on the beach."

"Sire, in Athens I have several times spoken to some of the refugees you mention. Even if one discounted nine-tenths of their stories, something extraordinary indeed must be happening on Thera. And whatever it is must have been going on for more than twenty years."

"Do gods dwell there, Daedalus?" the King of Crete asked me flatly. "In the sense that I and you dwell in this room? And might a man who went to that island find himself confronting them face to face?"

"Majesty, I am no philosopher or seer. And it seems to me that only one who—"

"I have seers and philosophers at my call. A whole stable of them. And they can tell me nothing, really. But you are famed as a practical man. What can you tell me? What do you think?"

I hesitated to answer, but I had to at last. "Sire, I deal with practical matters, as you say. I know nothing about the gods. To my knowledge no outsider has visited Thera in the past twenty years or longer—of course I would not be surprised to hear that there had been a few Phoenicians, who will go anywhere. But that last is only my surmise."

The king considered my reply. Then for a time he sipped absently at his wine, gazing at the painted wall as his thoughts led him elsewhere. But presently his attention came back to me. "I question every intelligent traveler on that subject, Daedalus, when I have the chance. I suppose there is no reason to expect you to be able to provide answers where others have failed. You are, as you say, only an artisan."

"Indeed, sire, that is what I am. I find that my own field of endeavor offers more than enough problems for me to solve. My thought is that if there are gods, on Thera or elsewhere, I will leave them alone, and hope that they will do the same for me."

The king smiled. "Most men are content to think of the matter that way. And most of the time I agree with them." Then Minos shook his massive head, like a man emerging from water. In a brisker and more businesslike voice he said: "I would like some plumbing installed in my palace. I've heard there are some great Greek houses where fresh water, good to drink, runs in through pipes, while other pipes carry off the sewage."

I nodded. "I have seen one or two such on the mainland, sire. They are very convenient though for some reason there is no great demand for them over there. And I think I can improve on the ones I've seen. Much depends, of course, on the ready availability of water," I added cautiously, though it seemed a safe assumption that no palace this size would have been built far from a good source.

"Of course, of course—you can look over the whole place tomorrow. By the way, did anyone come with you?"

"Only one concubine, sire, a girl I dearly love. And our child. Kalliste's half a year into her second pregnancy, and I—"

"Hah, concerned about her, are you? Never mind, I'll make sure a good physician looks at her tomorrow. You'll want her with you tonight, I suppose. So, let that be enough discussion for tonight. Get a good night's rest, and we'll work out the details for your employment in the morning." The king got to his feet, frowning at his wine cup as if surprised to see that it was empty.

That night I slept snugly, installed with my woman and my child in quarters even finer than those we had enjoyed in Athens, when I had been at the peak of my favor at the Athenian court.

Kalliste and Icarus were both exhausted, and they were still fast asleep when I arose shortly after dawn. Three or four slaves had already been assigned to serve us, and these servants came in at first light to introduce themselves, bowing and scraping and bringing new clothing, gifts from King Minos for their new master and his woman.

One of these slaves was a calm and rather deaf old man, another a dull boy. I have forgotten their names. The third was a red-haired

barbarian girl of about sixteen, who, in response
to my curious questions, told me that she had
been brought as a small child from some distant
land to the far north. She was called "Thorhild,"
a barbaric sound indeed.

I questioned Thorhild further while I splashed
my face with water. "Is His Majesty still sleeping? I was to speak with him this morning."

She was moving about the apartment, clean-
ing and arranging energetically. "Sir, His Majesty has been up for half an hour, and has gone,
as he often does, to a shrine by the sea, to offer
sacrifice to Poseidon."

"Then let me hurry after him. I wish to appear alert and ready to serve him."

One of my servants provided me with a mount,
and another informed me as to which path I
should take. The shrine was on a rugged crag
overlooking the sea, a brief walk along the coast
from Heraklion. I left my horse, borrowed from
the king's stables, with the man who was holding the king's own mount, and walked on slowly
toward the place where Minos was standing with
only three or four attendants.

A young spotted bull was about to be sacrificed, and, looking down at the sea, I decided
that those making the offering were probably
waiting for what they judged to be the moment
of high tide. While gulls wheeled and cried
above, waves mumbled and spoke around the
rocks below, a voice-like roar resulting from the
recurrent drainage of water between two sharp
angles of rock. A man determined to hear some
message from a god, I thought, could hardly fail
to perceive words in that noise.

On a crag overlooking the tidal vortex of the waves, two priests held the bullock bellowing, while the king with an ancient obsidian knife managed with three stabs to open one of the great blood vessels in the side of the beast's neck. I observed this bloodiness with respectful attention, but mild distaste. Nor did it appear to me that Minos was enjoying himself, but he pressed on with the butchery. When it was done he accepted a white towel on which to wipe his hands, then submitted to a more thorough cleansing. One helper provided more towels, while another poured water into a silver basin.

Turning his head at last, he saw me watching and called to me: "I do what you see me do here, Daedalus, because of an old prophecy. You've probably heard it."

I approached the royal presence respectfully. "I have heard one, sire, about a bull, a gift from the gods, coming to this island from the sea."

Minos nodded. "I suppose no one on the island any longer really expects the sea to cast up a white bull on our shores. Now it's enough for the people that the king discharge his obligation to Poseidon by a regular performance of the sacrifice." And now the dead bullock was being pushed into the sea, which I had never known to be significantly reddened by any amount of blood, animal or human.

Not knowing what comment I ought to make, I remained silent, until the king threw down the towels, which were no longer white, and started to talk about the plumbing system he wished to have.

* * *

After conversing on that subject for half an
hour with the king while we rode unhurriedly
back to the House of the Double Axe, I spent
another hour in a preliminary survey of the
present water supply serving the palace and the
town. When I got back to my new quarters I
found a physician examining Kalliste. I had now
been in Crete less than a day, but I was no
longer in the least surprised to see that the
physician was a woman. Beginning to feel rather
secure in the king's favor, I said as much to her
when we were talking.

"Women are not property here, sir, unless of
course they are slaves." As the doctor spoke,
her bare breasts were aimed at me as boldly and
provocatively as any courtesan's. "Your girl here
is doing fine. I'll be back to see her in a month."

That evening, Kalliste and I had our first real
chance for a private conversation since our arrival. Little Icarus had already made friends
with a steward's children, and the three of them
were playing together on a patio nearby.

Kalliste had already heard the rumors of Queen
Pasiphaë's lustfulness, which was said to know
no bounds, and now she spoke about them
worriedly. "They say she can be very cruel to
those she takes as lovers."

I was amused, and tried to relieve her fears,
which seemed to me then endearingly unrea-
sonable. "I doubt the king would put up with
her taking lovers. He doesn't seem the type to
stand for that kind of nonsense. And I haven't
even met the queen officially as yet. Anyway, I

doubt she's going to be very interested in me. I'm an old man, with failing powers."

"You're not yet forty! And, anyway, you're a famous man, and that intrigues some women greatly."

I grunted noncommittally, having long ago had reason to know the truth of that.

"And you are—as I have reason to know—a very strong man still. Stronger than some of these young athletes, I'd wager." Kalliste's eyes flashed wickedly. "In some members of your body, anyway."

"Come here. At last you need have no fear that I am going to want the queen. Or any other, while I have you with me."

In designing the new waterworks, the first part of my job was to make sure of the fountainhead. At present, several sources were in use, with water being hauled by wagon to the town and palace. I went up into the foothills, where there were springs here and there, if you could find them among the rocks. I looked into the highest valleys, where lay well-nigh permanent snows, whose melting through the long summer provided another possible fount. Any of these supplies would be hard to tap. And it was going to be a long pipeline indeed from here down to the palace—long, but not impossible.

Having decided to use the springs, I needed a few days to draw up a plan for the new works, and a few more to design clay pipe in different diameters and lengths. Each length of terra cotta pipe was to be made flared at one end, narrowed at the other, so that several lengths, or

hundreds if need be, could be sealed together
into one long conduit with a minimal prospect
of leakage.

I was surveying my way back down from the
springs one day in late afternoon, deciding on
the best path for the long acqueduct, when my
life changed forever. Someone—I shall never
know who—went hurrying past me, headed uphill. As this man or youth passed me, he called
out in a choked voice that a white bull had just
come out of the sea.

For a moment I did not even look up from
my work. Then I did, and stood staring after the
messenger in silence. By now I had been well
over a month in Crete, more than long enough
to begin to appreciate the local power of the
ancient prophecy.

Next I turned to my assistant who had been
working with me, meaning to leave this man in
charge of the surveying while I myself went
down to the shore to investigate this strange
report. But my assistant was already gone; I was
just able to see him in the distance, bounding
down the hillside.

By dint of walking quickly, and trotting a
little now and then, I was soon approaching the
shoreline, and in less than half an hour I had got
close enough to see that a strange kind of confrontation was going on. Presently I was running forward in my eagerness to see more.

I did not slow to a stop until I was within a
stone's throw of the principals. These were arranged in two small groups, one to my left and
one to my right. And the pair who stood on my

right were the most outlandish sight that I had ever seen in all my life.

The group on my left was much more ordinary, consisting only of a king and a small handful of high counselors, including a couple of soldiers—the queen was absent, for whatever reason. Minos and the men and women with him were standing so close to the waves that sometimes their sandalled feet were wetted. The two military officers were gripping the hilts of their bronze swords, and as I watched them I had the feeling they wanted to draw their weapons but the king had already ordered them not to do so.

On my right, also at the very water's edge, and facing the king and his entourage, stood the two figures who were so much more remarkable than mere royalty.

The least astonishing of this pair appeared to be a man, somewhat deformed perhaps in the proportions of his body, and outfitted from head to toe in a marvelously smooth and seamless suit of bronze armor. Actually the color of the metal was odd for bronze; it was far from matching that of the swords and breastplates opposite. But on Crete a hundred shades of bronze alloy were in common use, some of them containing traces of substances other than tin and copper, and so the color in itself was not so strange. Wondrously stranger was the way in which the armor had been made, with scarcely a seam or a joint visible, amazingly sexless and still extremely well-fitting. At the moment the man—or woman —who must be inside the armor was standing almost perfectly still. Only a slow movement of the figure's head, turning to aim a glassy visor at some of the gathering spectators, showed that it was not a statue.

And yet it was the other figure, the bronze man's companion, that drew my gaze almost immediately, and held it. There was no question of this one's being a statue; still, my first reaction on beholding it was simply: *That cannot be.*

Yet there it was.

Not a man, woman, or child, but a two-legged beast, though the arms and shoulders and torso were strongly human. No human legs, however deformed, could have fit into those shaggy, lean, mis-jointed looking lower limbs. No human feet were hidden inside those undoubted hooves. And the head—the head was somewhat human, somewhat beastlike, the factors of inhumanity strongly emphasized by the hornlike projections that curved up from the temples on either side.

And the creature, whatever it was, was white, white all over, or at least an off-white, mottled gray. Whitish fur grew in a mane down even the most human portion of the back, and from the bottom of the back there sprouted a very bull-like tail. Between the legs in front the growth of fur was at its thickest, but there was movement there among the hair, a faint but heavy swaying when the thing's hips moved, suggesting a bull-like potency.

In its two not-quite human hands, the Bull was holding something, some small object whose nature, I, from my little distance away, could not quite make out.

At the moment of my arrival on the scene, the king was talking and the two strange figures opposite him were listening, or at least so their attitudes suggested.

All up and down the visible stretch of seacoast, other human onlookers besides myself had appeared and were still appearing. These made up a representative assortment of Minos's subjects, from naked fisherboys to bewigged matrons. Singly and in small groups these folk appeared and began to approach the place of confrontation. Always they would stop before coming too near, struck by the strangeness of what they beheld. Then sometimes they moved again, in silence, creeping yet a little closer, their curiosity proving stronger than their fear.

All these other people must think, I said to myself, that we are beholding a visitation of a god. The gift of Poseidon, the answer to our monarch's patient prayers, the White Bull from the sea. But in my own mind I was not at all sure. For whatever reason, I simply did not know what to think. I had long been skeptical of gods, but at the moment I had before me a sight most skeptics would have accepted as persuasive evidence.

"Where did they come from?" I whispered, to someone's slack-jawed slave who had come to stand beside me, goggling at the spectacle.

"There was a small boat," the man responded, whispering also. He made a gesture that expressed confusion. "A strange-looking boat. It brought them, the bull-god and the bronze man, to the beach. But then the boat went out again, with no one in it, and now it's gone. I saw it sink beneath the waves."

"Brought them to the beach? From where?"

But the slave had already moved away from me, and I had no answer.

Again I focused my attention on what the king was doing. At the moment Minos was speaking, to his peculiar visitors and the world in general, pronouncing reverent generalities about the gods in general and Poseidon, lord of the sea, in particular. To me it sounded as if the king never doubted that in his strange visitors he was addressing some kind of god, or gods, but was at a loss to know their identities or how to deal with them. One thing the king would never lose sight of, I was sure, was that he was a king now performing in front of his subjects, who must never be left in the least doubt of his right to rule.

Minos was saying loudly: "Oh Bull, it seems then that you have come to me from Poseidon himself. He has sent you to me in answer to my long-repeated prayers."

"But I have not come as a sac-ri-fice, King Min-os." The bull-creature's voice, which I heard now for the first time, was appropriately deep; it was nothing at all like the lowing of cattle. But also it differed greatly from any human utterance that I had ever heard. On certain sounds that voice reverberated with a kind of internal echo, and on long words it tended to break, as if the mechanism of the throat in which it was produced was unable to slide easily from one syllable to another.

"For what, then, have you come?" the king asked.

"App-roach me close-ly, King Min-os. In-to your ears alone I will speak the truth."

No king has ever come to power or maintained his power long by behaving timidly in front of his people. Unhurriedly Minos made his decision. Then, moving slowly but without the least outward show of fear, he signalled his supporters to stay back, and walked majestically toward the pair of monsters who stood facing him.

The beast, the breathing, fleshly creature, was perhaps half a head taller than the man, as I could see when the two were standing close to each other; and Minos was a man of ordinary height.

Just at this point I was distracted by the arrival of Kalliste; she slid so gently and silently into her established place beside me, that my arm had gone automatically around her almost before I realized that she was there.

"What is it?" she whispered, quietly marveling at the amazing scene before us.

"Wait. Watch and listen. I don't know yet what it all means."

Whatever secrets this Bull-man had brought with him from the sea, they did not take long to impart to the king, or else this revelation was only partial. In another moment Minos had turned away again from that strange figure and was walking back toward his men, meanwhile signalling to them to stand easy. The king's face had a new look of contentment.

A faint, uncertain murmur ran through the rough ring of fifty or so onlookers. Gradually the small gathering had molded itself into a semicircle, and this formation was still thickening with the trickle of new arrivals. A formal addition of

military strength, some twenty or thirty men,
had been brought up by now, but one of the
officers at the king's side ran to intercept the
marching formation and post it behind a hillock,
where it remained out of sight of the chief parti-
cipants in the discussion on the beach.

Only now did the king appear to become fully
aware of how great an audience had gathered,
and was still gathering. He scanned the rows of
faces on the upper edge of the beach, and his
own face lighted up when his gaze fell upon his
new artisan.

"Daedalus! Come down here. There are matters we have to discuss at once."

I gave Kalliste's hand a squeeze, and obeyed
at once. In a moment the king was leading me
forward to confront the Bull from the Sea. And
then I found myself for the first time looking
closely into those large, brown cow-like eyes—I
could not help that the comparison occurred to
me immediately. In those eyes I beheld considerable intelligence, which I assure you is fright-
ening the first time it is seen in a non-human
face.

"Dae-dal-us," drawled the Bull's low voice.
"That is the name of the famed art-i-san of
Athens."

"I am Daedalus the artisan, oh god-sent one.
Formerly I was of Athens. For the past several
months, King Minos here has been my most
generous patron." In my words and actions I
was careful to take my cue from my king; I
would not treat this being, whatever and who-
ever it might truly be, as if it were a god. There
would be no falling down to worship it—not

unless my king bent his knees to it first. But at the same time I could not keep from wondering. Certainly this bull-thing was no human artist's trickery, no disguise. The hair, the horns, the face, the inhuman shape—these were all unarguably real.

But the Bronze Man, now . . . when I got my first close look at that, I was left only more impressed and mystified than before. Seen at close range, that figure was certainly not a human being in armor. The whole shape was subtly, impossibly wrong for that. There was a visor over the Bronze Man's eyes, reminding me of a small bright mirror in the sun.

I remembered to bid both creatures welcome to Crete, having heard King Minos do as much.

Only the Bull-man answered me. "I thank you for your wel-come."

"Daedalus." The king had business to discuss, and beckoned me to step back with him, until we were a dozen paces from the visitors. "Our guest is going to remain with us indefinitely, and he requires special lodging—indeed he tells me that a certain kind of housing is very important to him. So I want you to design a house, to be constructed in the close vicinity of the House of the Axe at Knossos. This new house is to be a . . ." Minos, using both hands to grope for words, turned back to his monstrous guest for help.

"A maze. That is the clos-est de-scrip-tion in your lang-uage. A large maze. This will be ne-cess-ary for the health of my soul."

"Then a large maze you shall have. Hey, Daedalus?"

"Just as you say, sire." And I wondered about

the Bronze Man, whose wishes were not being
consulted. Was he merely a servant, perhaps? A
device given life by true magic? Or—?

All my life, like everyone else, I had been
hearing stories of gods and other prodigies visiting the earth. But over the years I had grown
skeptical, because never until now had I seen
for myself anything that might represent such a
reality. Now, however . . .

There came a renewed murmuring among the
spectators, and their rough ring parted. Queen
Pasiphaë, with a few female attendants, came
sweeping upon the scene. Already I had learned
that the queen was shrewd enough when there
was need to be. Now she observed her husband
carefully as she approached, and took her cue
from him as to exactly what her own demeanor
ought to be in this unprecedented situation.
Still I thought she could not refrain from staring
for an extra moment at the white matted hair
that bushed between the Bull-man's thighs, and
at the bullhood only partially concealed there.

Half an hour later, the whole official party
was climbing the hill on foot toward the House
of the Axe, followed by a constantly increasing
horde of spectators. En route the king still hovered 'round his chief guest, treating him as he
might have treated some visiting monarch paying
an unexpected visit. Some monarch of great
importance, Pharaoh himself, perhaps, if any
visit of that kind were conceivable.

In a hasty and informal conference we had
come to an agreement with our guest the White
Bull—some kind of temporary maze shelter

was to be thrown up for the night. The visitor insisted that he would much prefer that to being lodged in any ordinary room, even as he preferred walking to any other kind of available transportation.

The Bull had shown no evidence of concern at being thus separated from the sea—which was presumably his home, if he were indeed sent from Poseidon. Still, at the moment of sunset, he did pause in the long climb to look back at the sea from which he had come, and to stare into the distance to the north. Then I saw him put back his head and gaze for a time up into the night sky, as if he were looking for something there, or merely wondering as a man might wonder at the stars. But in a few moments he went along meekly at the king's courteous urging.

Meanwhile, in haste and confusion, the temporary housing project was already being begun. Squads of workmen, impressed at a moment's notice from other tasks, were approaching through the dusk, converging on the palace. They were talking among themselves about the rumored wonders, then falling silent when the true wonders came in sight. Someone handed me a lantern, and I waved it back and forth to signal the workmen on their way.

LABORATORY WORK

On the king's orders I built the maze directly adjoining the palace. It was, I still believe, one of my more ingenious designs. After a month, though the full design was not yet manifest, the rambling structure was large and elaborate enough for the Bull to begin to feel genuinely comfortable in his private rooms, which were located at the center.

After the first month, construction continued on the project steadily, though at a slower rate. And by the time the Bull was satisfied, the maze had come to be called the Labyrinth, after the *labrys*, or axe, for which the adjoining House was named. Indeed, during the earliest period of construction, House and Labyrinth had started a process of growing into each other, as certain additions were made to each. As this interpenetration pleased both Minos and the Bull, it was allowed to continue almost at the convenience of the workmen and their architect.

In those days I was very busy. Not only was I architect and chief builder of the Labyrinth, but I had to keep pushing forward the previously ordained project of supplying the palace with water. Now the waterpipes and drains were also being run into the Labyrinth at the request of its occupant, and a small moat—of which more later—was being added near its center.

Meanwhile the Bull, though he had declined to oversee any of the actual construction of his new home, had been far from idle. The men and women whom Minos considered his wisest counselors in every field were constantly being summoned to meet, singly and in groups, with the king's visitor from afar. I felt proud, particularly as a newcomer, to be included in these councils.

Minos's enthusiasm for his inhuman visitor seemed to increase day by day. I gathered that our ruler expected to derive much wisdom from the Bull, to gain magical and other advantages that would give him an ever-increasing edge over his fellow monarchs in the world. What other king could boast of such divine assistance? In time, his domination of the whole world would be assured.

I, too, found this strange half-human being endlessly fascinating, though for different reasons; and I groaned with weariness on hearing that at least two new projects loomed large in the Bull's plans, and therefore, of course, in the new plans of the king. These were works in which I, Daedalus, would be expected to play a considerable part, without, of course, neglect-ing any of my other duties.

The first project that we discussed, and obvi-ously the dearest to the Bull's heart, was the establishment of a school.

"I mean it to be such a school, Dae-dal-us, as this island and this world have never be-fore seen. I hope that you your-self will be among its very first pu-pils."

I had not known what to expect when a new project was first mentioned; but certainly I had never expected this. And I protested. "There are many demands upon my time already, White Bull. Besides, I think I am too old to go to school."

The creature moved his head and shoulders strangely. By now I had come to understand such movements meant that he was irritated. He said to me: "That is an att-i-tude that must be ex-punged. No one is too old to learn."

"I must agree with that, sir." Perhaps this sounded to the Bull like an immediate reversal of my position, but it was not; what I had origi-nally meant was that going to school and learn-ing were not necessarily the same thing.

But the White Bull did not choose to ask me what I meant.

"Dae-dal-us."

"Sir?"

"I hope we can be friends. That we can work to-ge-ther. We are both exiles here."

"You are an exile too, White Bull?" If true, this was surprising news.

He signed assent. "I, too, know what it is to be far from home. And far from the com-pan-ionship of my own kind. But some things are more im-por-tant still." And with that he went back to talking about the proposed school.

When I was informed of the nature of the second project, I thought at first that I had failed to understand the explanation. But when the explanation was repeated, it turned out that I had basically understood it after all. On realizing that, I felt a foreboding of great evil. Hoping that I was wrong, I asked for still further clarification.

"Hear me, Dae-dal-us. If a jackass mates with a mare, what is born of the two species' un-i-on?"

"A mule, sir. I do not know if there are any mules here in Crete, but I have seen them elsewhere, used as beasts of burden."

"That is cor-rect."

Listening, I began to wonder if this creature ever asked a question to which it did not know the answer, or at least believe it knew.

The Bull was going on: "And if a bull were to mate with a mare, or a stallion with a cow, what off-spring would re-sult?"

"None at all, in my experience. No, it would be more accurate to put it this way: I have never heard of such matings as you describe. But if they were to take place, I would not expect any issue from them at all. Or if there were issue, surely it would be monstrous." And only at this point did my mind, engaged with the problem as it had been stated formally, hit on the rather obvious suspicion that the Bull himself was quite possibly the offspring of some similar mismatch.

But my would-be teacher was not in the least

offended. "Very good, Dae-dal-us! But go back a mom-ent to the mule. Here we see the poss-i-bil-i-ty of producing a hy-brid that is in some ways su-perior to either parent."

"In some ways," I agreed cautiously.

"It is the pro-per ob-jec-tive of sci-ence to find new poss-ibil-i-ties. Do you grasp what I mean by 'sci-ence,' Dae-dal-us?"

"By science we mean knowing—knowledge."

"Ve-ry good. And we mean al-so the sys-tem by which true knowledge is ex-pan-ded. It is ess-en-tial that my know-ledge—our know-ledge—about hu-man-i-ty be ex-pan-ded. You, hu-man-i-ty, are more im-portant to the un-iverse than you can yet be-gin to re-al-ize."

"The universe?"

"The en-tire world, seen and unseen. The world is al-most in-finite-ly larger than you can guess, Dae-dal-us."

I wondered if he could know how extravagant some of my guesses on that subject had been. It seemed to me that ever since my earliest child-hood thoughts I had been speculating in one way or another upon infinity. To me it seemed only natural that men should do so when they lived in the continuous presence of the sea and sky. And since meeting this creature of the gods I had been waiting, hoping, to hear some words of natural philosophy from him.

"Sire, will you tell me more about the uni-verse?" I pleaded in a low voice, and took a step closer.

"All in good time, Dae-dal-us. And one step at a time. You cannot run be-fore you learn to walk. To return to the ques-tions of breed-ing

new kinds of off-spring. I am of a dif-fer-ent race
than yours—far more dif-ferent than you know."

Our differences were quite obvious, I thought.
But that this being claimed membership in a
race was news of some importance to me.

"You are not one of a kind, then," I breathed,
and then fell silent in fear of my own boldness.

"No, though I know ma-ny of your peo-ple
think I am. There is indeed a race of be-ings
like my-self. We are not gods, only ol-der than
you and more learn-ed. A few of my kind are as
close to us as the isle of Ther-a. But most are
ve-ry, ve-ry much far-ther a-way."

I bowed in silence.

"And yet," the Bull went on, "it will be de-
sir-a-ble—it must be made pos-si-ble—for a male
of my race—for me, be-cause there is no one
else—to breed with wo-men of your spe-cies."

From the moment that suggestion fell upon
my ears, I found the thought of it uncomfortable. "If you say so, sire, it must be so."

"You are think-ing it is un-likely, and in that
you are co-rrect. As I have said, such a breeding is more un-like-ly than you, Dae-dal-us,
can well im-agine. And yet with the sci-ence I
bring to this world even this can be made poss-i-
ble. E-ven as a hus-band-man grafts the branch
of one kind of fruit tree u-pon the stock of
an-o-ther. For the sake of your pe-ople and
mine, it must be done."

I bowed silently, not knowing what to say.
My heart and my mind were united in silent
protest against the whole idea.

"You are so in-tel-li-gent, Dae-dal-us. I want
you to be-come my first off-i-cial pup-il."

"That would be a tremendous honor." And at that point I, thinking that I ought to make some further response but unable to find any favorable words, went down on one knee.

"I could not be-stow an hon-or up-on any-one more wor-thy. But get up." The Bull looked at me with an expression that I interpreted as sudden concern. "The time is near, I be-lieve, for your mate to be de-liv-ered of a child."

"That is true." I got to my feet.

"What say the phy-si-cians of her case? Do they pre-dict a nor-mal birth?"

"Yes. Yes, sire. She—Kalliste—is somewhat narrow through the hips, which sometimes causes difficulty in childbirth. But so far all the signs from the gods are favorable." That was how the physicians had expressed their opinion.

"Dae-dal-us." Now I thought that the Bull was looking at me very solemnly, though I had not yet learned to read with any assurance the expressions of that inhuman face. "When you think as a sci-en-tist, you know that there are no gods."

I supposed that I was being somehow tested again. I thought again about the great question, as I had a million times before I ever met the Bull, and came to the same conclusion that I had held through my mature years.

I said: "Whether there are gods or not is not a decision that is up to me to make."

My would-be teacher paused. "Then ne-ver mind. La-ter we will deal with the gods. Right now are mat-ters more prac-ti-cal in plen-ty to keep us bu-sy. Send your mate to me. The phy-si-cians I am be-ginning to train will en-roll

her in a sci-en-tif-ic program, ded-i-ca-ted to
the im-prove-ment of ma-ter-nal health in childbirth."

And I was filled with joy at this sign of the
favor of this supposed emissary of the gods, who
denied their existence. I expressed my joy and
gratitude to the Bull as best I could, and then
the two of us went on to talk of building
classrooms.

When I got back to our quarters I discussed
with Kalliste the matter of the new physicians,
by which we meant those who were already
being trained by the White Bull. She was at
first reluctant, still fearful of anything having to
do with the Bull. Patiently I overrode her objections, and next day she was enrolled in the
maternity program, along with a number of
Cretan women of different classes.

Meanwhile, my work on the various projects
for both king and Bull went on apace. The workers, some slave and some free, feared the Bull,
and for the most part behaved in a subdued way
when on the job, and worked hard that they
might be finished sooner. They were well content that the Bull chose to stay almost always
out of their sight and out of their way while they
were working.

But these workers cared even less for the
Bronze Man, who frequently came and stood as
if he were watching them while they toiled.
Never did that particular figure utter a word.
Somehow Minos, in one of his infrequent attempts to be humorous, had named the speechless thing Talus, after my late Athenian nephew

who had been known for this taciturnity. Naturally a name bestowed by Minos was certain to be adopted by everyone. There was nothing I could do about it. I was able to smile at the king's jest—I had to admit the naming was apposite—and go along.

The Bull, when I mentioned this incident to him, seemed to be irritated. He insisted that the bronze thing did not and should not have a name. "It is a tool, Dae-da-lus. It is not a-live."

"A tool only? A mere tool, that walks and speaks and follows orders? Surely such a tool has never before been seen anywhere on earth."

"That is cor-rect, on earth, no-where. Except for this is-land and Ther-a."

"You told me once, sir, that others of your race live on the isle of Thera."

"That is true."

"Will you tell me more about them, sir?"

"Tea-ching should be sys-tem-a-tic, Dae-dal-us. When school begins in ear-nest for you, my wor-thy pu-pil, you will have much to learn."

I felt definitely relieved when, a few days later, the Bull informed me that the project of interracial breeding was indefinitely postponed: during our tentative discussions I learned that it would have involved the Bull's mating—perhaps some transfer of the seed would have been accomplished by artificial means—with a number of young female slaves. I had been warned by the Bull himself to discuss this project with no one else, and I had spoken of it only to Kalliste. She too was vaguely horrified, and privately voiced her objections.

*   *   *

One day when I was busily at work supervising the installation of one of the more remote portions of the main pipeline, word was brought to me that Kalliste was in labor. I dropped everything at once and did my best to hurry to her. But I had been working well up in the foothills, at a considerable distance from the Labyrinth, in some rooms of which the new medical school treated its patients.

My hurrying was all in vain, because Kalliste was dead before I reached her, although the newborn baby lived. Eventually I came to realize that there was nothing particularly strange about her death; she had simply died, as so many other women did, and still do, in childbirth.

The new physicians, trained by the White Bull, were as professionally regretful as any doctors of the old school would have been, and as essentially detached. And the Bull himself was not available for comment, being in conference with Minos and others on the great subject of his school.

I stood dumb, for a long time, beside the lifeless clay that I had loved when Kalliste's spirit lived in it. Around me the life of the living women there continued, some of them nursing their newborns, others still awaiting the start of labor.

More sympathetic than the doctors, the nurses showed me my newborn son, already attached to the breast of a woman whose own infant had just died.

FULL SCHOLARSHIP

One day some four years after Kalliste's death—
and the death of our newborn infant, who had
followed her very quickly into the underworld—I
was once more up on the high ridge above the
House of the Axe. This time I was ostensibly
inspecting the plumbing with a view to expand-
ing the system, but in fact I was only half-
heartedly pretending to work on that. Such work
indeed proceeded, and sometimes my personal
direction was required. But less and less did
these Cretan waterworks, or any of the other
routine projects requested by king or Bull, have
any meaning for the designer. Rather I was
sitting with my attention fixed on the white
gulls, who rode in so effortlessly over the land
from the bright sea.

I was pondering how the birds always came to
be borne up as if by magic as soon as the sun-
dazzled landscape began to rise beneath them,

when in the gray sea-distance beyond the birds I caught my first glimpse of the black-sailed ship, inbound to the port.

Standing, I raised a hand to brush aside my hair—notably grayer than it had been four years ago—and shade my eyes. The ship was Athenian, I thought, studying her as best as I could at the distance. But her sail was black. The only meaning I could assign to such an ominous display was that King Aegeus of Athens must be dead.

If that was true, then perhaps, just perhaps, my need for a refuge away from Athens might be over. I was not sure how I felt about that.

I grabbed up and threw over my shoulder the cloak with which I had padded rock into a more or less comfortable chair. Then I started down the hill.

For more than an hour I picked my way cautiously down the rocky slope before coming to an easy road. Once on the road my stride lengthened and my speed increased correspondingly. Half an hour more, and the harbor of Heraklion had surrounded me with its customary noise and activity. There was the usual confusion of naval ships and cargo vessels, half of them at any time, it seemed, undergoing some kind of repair. Others were unloading or taking on cargo. Relatively few were simply riding at anchor or tied up at dockside; everyone knew how the King of Crete disapproved of idleness. There were, of course, worse sins. On Execution Dock the sun-dried carcasses of pirates, looking like clumsily-made statues, were shriveling atop tall poles, testimony to an extreme form of royal disapproval.

The black-sailed ship was tied up at a dock now, between a Cypriot merchantman and a Canaanite, and I paused in order to observe her from a cautious distance. A number of her passengers had disembarked, and appeared to have stepped right into what looked like some kind of debate or argument on the dock. Meanwhile a brightly-painted wagon, pulled by two white horses, had come down from the House of the Double Axe to meet the ship; thus important embassies, from Athens or elsewhere, were often met. But this time none of the arrivals had yet moved to get into the wagon. This was no common diplomatic mission.

For one thing, the new arrivals standing on the wharf looked unusually young. With a little patience I was able to count fourteen youths and maids wearing what looked like good mainland clothes, that seemed to have been deliberately torn and dirtied. Also the faces of these young people had been smeared with soot and ashes as if they were in mourning, and to make the situation really puzzling at least some of them looked somewhat the worse for wine.

This youthful delegation from Greece were confronting and arguing with a couple of minor officials of the House, who had doubtless come down with the wagon to meet the ship. Backing up the officials was a small honor guard of soldiery, who managed to look both bored and worried by the protracted delay.

At last I concluded that these people from the black-sailed ship must be young Athenians come to attend the school of the White Bull. But why the mourning, and the drunkenness?

Eventually I allowed my curiosity to draw me closer. I was especially unable to resist the sight of one young man who stood arguing in the forefront of the Athenian group. He was not at all difficult to notice, being at least half a head taller than anyone around him. If I was right about his identity, he had not been nearly so tall when last I had seen him five years earlier.

Presently I came pushing my way in through the little crowd of onlookers that had gathered around the argument. None of the Athenians took much notice of me at first; by now I was to all appearances a gray, middle-aged Cretan with the heavy calloused hands of a hardworking artisan—though I did wear certain signs of the king's continuing favor, in the form of heavy gold and silver ornaments on my fine white loincloth.

A soldier looked around resentfully as I pushed on his shoulder to urge him from my path; then he recognized the pusher, closed his mouth, and stepped aside.

"Prince Theseus," I said, standing at last before the tall youth. My hands went out in a gesture of deferential greeting, long unpracticed. "I rejoice that the gods have brought you safe again before my eyes after so many years. How goes it with your royal father?"

Rather slowly the tall young man swung his dark gaze around, bringing it gradually into focus upon my face. Some of the sullen anger left the princely countenance.

"Daedalus," he acknowledged. His nod, a gesture giving back unforced respect, became almost a bow as the strong, broad-shouldered body threatened momentarily to overbalance. "Daedalus, how many years has it been?"

"Four years now, prince, since I fled your father's court—how is His Majesty?"

Theseus belched faintly, and considered. "King Aegeus does well enough."

"I am relieved to hear it." When I heard myself speak those words I realized that there was more than a little truth in them; Aegeus might have felt compelled to hang the slayer of his nephew, should that offender ever fall into his hands, but I had never thought that the King of Athens was actively my enemy. "When I saw your ship's black sails, I feared that they might bear news of tragedy. And you and your companions show some signs of being in mourning."

"All m'family are healthy as war horses, Daedalus. Or they were when we sailed. The mourning is for ourselves. For our approaching . . ." With his big hands Theseus groped hopelessly for a word.

"Immolation," cheerfully supplied one of the other young ash-smeared men.

"Our immolation in the school. That's it." The heir to the Athenian throne smiled faintly at me. "So you may tell these officers that we are going to wear what we please to our own welcoming ceremony." He turned slightly and his dulled black eyes went roaming up the great stair-steps formed by the harbor town's white houses and warehouses and whorehouses, to fasten at last upon an outlying flank of the great complex formed by Labyrinth and House, just visible beyond a grove of cedars at the top of the first real ridge. "Where is the school?"

"Up there where you are looking, prince. Not far beyond the portion of the House that you can see. Say an hour's walk from where we are standing." I observed the young man with sympathy. "So, I take it that you find the prospect of a student's life in Crete not much to your liking." By now, everyone around the two of us was attending to our dialogue, and all the other branches of the argument between Cretan officials and Athenian youth had ceased.

"It's four years my father wants me to spend here, Daedalus." I knew the curriculum had just been expanded to that length. The princely cheeks, one of them already scarred with an old sword-wound like that of a veteran of forty, puffed out in another winey belch. "Four years. To get some kind of a piece of paper saying that I have achieved learning. That I am educated. Four god-blasted years, without any real break. I'm nineteen years old now." That last statement was uttered in despair, looking forward to a hopelessly distant twenty-three.

"I know, I know." I grimaced in sympathy. Almost I put out a hand to take my young friend's arm; but that would be a little too familiar a way to treat royalty in public, even here in easy-going Crete. "Prince Theseus, will you walk up the hill with me? King Minos will want to know that you've arrived, and to see you promptly, I expect."

"I bear him greetings from m'father."

"Of course you do."

"Daedalus, who is this White Bull we hear so much about, who wants to educate us all? Is he a real god, or what?"

"Most people think so. I will try to explain about him later. Meanwhile, these officers here will help your shipmates on their way to find your quarters. What of the ship's crew? Are they returning to Athens at once, or—"

"Ship and crew are mine. They stay here in Crete till I tell 'em different."

"I see." And I turned my head to shoot a warning glance at the officer who had been ready to make an issue of proper attire and demeanor for arriving students; and that officer, now grateful for my intervention, nodded.

Thus our ascent from the harbor at Heraklion began. Immediately it turned into an informal procession, led by Theseus and myself walking together. Close behind us paced the two court officials, and just behind them a small honor guard of soldiers. This honor guard was sometimes accompanied and sometimes followed by the remaining thirteen new arrivals, who looked about them uncertainly and no doubt were confused by the lack of ceremony here. The seven girls, I was certain, would be already whispering among themselves at the evident freedom of the Cretan women they could observe on every side, females who appeared eminently respectable except for the bold way they strode about, casually unescorted, looking strange men in the face and aiming their bared nipples proudly at the world. *All very well*, I wanted to caution the young Athenians; *but don't luxuriate in freedom yet. Wait until you get to school.*

At a little distance behind this pedestrian procession of ours, the gaily decorated wagon rumbled along, loud with its continued emptiness.

The pair of horses pulling it uphill looked grateful that it was not loaded with fourteen people. The bright paint and colorful cloth streamers of the wagon jarred with the mock-mourning of the people walking just ahead of it.

After we had climbed half the distance through the town, I gently suggested to my companion that the imitation mourning would really be in especially bad taste at court today. A real funeral was going to take place in the afternoon.

The tall youth blinked. "Someone in Minos's family?"

"No, not that bad. One who would have been your fellow student had he lived; in his third year at school. A Lapith. But still."

"Oh." Theseus slowed his long but slightly wobbly strides. He rubbed a hand across his blackened forehead, looking at the fingers afterward. "Now what do I do?"

"A good question. Let us not, after all, take you to see Minos quite immediately." I turned and with a gesture called one of the court officials forward, saying to him: "Arrange some quarters for Prince Theseus that are better than those customarily given the new students, and conduct him to those quarters now. He and his shipmates will need some time to make themselves presentable before they see the king. Meanwhile I will immediately seek out Minos myself and offer explanations."

The officer's face, and the quickness of his salute, showed his relief.

"Daedalus." King Minos's voice in greeting was pleasant, and his manner businesslike as he welcomed his chief engineer. I had found the monarch in a pleasant, white-walled room where, at the moment, the royal tax-gatherers were arguing over a number of scrolls they had unrolled upon stone tables and pinned in place with small stone weights. In one direction an open colonnade gave a fine view of startlingly blue sea and blank horizon; in the other, Mount Ida, almost snowless now in summer, crowned the skyline of the inland peaks.

Minos, despite the evident dispute among his financiers, was in a good mood. "How can I help you today, workman? How goes your effort on the rock-throwing machine?" One of the tasks that he had recently assigned to me was that of trying to create with known materials a machine capable of duplicating some of the feats performed by the Bronze Man, Talus. Today I could only shake my head in response to that question.

The king's hair, that had been still raven black when I first encountered him four years before, was starting to gray now, and his bare paunch stood out honestly and comfortably over the waistband of his linen loincloth. But his hairy arms within their circlets of heavy gold looked as strong as ever, and his eyes were still keen and penetrating.

From the way the king was looking at me I felt sure that a mere head-shake was not going to suffice as an answer. And so I said: "The work on the catapult is going as well as can be expected, sire. I await the arrival of the cattle-hides from Thrace, that are to be twisted into the sling." Someone had suggested that Thracian leather had some special qualities. "And while waiting I improve my time by overseeing the construction of the new bronze shields." By a long series of experiments my personally trained metalworkers and I had achieved a somewhat tougher alloy than any previously made by men, though even at that time I suspected our best product was still nothing like the Bronze Man's metal.

By now the royal Cretan smiths and smelter-workers had been trained as well as I could train them, and needed but little of my supervision. So I had time for thought on other subjects whilst gazing into the flames of forge or furnace; time to see again and again those effortless gull-flights, as my attentive eye and memory had captured them. During the last few years my attention had been drawn more and more to the miraculous abilities of birds. Now I had time to dream one of the greatest of all dreams . . . but right now that would have to wait.

"Today, King Minos, I come before you with another matter, one that I am afraid will not wait." And I began to relate to Minos the circumstances of the arrival of the Prince of Athens. I left out neither the black sail nor the drunkenness, though they were mere details compared with the great fact of Theseus's coming to be enrolled in the Bull's school—that would surely mean a great boost for the prestige of Minos, in all the civilized lands of earth.

As soon as Minos understood what the general burden of my recital was going to be, he made me pause, and led me, his arm around my shoulders, into another room, where it seemed

we might be out of earshot of the tax-gatherers.
There the king, frowning, heard my story through
in detail. As he listened, he paced the floor
restlessly, pausing now and then to look out of a
window into a courtyard where preparations were
under way for the afternoon's funeral games.

In a short time my relation was finished.

"So it is going to happen," the king said, "as
the Bull foretold."

"It would seem so, sire," I offered cautiously.

"If the son of Aegeus himself seeks to enter
our school, then who will any longer be reluctant to do so? That first group of two-year graduates must have made a good impression when
they returned home—it would seem that the
word has gone about the sure way to success
and power is to attend our school."

"So it would seem."

"You've never thought much of it, though,
have you, Daedalus?"

"Sire?"

"The school. For yourself, I mean."

"Sire, my only son is now enrolled, in the
primary division."

"Yes, of course—Icarus." Minos frowned,
trying to remember. "How old is the lad now?"

"He's ten, Your Majesty."

"Is he, by the gods? How time flies by. My
own daughters are well-nigh grown up—yes, I
recall now! You yourself *were* enrolled as a student when the school began—but then for some
reason you very quickly dropped out."

I hesitated. "That is so, sire."

"I suppose you were too busy—what word is
there from Athens of King Aegeus, by the way?"

"Prince Theseus reports his esteemed father in excellent health."

"Good." Minos heaved a great sigh, and frowned. "Daedalus, as gratifying as it is to have the crown prince of Athens here as a student, there are potential problems that we must consider. It would not do for the son of King Aegeus to go home with his brains addled, any more than they are already. We must admit that has happened a few times to other students of the Bull."

"I could not agree more, Majesty."

"Good. Daedalus, I myself have many claims on my attention, particularly in foreign affairs."

"I can appreciate that, sire."

"Good . . . so I am unable to take charge personally . . . most especially, it would not do for the son of Aegeus to be driven to such madness in the school that he leaps from a tower and dashes out his brains, like this young man we're burying today. Fortunately only a very few students have been so strongly affected. So far no one of any real importance."

"Yes sire, fortunately. And I strongly doubt that the prince would ever be moved to dash out his own brains. But no more, I suppose, would it be desirable for him to fail at an assigned task, even if the task is nothing more glorious than obtaining a certificate of achievement from a school."

"Your words are rich with wisdom, counselor." Minos paused, and suddenly looked at me as if he were measuring me. "You're always in and about the school a good deal. Why *did* you drop out, Daedalus? Why are you not currently enrolled?"

"As you said yourself, sire, I was too busy with other affairs. I still am."

The king shook his head doubtfully. "But I know you, Daedalus. If it were something you really wanted to do, you'd find a way, you'd make the time. No, I have the feeling that even if you were not at all busy with your other work, you'd still hesitate to go to that school, despite your well-known thirst for knowledge."

I drew a deep breath. "Yes, King Minos, I would hesitate."

"Why? Afraid of having your brains addled? That risk would seem to be small."

I hesitated with my answer, while Minos, as was usually his way, waited patiently. It was not that I feared to speak to the king in this matter, but that I was unsure what the real answer was.

"It may be," I said to the king at last, "only the rivalry between two scholars, the Bull and myself. Two teachers, who see the world so differently. It may be that I hesitate to submit myself to my rival in anything at all."

"Or might it be that the wound of Kalliste's death is not yet healed? And that you blame the physicians trained by the Bull?" Sometimes Minos could be surprisingly sensitive to what was going on in the souls of lesser mortals.

I thought about it and shook my head. "That would not stop me from trying to learn, sire. I know those same physicians have healed others, whom everyone expected to perish. The gods know women die every day in childbirth, as the

Bull says. And she was never promised safety in his school of medicine."

"Then what is your objection to being a student?"

"I don't know, sire. A feeling."

The king grunted. "Yes. Well." Then to my relief he let that line of questioning drop. "Whatever your personal feelings about the school, Theseus is the problem at the moment. *Our* problem, I repeat, yours as well as mine. We both know the prince, and we both know what the school is like—you even better than I, I suppose. I could have Phaedra try to keep an eye on him, I suppose—didn't you know? She'll be enrolling this semester too; I thought she'd be first of any royal house to do so."

Ariadne, who stood next in line to inherit the throne, was presumably too busy with other kinds of training. The king went on: "Not that Phaedra has her sister's brains, but a dose of this 'education' may do her some good. People do learn things in the school, you know. And of course she'll be living at home, so we can disenroll her quickly if it looks like anything is going to drive her to distraction—though in her case it might not be that easy to tell—"

Minos drew a deep breath and forced himself back to the point. "The prince is still as stalwart and handsome as ever, I suppose?"

"More so, Your Majesty. He was no more than fifteen, I suppose, when last I saw him on the mainland."

"Well, I have seen him since then. And no doubt my younger daughter will have her eye on him in any case."

Thinking aloud again, with his arms folded across his chest and a frown on his royal face, Minos came closer to me, until an observer unacquainted with either of us might have thought that the monarch was threatening his chief engineer.

The king went on: "I had no thought that Aegeus was about to send his own son. But I suppose he didn't like the idea of his nobles' children displaying any honors, even these new academic things, that could not be matched in his own house. And Theseus. Oh, if he'd been a scholarly boy, given to hanging around with graybeard sages, then I wouldn't be surprised. I might even have issued a specific invitation. But, in fact, given the prince's nature . . ."

Minos unfolded his arms, but kept his eyes fixed firmly on his waiting subject. "Daedalus, you are a friend of Theseus, from your long sojourn at the Athenian court. I take it your little difficulty there, that forced you to leave, has not made too much difference in the relationship between you and the prince? Good. And also you have first-hand experience of the school. On top of that you are a man of considerable practical sense. Therefore I now expect you to do two things."

I bowed.

"First, you are to stand ready to offer Prince Theseus your services as a tutor, as they may be required."

"Of course, sire."

"Secondly, I want you to go and see the Bull, today, and try to talk to him. My authority as king does not extend to him—do you see that?"

I bowed again, thinking that the king must certainly believe the Bull-man to be a god. As for myself, I still did not know what I saw, or what to think.

"Sometimes, Daedalus, I can persuade the Bull to do things and sometimes I cannot. I hope that you can influence him to see—reason. I suspect he may care more for his academic standards than for any problems in diplomacy that those standards might pose me if they were too rigidly enforced."

"I understand, sire." I thought I did, in part at least. "I will of course go and talk to the White Bull if you wish it. But it seems to me that I may not be the best person to send on such a mission."

"Oh? Then who would you nominate for the job?"

I was silent.

"There, you see? You, my friend, have talked to the Bull more than anyone else whom I can trust, even though the two of you are in some sense rivals. Despite that rivalry I can see that there's also a mutual respect between you. So do what you can toward explaining the diplomatic situation to him, and report back to me when you have done so."

I bowed. I hoped there was respect between the Bull and me.

Clouds had gathered, and a thunderstorm was threatening, as I made my way toward the Labyrinth, in which the Bull's living quarters were deeply embedded—still near the center, in fact, for the surrounding growth had been approximately symmetrical. Detouring slightly, I chose a path that would let me peer into the windows of the elementary school. This school, like most other governmental departments, occupied its own corner of the vast, sprawling House. Finding the window I wanted, I stopped just outside, shading my eyes that I might be able to see into the relative gloom of the interior.

There perched Icarus, his wiry sunburnt legs entangled with the plain wooden sticks of a three-legged stool, surrounded by a gaggle of other boys and girls similarly mounted. My son was holding a stylus, rather awkwardly, in his right hand, and his dark head was bent over the table in front of him, where lay several wax tablets more or less covered with symbols. The teacher of this class, an earnest young Cretan woman, was pacing among her pupils most of whom were chanting grammar. I recognized the teacher as one of the most recent graduates of the upper school, the one to which Theseus was now bound. As far as I was able to tell by observing her through the window now, the experience of higher education had not driven her mad. On the other hand, it did not seem to have conferred upon her any visible benefit. She did not appear to be doing anything more to her pupils, or for them, than other schoolmasters had done with theirs since time immemorial.

At least Icarus, as far as his vigilant father could tell, was not taking any harm from her treatment. And the boy had, I thought, recovered as well as could be expected from his mother's death four years ago.

With a last lingering glance at my son, I

started to walk away from the window, then
delayed for another moment. In my mind's eye
arose a vision of a newly-graduated Theseus four
years hence, a caged lion pacing about in this
classroom, trying to teach these children grammar. That was hardly any madder a vision, I
supposed, than one of the prince sitting down to
study. After yet one more look at my fidgeting
son—Icarus was bright enough, but didn't seem
to want to apply himself to any sort of learning
yet—I walked on.

Now, passing along one outer flank of the vast
House, this particular surface a rock wall of
many turns and angles, I glanced in the direction of a field of rock-hewn tombs nearby. In
that direction I could see a small procession
returning across the bridge that spanned the
ravine between House and cemetery. They would
be coming back to the House for the funeral
games, the acrobatic bull-dancing with half-tamed
animals that had so lately become popular, and
the wrestling that should please the gods.

When my way led me past the small arena
where the games were about to be held, I paused
in a cloistered walk for a few moments to observe. While standing there I pondered briefly
the fact that Minos himself had not taken time
out to attend today's funeral, nor, apparently,
was he going to attend the games. There was
Queen Pasiphaë, though, occupying the seat of
honor in the king's absence. Pasiphaë, as usual
these days, had rouged and wigged herself in an
ever more serious attempt to deny her age. Her
tight girdle was new, painstakingly designed—
though not by me—artfully braced so that it

thrust up her full bare breasts in a passable imitation of youth. And now, here came the fair Princess Ariadne, looking cool and serene as usual, mounting the royal bench, taking the position of Master of the Games, as befitted her status of eldest surviving child. And here was Phaedra—how old was she now? Fourteen? —darker and fuller-bosomed than her sister, and quite the prettiest girl in sight.

I had thought that by now Theseus would probably be sleeping off the debauch of his matriculation-mourning, but evidently the powers of recuperation in the Athenian royal family were even stronger than I remembered. The prince, his body cleansed by what must have been a complete bath and a thorough scraping, was just now vaulting into the ring for a wrestling turn. Theseus was stripped stark naked for the contest, except for a modest and genuine official band of mourning black round one of his massive biceps. He made an impressive figure indeed. I lingered just long enough to watch him earn a quick victory over his squat, powerful adversary, some Cretan champion, and then claim a wreath from Ariadne's hand.

It would not be wise to delay my distasteful duty any longer. I walked on.

On this side of the House, particularly, no sharp line of architectural demarcation showed where the business rooms and living quarters of the palace ended and the subtle Labyrinth itself began. But I, the architect and builder, knew that I had already entered the first phase, the outer fringe, of the great maze.

The Bull had wanted his Labyrinth to blend

with subtle borders into its environment, and I had met his requirements with a success in which I still took pride. A pointless passageway here, a blind room there. One stair went up, and another down, to nowhere. At the moment a man walking where I was had only columns around him, with an occasional entablature above. Now I stepped beneath a roof, and was firmly indoors, though the uninitiated person walking in my place might not yet have fully realized the fact. In ten more paces there were only a few windows to let me see the land outside, and in twenty more paces the last of these apertures was gone, taking with it my last view of the open sea and the mountains.

Now, for a little while as I proceeded, the roof of the Labyrinth was almost solid, cutting out the sky. Then roofed space once more became less common, and the light increased. At the same time the walls grew unscalably high and smooth, and the many branching passages, which had now entirely replaced rooms, grew narrower. There were steps and stairs to take the explorer up and down again, for no apparent reason. Soon the stranger walking here would no longer have a clue as to whether he was above or below the natural level of the ground. Only remote patches of sky, one of them now blue, one heavy gray with thundercloud, remained to give the explorer any light or perspective or mental hold upon the outside world.

And now I, the designer threading my way unerringly and thoughtlessly, had entered upon the precincts of the real school where I was an outsider, the school that Theseus was fated to attend. Now once more the traveler was surrounded by rooms. Behind closed wooden doors, taut silence reigned. And now, only now, did I pass underneath a sign warning in three languages that the real Labyrinth, the dangerous core of deceit and confusion, lay just ahead.

Scarcely had I proceeded fifty paces beyond the sign, turning in that distance half a dozen corners at different angles, before I was made aware by certain faint sounds that someone had now begun to follow me. A sudden stop and a quick glance back earned me one brief glimpse of long brown hair swinging from a girl's quick head, before she had dodged back around a corner, out of my sight.

I waited for a few moments, but the girl did not reappear. Everything in this corner of the Labyrinth was silent, except for the singing of some very distant workmen. The students of the school were immured in their silent rooms like bees in cells of wax.

There was no further sign of the girl. Presently I turned and went on my way again, at which point the furtive shuffle of those following feet resumed.

With a sigh, I stopped and turned again. Seeing no one behind me, I called softly. "Just stay where you are, and I promise I won't hurt you." Then I walked back and peered around a corner.

As I had expected, my follower was a student. A slender Athenian girl of about eighteen was leaning against the smooth stone wall, looking exhausted and defensive. I wondered how long she had been lost. Vaguely I thought that I could recall seeing this girl, at some time during the past year or two, among the score or so of the Bull's most advanced students.

I was not eager to interfere in what was doubtless some assignment of school work for advanced credit. But at the same time it seemed cruel and unsympathetic to walk away from her without speaking. "Follow me, if you like," I suggested. "Then you will come out in the apartments of the Bull himself. Is that what you are trying to do?"

The girl responded, weakly but quickly, with a gesture of denial.

Still I was unable to let matters go at that. "Can I help you in any other way?"

"No. Thank you, Master Daedalus. I have been assigned my own goal, and am supposed to find my own way, without help from anyone." She was not suffering deadly thirst or starvation—not yet, anyway—but I could see a great fear in her eyes. Not the sharp, immediate fear of a soldier entering battle, or a captive going to execution, but deep and vital all the same. Death was not in prospect, only failure, but abysmal failure could sometimes seem as dreadful as death, especially to the young.

The two of us had nothing more to say to each other. I turned from her and went on my way, and heard no more of furtive feet behind me. Soon I came to the place where a large waterpipe, one of the main conduits bringing water down to the House, crossed overhead. The pipe was well masked by concealing brickwork, and most people passing beneath would not realize that it was there. But I knew that it was there, and that this wall just to my left now was as thick as four men's bodies lying head to toe. And just outside that wall, though you could never guess it from inside the Labyrinth, was a free, open sunny slope, at this season probably aglow with wildflowers.

Thunder grumbled, and the indirect daylight in the maze suddenly grew dimmer.

I had still a few more turns and branchings to negotiate; I, their designer, at each turn made the proper choice unthinkingly.

. . . and then I was emerging abruptly into the Labyrinth's central open space, a modest stone's throw across. Here the Bull could feel inwardly secure; his inhuman spirit was really at ease only when he knew he was surrounded by artificial complexity. The space was an easy stone's throw across, partially roofed by connected domes. On the far side of the broad stone dais, waist-high, that occupied the middle of the circular space there yawned the several dark mouths of the Bull's own private rooms, which I had never entered since their construction had been completed.

In the middle of the the dais, like the gnomon of a sundial, there stood in sunny space a big stone chair upon whose humped seat no human could comfortably have rested. On this chair the White Bull sat waiting, as if he had been expecting my arrival.

"Learn from me, Dae-da-lus." This had come to be the Bull's regular greeting to me, in place of any more conventional salutation. His speech had not improved noticeably since that first day about five years ago when we had first encountered each other on the seashore.

Silently I walked closer to the dais, which was surrounded by a gently flowing moat, a couple of strides wide and no more than about ankle-deep. The dweller in the Labyrinth had no physical need of such an open flow of water, but he loved it, as he loved the Labyrinth itself.

As I approached, the Bull, an almost manlike figure clothed in different lengths of silver hair, stood up to welcome me. His hands, extended in a learned gesture of greeting, were far from human, something I had failed to notice at our first meeting, bewildered by his overall strangeness as I was then. Each hand bore two thumbs on opposite sides of the palm, each thumb fully opposable to the four fingers. Yet fingers and thumbs looked clumsy and sometimes were. Each fingernail was so enlarged as to be almost a tiny hoof, a miniature of the real hooves that were the Bull's feet.

"Learn from me, Dae-dal-us," he said again, when I had reached the dais without speaking. I came to a stop leaning against the waist-high rim of stone, standing on the last of the short series of stepping-stones that enabled more fastidious human visitors to cross the moat easily without getting their feet wet. Rain was falling now, drumming on the roof and filling the nearby cisterns, trickling into the moat.

There was movement in the corner of my eye; Talus, the Bronze Man, had entered the circular space from a side passage, and was standing motionless, distant lightning reflecting dully on his metal skin.

"I have tried enrolling in your school," I replied to the Bull at last, my voice a heavy rasp. "The results were not pleasing to either of us."

"Learn." The deep voice somehow sounded more bull-like the more I listened to it. The voice could be as stubborn as a wall. "The secrets of the a-toms and the stars are mine to give."

"Then what need can you have for one more student, an aging craftsman like myself? There must be great numbers of young minds ready and eager to learn from you. I understand your school is becoming a fad all across the eastern Mediterranean. More than a fad. From the Egyptians to the south to the barbarians far in the north, great numbers of the wealthy and powerful are coming to want your education for their children. Even today a fresh contingent of young people has arrived from Athens for your instruction."

"Dae-dal-us, you are not tru-ly old as yet. De-cades of strong life lie a-head of you. And if you tru-ly learn, you may be ab-le to ex-tend your life." The Bull, suddenly looking remarkably manlike, sat down in his chair again. Lightning flared nearby, close enough to set a human's teeth on edge, and simultaneously thunder smashed. Talus, who had started to move again, stood frozen for a moment, then quivered faintly before pacing on.

Backing away a little from the edge of the dais, I curtly signed refusal. I said: "For five years now I have watched the young men and women coming to be enrolled in your advanced school, and for the past year or so I have seen the graduates come out. I have spoken with them, and I do not know that I wish to be taught whatever it is that they are learning. Not one of them has whispered to me of the stars' or the atoms' secrets."

"Some might have done so. But compared to you, Dae-dal-us, all my students thus far have been fra-gile ves-sels of lim-i-ted ca-pa-ci-ty. Lim-i-ted ves-sels can hold only so much. Some-times they crack. And, once cracked, are good only as ob-jects of stu-dy."

"Objects of study?"

"To find out how they are made." Now the Bull leaned forward on his chair, until I was able to smell his breath—a not unpleasant smell, like moist dead leaves. The creature ate only vegetables and fruits, and scattered about it on the dais now was a light litter of dried husks and shriveled leaves.

He went on: "But for such a mind as yours, I bring ful-fill-ment, ne-ver bur-sting."

In those days always the same arguments, with some variations, were passed back and forth between the two of us. "Are there no sturdy, capacious vessels among your students?"

"Not one in a thous-and of them will have your mind, Dae-dal-us. Not one in ten thou-sand."

"But I tried enrolling once, as you well know. The experience was not good for me."

"Of course I re-mem-ber. But you gave up too ea-sily. You must try a-gain."

There were moments when the temptation of the wealth of knowledge became very strong. I knew that wealth existed, and that some doorway to it opened here.

Drawing a deep breath, I entered new ground. "What I would really like to learn is something quite specific."

"And what is that?"

Almost involuntarily I looked around me, to make sure that no one else was listening. The Bronze Man, standing as if still mesmerized by lightning, did not count.

When I spoke again my voice was lower. "Can you teach me to fly? Show me how the wings should be constructed to support a man? I am sure there must be a way."

The Bull, as if startled by this request, sat back in his chair and was silent for a few breaths. His half-human face was as difficult for me to read as ever.

At last he said: "The mat-ter is not that sim-ple, Dae-dal-us. But if *you* stu-dy in my school four years, you will be ab-le to build wings for your-self. I prom-ise you. Would you learn how to cre-ate a flock of birds? E-ven that is not im-poss-i-ble."

The temptation, the promise of knowledge, was growing very great, but still I would not yield. I clenched my calloused hands. "How can it take me four years to learn to build a wing? If I can learn a thing at all, the idea of it should take root within my mind inside four days, and any needed skill should come into my fingers within four months. The knowledge might take longer to perfect, of course. And the process of perfection might go on endlessly. But I do not ask to be able to build a flock of birds complete with beaks and claws, and breathe life into them and set them to catching fish and laying eggs. No, all I want are a few functional feathers for myself."

"En-roll a-gain, Dae-dal-us." The voice of the Bull, solemn and stubborn, maintained its muted and inhuman roar. "You will be-come a tru-ly ed-u-ca-ted man. Hor-i-zons that you can-not guess will o-pen for you."

"You mean, I think, that you plan to teach me not what I want to learn, but rather to learn to want something else instead. To make my life depend and pivot on your teaching." Yes, here we were again, getting bogged down in the same old unwinnable dispute, even when I had come here on another errand entirely.

Why did I keep at it, the arguing? Because there were moments when I hoped that the Bull was right, when I seemed to myself insane for rejecting the chance to gain the undoubted wealth of knowledge that the Bull had somehow at his disposal.

And yet at the same time in my heart I was stubbornly sure that I was right in my rejection.

"Bull, what good would it do you to have me come and sit at your feet and learn? There has to be something that you want out of it."

"In-deed there is. My rea-son for be-ing is to teach." The tall figure on its high chair nodded down solemnly at me where I stood below. Then it crossed its legs, suddenly making itself look like the statue of the Goat-God. "For the sake of teach-ing and learn-ing have I and o-thers of my peo-ple crossed o-ceans un-i-mag-i-na-ble be-tween the stars. For the sake of pro-per ed-u-ca-tion have I come here to Crete, accept-ing ex-ile from my mis-gui-ded com-rades in the base on The-ra."

Now my curiosity would not be controlled. "These comrades of yours, sir. Do you mean your kinfolk, who as you once told me still live on the isle of Thera? And do you tell me that they are misguided?"

"They are in-deed. I mean those of my race who came with me from be-yond the stars. I have cut my-self off from their so-ci-e-ty, be-cause my purpose in com-ing to your world was to teach, and pro-per teach-ing they would not al-low. When I am a-ble to con-vey my teach-ings to minds ca-pa-ble of hold-ing them, on-ly then will I know peace and be ful-filled."

I stared at him, trembling.

The Bull, sensing my resolve was shaken, pressed on: "Shall I tell King Min-os that you still re-fuse to learn from me? That there are wea-pons great-er than cat-a-pults that you could make for him, but you re-fuse to learn?"

"The king thinks that the Bronze Man will fight for him against his enemies if the need arises." I had heard Minos speculating on what might be done with such a tool, or weapon, in combat. But I had never before heard the Bull utter a word on the subject.

"It will help him to de-fend this island, if need arises. Yes, I have prom-ised the king that. As long as I am giv-en free rein with the school. What you call the Bronze Man was not de-signed as a weap-on, but on this world it will serve."

With an effort I had regained something of

my composure. And now I pulled myself up
onto the dais, where I stood at my full height
before the Bull.

Then I said: "I doubt you will tell the king
anything about my refusal to enter your school.
It may be that he will not speak to you any
more. He might have come here himself today,
or had you brought before him, but instead he
sent me to talk to you."

The Bull was silent, his face impossible to
read.

Boldly I went on: "How long is it since the
king has been here to visit you? Or invited you
to that part of the House in which he lives and
works?" Not that the Bull had ever seemed
happy to leave his own quarters.

"You mean, that I have dis-pleased him?"

What I meant, but did not care to put into so
many words, was that Minos seemed to be getting
increasingly afraid of his pet monster. Perhaps it
was only natural, and men and gods would never
be able to live on such intimate terms for a*y
length of time. Perhaps there was some other
reason.

But Minos, though he feared him, was unable
to evict or kill any creature so vested with su-
pernatural power and authority, whose school
was so popular with all his neighbors, whose
treasury of knowledge might any day now provide the sea-king with some technical advantage
that would seal his superiority over his neighbors for good and all—and who controlled the
Bronze Man, a weapon of mysterious and no
doubt tremendous power. I had seen the strength
of Talus, far more than human, employed in

lifting some of the huge stones of the Labyrinth into place.

And it was very likely, I thought, that the king, afraid, did not want to admit his own fear even to himself.

The Bull considered the idea of the king's displeasure, and appeared to be able to accept it with serenity. "In time Min-os will un-der-stand what great trea-sures I have brought him. But up-on what er-rand did he send you to-day?"

"Certainly it was not to renew old arguments." Trying to make myself relax, I sat down on the edge of the dais. Turning my head, I spat into the White Bull's moat, then watched critically as the spittle along with an infusion of raindrops was borne along slowly but steadily toward the drain. I was, and am still, proud of all my constructions—yes, even the Labyrinth—and I like to see that they are working properly.

Turning back to face the Bull, I said: "Among today's fresh crop of Athenians is one young man whose coming here to the school poses problems for us all."

Briefly I went on to identify Theseus, and to outline the concern felt by Minos for his some-what shaky alliance with Aegeus. "And the young man is probably here at least in part because his father wants him kept out of possible intrigues at home. Not that Minos said anything of the kind to me; but I thought I could hear it be-tween the words of what he said."

"I think I un-der-stand, Dae-dal-us. Yet I can but en-roll this prince of Ath-ens with o-thers in the school, and then try to im-part know-ledge to him. If he can-not or will not learn, he must go to the rem-ed-i-al class, or be ex-pelled if all else fails. I can-not cer-ti-fy that he has learned if he has not; he is a prince, not of a dis-ad-van-taged race or class."

"In this case, surely, an exception might be made." Even as I spoke, I detested the pleading tone that I could hear in my own voice.

We argued this point for a while, I getting nowhere. Then something occurred that I might have foreseen, but did not. The White Bull suddenly offered that something might be done to make Prince Theseus's way easier, if I myself were to enroll as a student again.

On hearing this I was suddenly angry, proba-bly at my own failure to anticipate this develop-ment. I said: "Minos will really be displeased with you if I bear back the message that you want me to spend my next four years studying rather than working for my king."

"As I am sure you re-mem-ber, Dae-dal-us, we solved that prob-lem at the time of your last en-roll-ment. You will be a part time stu-dent. Even so, one with a mind like yours may learn in three years what a mere-ly ex-cell-ent stu-dent learns in four."

That, I supposed, might be true enough. Si-lently I hopped down off the dais and stood in the moat, oblivious to the water curling about my ankles. Trying to think of a way out, I paced a few steps this way and that, meanwhile avoid-ing looking at the Bull. At last I came to a stop and stood there, silent, holding in, like bronze Talus, like an old soldier at attention, staring at a wall, at the temptation of knowledge that might lie behind it.

"Why do you al-ways re-sist me, Dae-dal-us? Not really be-cause you fear your mind will crack be-neath the bur-den of my teach-ing. Not many even of the poor-er stu-dents have that hap-pen."

Gradually I was able to relax somewhat. The wisdom born of experience came to my aid, assuring me that going to school again was not likely to be fatal. I sat down on the fine stone pavement, beside the chuckling moat. Eventually I was even able to smile myself.

"As I may have already told you, oh great White Bull, whenever I see someone approaching to do me a favor—be it man or woman, god or goddess—I generally do myself a favor first and turn around and flee in the other direction. Through experience I have acquired this habit, and it lies near the root of whatever modest stock of wisdom I may possess."

There was at first no answer from the crea-ture seated on the high inhuman chair, and I pressed on. "Because I *can* learn something, does that mean that I must? Should I not count the price?"

"There is no price, for you. I per-son-ally award you a full scho-lar-ship."

"Baah!" But at the same time I was somewhat impressed. I knew that the Bull delighted as much as any human miser in gold and gems, and that a good stock of such accumulated tu-ition lay hidden somewhere in his private rooms. I had once heard him vow that this wealth was meant only to further the cause of ed-u-ca-tion.

Now he was saying sternly to me: "You should dem-on-strate re-spect. What is the price for one who stum-bles u-pon great trea-sure, if he sim-ply bend and pick it up?"

"A good question. I will think upon it."

"But the cost to him is all the trea-sure, if he re-fuse e-ven to bend."

CRAMMING

Painful experience had long ago convinced me that I had no particular skill in intrigue, and I was afraid to do anything but carry the whole truth back to Minos. When I did so, the king of course gave me no way out; I was going to have to enroll in the school again.

Our interview at this time confirmed my private theory that the king was really afraid of the Bull but reluctant to admit it even to himself.

"What did the White Bull say to you?" Minos demanded. I had reached the monarch in his new bathroom, where steam bedewed the marble walls. He paced back and forth uneasily, muffled in huge towels, dabbing at his forehead with the end of one of them.

I recounted our conversation in the Labyrinth as best I could.

"Then let it be done as the Bull says," was the only comment Minos made at the end.

Next day I was forced to register as a student. I had no black sail to hoist, and wanted to get the matter over with as quickly as possible. So I simply walked to the White Bull's apartments again and announced: "Well, here I am."

"Good." It was impossible for me to tell whether or not the Bull was gloating over my defeat. Then he frowned. "First you must of course fill out the pro-per forms of app-li-cation to be ad-mit-ted—"

"I filled out an incredible number of forms last time. Since you want me as a student so badly, I am surprised that you have thrown them all away."

"Whe-ther the prev-ious forms have been thrown a-way is ir-rel-e-vant, Dae-dal-us . . . and when the forms have been pre-pared, you will be ad-min-is-tered some place-ment tests."

This only made me protest the more. "I have also taken those tests before. Surely there is no need for me to waste my time on that again."

But of course my protests availed nothing. Filling out new copies of the old forms, and taking the old tests over again—they were as incomprehensible as I remembered them—did indeed consume a considerable amount of time. It was afternoon before I found myself walking into a classroom where Theseus and Phaedra were sitting side by side, surrounded by some fifteen or sixteen other young folk from around the civilized world, every edge of the Mediterranean.

The royal pair had evidently heard of my re-enrollment and were not surprised to see me; the prince looked openly relieved. I took my place on a rear bench, endured some curious

glances at my grizzled locks, and waited, feeling
gnarled and old and incongruous, until the Bull
himself entered and began to teach.

There was very little preamble. "Yes-ter-day
we be-gan up-on the sci-ence of ge-og-ra-phy,"
the Bull said to the assemblage of students seated
before him. "To-day we will app-roach it for the
first time in a new way."

And it was soon apparent to me that this was
not going to be like any kind of instruction that
I had ever encountered before, in the Bull's
school or elsewhere. The Bull began to do
something—how, I could not tell—directly to
our thoughts, and to our eyes. I knew that I and
my fellow students were still sitting on our
benches, and now and then, with all the imper-
fection of vision in a cloudy glass, I could still
catch a glimpse of the Bull still standing in the
front of the classroom before us. But far more
vividly than these glimpses, there came an inward vision that dominated all else, with the
sudden clarity and precision of objects seen in a
flash of lightning.

On the one hand I understood that my body
still sat in the classroom. And on the other it
seemed to me that I and my fellow students
together had sprung upward somehow from the
ground, and that we were flying at more than
arrow-speed into the blue. The Labyrinth, the
school, and the whole House of the Double Axe
had dropped clear away. In one direction,
downslope, I could see the harbor of Heraklion,
and in the opposite direction, to the south, the
sharp hills rising.

The speed with which we seemed to rise was

quite insane, divine, miraculous. Before I had ceased to hold my breath, my field of vision encompassed the whole fair isle of Crete. Even its snow-capped mountains were dwindling and flattening beneath me now, becoming almost on a level with the fields and groves and villages, while other islands to the north, large cone-topped Thera and a score of smaller specks, popped into view. The sky and air were very clear.

Our mad ascent toward the uppermost vault of sky continued. By now my field of vision encompassed even the eastern and western tips of the isle of Crete. To the northwest I could see mainland Greece, to the north innumerable islands, the farthest of them shrouded in cloud, and to the south the very rim of Africa beyond the sea. I uttered frantic words, then bit my lip to keep from crying out aloud. Recoiling from the vision in momentary terror, I shut my eyes, clutching at the bench on which I sat. It was not only the strangeness of what I saw that terrified me, but the simultaneous conviction that the vision represented truth.

The experience was proving too much for some of my fellow students. Around me there were louder outcries than my own, and faintings—if I tried hard to externalize my own vision again I could see the falling bodies and the prostrate students on the classroom floor.

Somewhat more slowly than it had been imposed upon us, the vision faded.

Why did the White Bull do that to us? was for a short time the only clear thought my mind could formulate. Then I thought: *Why, there at*

the highest place near heaven, I was able to see
the roundness of the earth.

"Dae-dal-us?" The Bull, in the front of the classroom, was calling on me, though I was not aware that any question had been asked.

Around me, the haggard faces of my fellow students, most of them now nearly recovered from their experience, turned in my direction as I got to my feet. "Sir?"

"Please tell the class what you man-aged to learn from that pre-sen-ta-tion."

I answered slowly. "I have learned, sir, something about the school." But that would not be the desired answer. "And something about the world around the school." I paused. "That world is more of one piece than I ever thought it was."

I thought the Bull was pleased. He made some noncommittal comment, and the class, showing either an unexpected resilience or an amazing numbness, passed on to a much more mundane lesson in geography. Some of that day's routine lesson was new to me, and I supposed I might find the information useful someday.

Eventually the first day of my renewed enrollment was over, leaving me rather more to think about than I had expected. In due time the second and third days had passed as well. Throughout these days rather ordinary lessons were presented to my class, by the Bull himself or one of his teaching staff of human graduate students, not in accordance with any obvious plan. The drama of that first soaring mental flight was not repeated. Most of the information presented appeared on scrolls, hand-copied by some previous class of students. There were wax tablets, too.

And then there were the written tests. I believe I can still remember a typical example.

QUESTION: The world inhabited by men, women, and children is:
A: Bigger than the island of Crete.
B: Approximately spherical in shape.
C: In need of cultivation and care, that can only be accomplished through education, if it is eventually to support adequately a population of billions of intelligent beings.
D: All of the above.

"White Bull, are these the secrets of the stars and atoms?" When I dared to ask that question the two of us were alone in a classroom, after class.

"Did you an-swer all the ques-tions on the test cor-rec-tly, Dae-dal-us?"

"I received a perfect grade." The wax tablets had already been graded. "And it wasn't very hard to do that. Look at this question. Anyone might be expected to realize that the world is bigger than one island it contains. And I have not doubted for a long time that the earth is spherical. Few intelligent people doubt that, once they begin to think about it. One need only look at the earth's shadow on the moon during an eclipse. And if answers A and B are both true, then it must be intended that I accept C as truthful also, though I confess C really makes no sense to me."

The teacher was silent, as if ruminating. As if I had somehow put him on the defensive.

I was not content to let him remain silent. "Are these the secrets of the stars and atoms? Do these questions represent any kind of step on the way to learning how to fly?"

"Pa-tience, Dae-dal-us. One step at a time. The ad-vanced the-o-ries of ped-a-gog-y hall-ow this mode of tea-ching."

"Bah!"

"Now you are once more a stu-dent, dis-re-spect low-ers your grade and slows your pro-gress."

According to the agreement, I was to attend school for half a day, every day except on the rare holidays. But it was also understood be-tween the Bull and Minos that I, as a student, would be able to keep a somewhat flexible sched-ule. At least I hoped that they shared such an understanding. My two masters no longer met each other face to face, so it was up to me to do what I could to convey this idea to them both.

Meanwhile I found myself still compelled to spend varying amounts of time on the king's various projects —the building, the catapults, the life-like moving statues (not much hope of success there) and to keep them all progressing as well as possible. Naturally the Bull declined to give direct assistance on any of them. My days were more than full, though half a brain would have sufficed to do all the schoolwork that had so far been required of me.

At least, as far as I could tell, the White Bull was keeping his part of the bargain. One of his chief acolytes and assistant administrators, an earnest mainland youth named Stomargos, explained proudly to me how Theseus was being shunted into a special program.

"The Prince of Athens will be allowed to choose both his Greater and Lesser Branches of learning from courses that have not previously been given for credit," announced this young man, whose own Greater was, as he had proudly informed me, the Transmission of Learning itself. "Since Prince Theseus seems fated to spend most of his life as a warrior, the Bull is preparing for him courses in Strategic Decision, Command Presence, and Tactical Leadership—these, of course, in addition to those in Language, Number, and the Values of Thinking Beings, that are required of all first-year students." Stomargos, frail and clumsy at the same time, stood teetering proudly on his toes, his hands clasped behind him.

"I wish the royal student well," said I with feeling. Then I paused for thought. "It may be foolish of me to ask, but I cannot forbear; where and how is the course on Tactical Leadership to be conducted?"

"All courses are conducted within the student's mind." This answer, especially in the tone used by Stomargos to impart it to a first-year student, sounded somewhat condescending. But I maintained my patience and pursued the matter. I was able to discover that part of the Labyrinth itself was to be the military training ground, which was no surprise. Beyond that Stomargos could not—or would not—tell me much.

On returning to my workshop that afternoon,

I found a tablet-message from Icarus's teacher awaiting me. The boy had run off somewhere, playing truant. It was the third time within a month that this had happened. And scarcely had I had time to grumble at this message and put it aside to take up my real work, when Icarus himself came dawdling in, an elbow scraped raw, arm messy with dried blood from some mishap during the day.

Waving the teacher's tablet at my son, I growled and lectured. But in that boy's face I could always see Kalliste, and I could not be really harsh. I ordered a servant to take Icarus home, treat his injury, and keep him confined to quarters for the remainder of the day.

Then, at least, I had a little time alone. Time in which to part the curtain at the rear of my more or less public workshop, and move into the private regions beyond. Only now and then did I allow a single helper to enter these precincts. At the rear of this private section there was a secret door beyond which no helper had yet passed. The door was a panel in a wall that I had fashioned with my own hands. The panel looked like nothing more than dead, dull wood, yet it slid out of the way as if by silent magic when you knew how to make it move. In moving, the panel carried with it what had looked like an awkward, obstructing pile of trash.

Now there was time for me to step through one more door, and close the panel again, and then crank open a secret skylight above this secret room. And then to look by daylight at the great man-wings spread out on a long bench.

I had long ago given up on real feathers as

totally impractical. Now I worked mostly with thin canvas and thin leather, using light padding of Egyptian cotton to add shape. But the work had been lagging lately, and not only because of the demands of other projects. I could feel in my bones that more thought, a new approach, were needed. If the trick of designing wings were as easy as it appeared it might be, it would have been accomplished long ago by someone else.

When, using straps at waist and shoulder, I fastened on one of the half-finished wings and beat it downward through the air, the effect was essentially no better than waving a fan; there was no suggestion of my body being impelled toward the sky.

Yes, there were obviously essential secrets still to be discovered. And I comforted myself by thinking that it would be much more satisfying to discover those secrets on my own than it would be to learn them from the Bull. Not that any enlightenment from that source seemed likely at any time soon.

I did not return to my living quarters until late at night. Looking in on Icarus I found him sleeping peacefully in his own small room. Then I grabbed a mouthful of fruit and one of cheese, drank half a cup of wine, shooed a bored and sleepy concubine out of my way, and dropped on my own soft but simple bed to rest.

It seemed that scarcely had my eyes closed before I heard the voices of soldiers, loudly bullying a servant at my door.

One raucous voice came bellowing in: "—orders to bring Daedalus at once before the king!"

By now the hour was very late indeed. This was not the usual way for civilized Minos to summon one of his most trusted and respected advisors. I knew fear as, shivering, I went with the soldiers out under the late, cold stars.

Fortunately, the lieutenant in charge of the small squad, an old acquaintance, took pity on me. "The problem's not primarily about you, sir, but about Prince Theseus. The king is . . ." The soldier shook his head, and let his words trail off in a puffed sigh of awe.

It was the formal audience chamber to which the soldiers conducted me—definitely a bad sign, I thought. There were two people in the chamber already when we arrived. At the king's nod my military escort saluted and backed out, leaving three of us there including the king. I went to stand before the throne, where Theseus moved over a little on the narrow carpet to make room for me.

Minos, seated on his own tall chair between the famous painted griffins, ignored me for the moment and continued a merciless chewing-out of the young prince. The flames of the several oil lamps now and then trembled as if in awe. The tone of the king's voice was settled, almost weary, suggesting to me that this tongue-lashing had been going on for quite some time.

Sneaking a glance now and then at Theseus, I decided that the prince had been drunk recently, but was drunk no longer. Scratches on the sullen, handsome face, and a large bruise on one bare shoulder—Theseus was now attired in the Cretan gentleman's elegant loincloth—suggested a recent bout of strenuous activity. And the king's words filled in the story.

Icarus had not been the only student playing truant yesterday, and Theseus would have been wiser to bruise himself in some activity as innocent as seeking birds' eggs on the crags. Instead he had led a few of his more adventurous male classmates on an escapade in town. Practicing his Tactical Leadership, I could not help but think, even while I kept my face impeccably grave and my eyes properly downcast in the face of Minosan wrath.

The catalogue of charges was enough to stifle laughter. Violence against citizens of Crete and their valuable slaves. Unprincipled destruction of property. Shameful public drunkenness, bringing disrepute upon House and School alike, not to mention the royal family of Athens. All these offenses topped off by the attempted outrage of the daughters of some merchant families who were too important to be so treated with impunity.

Through most of this recital, Theseus held his hands behind him, sometimes tightening them into fists, sometimes playing like an idiot with his own massive fingers. His heavy but well-shaped features were set now in disciplined silence. For him this was probably very much like being home again and listening to his father.

"—classmates involved will be expelled and sent home in disgrace," the king was saying. There followed the longest pause he had made since his chief engineer's arrival. "To do the same to you would of course be an insult to your father and a danger to our alliance. Daedalus, did I not set you in charge of this young block-head's schooling?"

Strictly speaking this claim was not accurate; but I merely bowed my head a little lower. Now was not the moment for any philosopher's insistence upon precise Truth; rather, the great fact that Minos was in a rage easily took precedence over Truth in any of its lesser forms.

"His schooling, Daedalus, is not proceeding satisfactorily."

The king's chief artisan bowed his head somewhat lower yet.

"And as for you, *prince*—now you may speak. What have you to say for yourself?"

Theseus shifted his weight on his big feet, and spoke up calmly enough. "Sire, that school is driving me to drink and madness."

Now Minos, too, was calm. The royal rage had been used up. Or else it could, on the proper occasions, be turned on and off like the flow of water in one of the pipes I had provided for him.

"Prince Theseus, you are under house arrest until further notice, allowed out only to attend school. I intend to station six strong soldiers at your door, and you may assault them, or try to, should you feel the need for further recreation."

"I am sorry for what happened last night, King Minos." And it seemed he was. "But I can take no more of that school."

"You will take more of it. You must." Then the king's eye swung back again to his counselor. "Daedalus, what are we to do? I and the queen leave in three days for this damned round of state visits. We are going as far as Macedonia, and we will probably be gone for months."

"I fear I have been neglectful regarding the prince's problems, sire. Let me now make them my prime concern."

A few hours after being excused by King Minos, and shortly after dawn, I once more entered the White Bull's quarters. This time I found the dais unoccupied. Heedless of stepping-stones, I sloshed through the little moat and stood beside the odd-shaped chair. There was never any need to call, and I stood waiting silently.

In a few minutes the half-human figure appeared, more silvery and inhuman than ever in the early morning light. Before it took any notice of its caller it proceeded through a ritual splashing, bathing, in the moat. Then it climbed up on the dais to bid me welcome.

"Learn from me, Dae-dal-us! How are you learning?"

"White Bull, today I come to see you not on my own affairs, but on behalf of Prince Theseus. He is experiencing great difficulty in . . . no, let me speak more plainly than that. He tells me that his testing in the Labyrinth, in particular, is likely to drive him to violent madness. Knowing him, I believe him when he tells me that. He must not be allowed to fail in such a way."

"The course of stu-dy of Tac-tics, Dae-dal-us, is pre-scribed. In part the course de-scrip-tion is as fol-lows: the tea-cher shall e-lic-it from the stu-dents facts as to their a-bil-i-ty to de-ter-mine spa-tial lo-ca-tions—"

I couldn't stand it. "Oh great teacher! Master of the science and art of Transmission of Learning! I beg you—"

"Not Master, Dae-dal-us. My a-ca-dem-ic rank is that of Doc-tor, which is high-er."

"Master or Doctor or Divinity or what you will. You say that you are going to instruct the prince in the science of tactics. I suppose it means nothing that the fate of Theseus in battle, insofar as it is not determined by all the chance stupidities of war, is not at all likely to depend on his ability to grope his way out of a maze?"

"He has been all-owed to choose his course of stu-dy, Dae-dal-us. Be-yond that, spe-cial treat-ment can-not be ac-cord-ed any non-dis-ad-van-taged stu-dent."

"Well." There were times when I despaired of ever getting a direct answer to a question. "White Bull, *I* have never fought anyone with a sword. Have you?"

The figure on the high chair was silent. Per-haps it was outraged already that anyone dared to cast doubt upon its competence.

But I pressed on. "*I* have never bullied men and challenged them and cheered them on to get them into combat. But once, shortly before I left the mainland, watching them from the highest and safest place that I could reach, I saw Prince Theseus do these things. He must have been not quite fifteen years old at the time. Some vassal's uprising somehow got started against Athens, and Theseus put it down, al-most single-handedly, you might say. I think he would not be likely to learn much from me in the way of military science, were I to lecture on the subject. No doubt you, however, have some great skill and knowledge in the field to impart?"

The Bull showed no emotion, none at least that I could understand. "My qual-i-fi-ca-tions as tea-cher are be-yond your a-bil-i-ty to com-pre-hend, much less to ques-tion. Your own pro-gress in school should be your con-cern."

"White Bull!" I paused, raising both hands to my own grizzled hair; I felt like tearing handfuls of it out. Why, why, was I fated to spend so much of my life in this insane struggle with this inhuman creature? "Try to understand. If Theseus should fail here, fail spectacularly, then I may not be on hand to make any kind of progress through your school. Minos will be angry with me. And not with me alone."

"You are worth too much to Min-os for him to kill you."

"I am not at all sure of that. Am I worth more than an Athenian alliance? I think not. And how much do you think that you are worth to him?"

"*I?*" For once the Bull's voice had real tone in it. Surprise, I thought. "Ed-u-ca-tion is price-less."

Argue with the chief educator as I might, I was unable to get my princely ward excused from Tactical training and testing in the Laby-rinth. I returned to my own living quarters in a cloud of worry.

Still, for the next couple of days, the situation seemed to ease. The prince at least was attending school, and I thought he must be applying himself to his studies.

Foolishly I did nothing, and allowed my hopes to rise. Then, as I emerged one afternoon from my own classroom, I saw a page from the Inner House coming to get me, and I knew a sinking feeling. But the message was not quite what I had feared: it was the Princess Ariadne who required my presence in the audience chamber at once.

Going along with the page, now more puzzled than alarmed, I found Ariadne perched regally on the small throne. She greeted me formally, and dismissed the page and her other attendants. As soon as they were out of the room, the princess came down from the chair and spoke to me with her usual lack of ceremony.

"Daedalus, before my father's departure he told me—"

"Departure!—but I beg your pardon for interrupting, princess. Then your mother and father have already departed on their state tour?"

"Of course. Where have you been for the past two days, Daedalus, that you don't know what's going on?"

"In school—but never mind, Your Highness. What were you going to tell me?"

"My father has informed me that Prince Theseus has been having—difficulties—in school, and he impressed upon me the importance of this problem. Also I have—I have talked with the prince myself, and I find that the situation does not seem to be improving." Ariadne sounded nervous, vaguely distracted—as well she might,

I supposed, with the cares of a kingdom suddenly left upon her shoulders.

"I fear that you are right, princess, about the situation in the school," I began. Then, before I had time to say anything more, I was interrupted by the entrance of another page, come to announce the arrival of Theseus himself.

No escort of soldiers accompanied the prince when he walked in—evidently the princess had wasted no time in setting aside the house arrest ordered by her father. I thought that the exchange of greetings between the two young people sounded somewhat too stiffly formal, and I noted also that Ariadne scarcely looked at Theseus as she spoke to him. Certainly she had made no such effort to avoid looking at him when he entered the wrestling ring on the day of his arrival, or during the days that had passed since then. But now she did. And now, when the prince looked at her, his face was wooden.

For a few moments I entertained the idea that the two of them were quarreling, but I soon decided that the absolute opposite was much more likely. An affair, then, and they were naturally trying to hide it. What next? As if there were not problems enough already. Silently I breathed unpracticed prayers, addressed to any god who might deign to listen.

Theseus, in response to an awkward-sounding question from Ariadne, was now relating his continued difficulties in school. Their dialogue had a rehearsed quality.

Now she turned back to me, almost pleading, in a voice that sounded much more natural. "Daedalus, he will fail his Labyrinth tests again unless we do something, and perhaps he will be expelled. What are we to do? We must find *some* means of helping him."

And a glance flashed between the two young people. It was a very brief glance, but it was quite enough to make me feel certain of what was going on. My sinking feeling grew worse. Something told me that this affair was neither completely casual nor formalized by an official engagement—that would have been announced with such fanfare that even I, isolated from much of what went on at court, must have heard the news. No, then it must be Love—the cause of no end of trouble, especially among royalty.

Still, now that I had grasped the situation, I could almost begin to relax. I suppose I gazed at the two young people with something like a smile. I could only hope that the Princess Ariadne would not allow infatuation to lead her into any real craziness, such as trying to arrange a secret marriage. Meanwhile, it occurred to me, Theseus's problems might actually be easier to solve while Minos, with his secret fear of the Bull, was not around.

Was it even possible that Minos had planned his diplomatic trip, and taken his queen with him, in the hopes that someone would take care of the embarrassment for him while he was gone?

Conferring with the prince—while Ariadne hovered near and listened to our talk—I made sure that the key to the young man's worst difficulties was the maze itself. In his courses other than Tactics, all of them taught in ordinary classrooms, the prince might, probably could, do well enough to scrape by.

Having heard Theseus out, I took a charred stick from a sacrificial brazier nearby, and began to draw on the smooth stone floor beside the narrow rug. From memory I sketched there a crude plan of a key portion of the Labyrinth, the very area in which Tactical Training began each day. The painted griffins on the walls glared down balefully at the three people who squatted near the foot of the throne, like three children at some game.

Theseus, saying little, stared gloomily at the patterns as I drew them, and appeared to listen while I talked. Once the slender brown hand of Ariadne came over, forgetfully, to touch her lover's hand. Then her hand flew back, while her eyes jumped up to search my face. I affirmed that I had noticed nothing, by holding my own scowling concentration on the floor.

"Now, prince," I said, "I am going to reveal a secret that you must tell no one." I raised my gaze deliberately to meet the eyes of Theseus. "I hope you understand."

"Of course. I can keep a secret. What kind of secret is it that'll help me, though?"

"If you felt confident of being able to find your way completely out of that portion of the Labyrinth, anytime you wanted, *that* would help you, would it not?"

Theseus started to answer, then settled for drawing a deep breath. "Yes," he said at last.

I frowned at him. "One way is to take advantage of a gentle, very subtle slope of the floor, away from the center—but that may be hard to detect. The foolproof way is this: If you were in the center of the maze, trying to find your way out, the idea would be to let your right hand touch the wall at the start—hey? Follow me?"

"I think so. I can always tell my right hand from my left." The reassurance was offered to me quite seriously. "At least when I'm outside the Labyrinth. My right hand's the one in which I always—almost always—hold a sword. I just imagine myself picking one up." The Prince of Athens nodded grimly.

"Ah—yes. So, as I say, if you are trying to find your way outward from the center, or from any point inside, you must just let your right hand glide continuously along the wall as you move. You may not reach the exit by the shortest path, but you'll certainly get there."

The handsome, scarred face frowned. "If I'm carrying something in my right hand, though . . ."

"Well then, *imagine* your right hand gliding along the wall. Or use your right shoulder. Now, there is one important exception to this rule. If, in that section of the maze, you should find yourself climbing a stair, you must remember to switch at the top of the stair. Then you glide your left hand along the wall. Keep doing that *until* you have descended at least one step again, then switch back to using the right hand. Now, of course, if you should be trying to find your way *inward* from the entrance to the center, simply reverse—"

"Daedalus." The prince's voice was not very loud, but still it stopped me in mid-sentence. "Thanks for what you are trying to do. But I tell you, when I am put in there, I cannot help myself."

Theseus got to his feet, moving as if he were unconscious of the movement. His eyes were fixed on something in the distance, beyond the audience chamber's confining walls. "Once I get *in there* I forget all about left and right, except I know that the walls are crushing in on me, the doors are all sealing themselves off—" Ariadne, who now was standing too, put out a hand again, then drew it back. "—so there is nothing left but stone walls, all coming closer. I wish you had never told me that some of them are four men's bodies thick."

Theseus was shivering now, as if with cold, although the afternoon was warm. There was a look in the prince's eyes that I had seen there on only one occasion in the past, and now I too got to my feet, moving with deliberate care.

The prince said, without any particular feeling in the words: "If that god-blasted cow dares to lecture me on courage and per-sev-er-ance in my stu-dies one more time, I swear by all the real gods I'll break its neck."

"Very well, my friend." I laid a hand gently and briefly on the prince's shoulder. "Very well. We will do all that we can to help."

It was midafternoon on the day following that conference, and I, in my own classroom, half-hypnotized by the drone of an assistant teacher's voice, had fallen into a daydream of numbers that my stubborn mind kept trying to match with flying gulls. I was roused from this state by a hand shaking me.

Stomargos stood at my side, looking down at me with an expression of obscure triumph. "Daedalus, the White Bull wants to see you, at once."

I would not give him the satisfaction of asking why, although I knew a premonition of sickening fear. Getting to my feet in a silence of outward calm, I followed the educator from the classroom.

I had expected that when we reached the White Bull's private chambers, Stomargos would immediately be dismissed. But the Bull, who was waiting for us on its tall chair, made no gesture to send the young man away. And Stomargos, with a smug look on his face, remained standing at my side.

And today the Bull, for once, did not say *learn from me, Daedalus*. Rather it rumbled: "We have dis-co-vered the prince's cheat-ing, Dae-da-lus."

"Cheating? What do you mean?" But I had never been any good at trying to brazen out a lie.

"I mean the thread tied on his right wrist. In his pock-et, the ti-ny met-al balls, to bounce and roll and seek al-ways the down-ward slope of floor, how-ev-er gen-tle. How do you make a ball so smooth and round? Ex-act-ly spher-i-cal?"

I had dropped them molten from a tall tower, into water. I wondered if the Bull would be impressed to hear this method. "I see," I said, trying to be noncommittal and admitting nothing. "What do you intend to do now?"

There was a silence. Then the White Bull said at last, in a changed voice: "Leave us a-lone,

Sto-mar-gos." And then, when the two of us were finally alone, it said to me: "Now learn from me, Dae-dal-us. As you have sought to learn."

. . . and before I was able to sit down, I reeled and almost fell into the moat, with the painful power and clarity of the pictures that were being forced into my mind. There, in front of me, as if pinned up on air, were spread the wings of which I had long dreamed. These wings were not very greatly different in their gross structure from the ones I had pinned on my workbench; but in the fine structure there was a great difference between the two. The wings in the vision were pierced through in a thousand places with tiny, peculiarly curved channels. Presently, when the finest scale of the structure was enlarged so I could see it, I saw how the channels would have to be made. Each of them was a soft, sculpted cavity, that would enlarge just slightly each time the wing was beaten downward and air flowed into it. Then in my vision the wing finished its downward motion and the cavities all contracted, forcing air out of each channel at the bottom.

The strangest part of the cycle of operation was the way in which the air just below the wing, on encountering all the suddenly closed entrances, changed pressure wildly. A thin layer of that air, much broader than the wing itself, became momentarily almost as hard as wood. Somehow in the vision I was able to feel, as well as see, the fluid alterations . . . and I could see also, with no feeling of haste, no need to hurry, that the length and width of the pinions must be just *so*, in relation to the height and weight of the human being who was to wear them. And just *so* must be the variation in the different channels that pierced the different sections of the wing. . . .

It was all, in every least detail, burned into my brain. From that first learning I knew that there would be no forgetting this lesson, even if forgetfulness were someday willed. But the imprinting did not take long. Soon it was over.

I, Daedalus, feeling like a clay tablet on which someone's signet ring had just been impressed, got shakily to my feet and stood at my full height once more.

"Bull—why did you never before give me such a teaching?"

The soft brown eyes blinked at me, as if the Bull had been expecting a different kind of comment. "It will not make of you an ed-u-ca-ted man, Dae-dal-us."

"All right, then, it will not. I do not know what you think an educated man is like, or even whether I want to be one by your standards. I thank you for this teaching, though . . . you refused it to me before, why did you give it now?"

The Bull was no longer looking directly at me; its eyes and its face were human enough so that at least I could be sure of that. When it answered, its voice was almost soft.

"Because I think this tea-ching will re-move you from my pre-sence. In one way or a-nother. I see now you are not wor-thy of fine ed-u-ca-tion. One way or a-nother your dis-rup-tion of my school must stop."

"I see." But no, I did not really think about it. Because in my mind the plan for the new wings was burning, as urgent as a fire in my workshop.

Stomargos, his triumph fading into puzzlement when he beheld my elation, was my escort once again. But the image of the wings still burned before my eyes, blinding me to almost everything else, and I allowed myself to be marched away through the Labyrinth for a hundred paces or so before the realization came to me.

When that happened I stopped and grabbed Stomargos by his flabby arm. "And Prince Theseus? What of him?"

"I myself am a witness to the prince's attempt to cheat," said Stomargos, firmly and primly. "There is no doubt of his guilt, and the Bull has decided rightly that he must be expelled."

"But that cannot be!" My reaction was so strong that even the educator was shaken for a moment.

But for a moment only. "Oh, the Bull and I are quite agreed that expulsion is necessary. The prince is probably receiving his formal notification at this moment."

On hearing that I spun around in my tracks and ran, back toward the inner Labyrinth.

"Stay! Stay!" Stomargos shouted, running clumsily after me. "You have been expelled also. You are to leave the grounds of the school at once. . . ."

He was much younger than I, but still I outsped him easily. The voice of the educator faded behind me in the windings of the maze. From somewhere ahead, in the direction of the Bull's habitation, there came inhuman roaring noises and the sounds of physical struggle.

Moments later, I burst into the central room, to behold Theseus and the Bull grappling on the central dais, arms locked around each other's necks, the prince gripping a horn with one fist. Theseus was slightly taller. The heavy stone chair had already been overturned, and a Bull-meal of fresh fruit was scattered and trampled under their feet and hooves. In the broad back of the Prince of Athens—even now I can see it vividly—the great bronzed, cabled muscles stood out like structural arches new-glowing from the forge.

The end came even as I, yelling at the combatants, splashed through the moat, running to reach them before it was too late. I heard the sickening bony crack, and the Bull's hoarse warbling cry at the same instant. I saw the prince move staggering back, and then stand motionless, staring down at what his hands had done. At his feet lay a gray-white mound of fur, suddenly no more human than a dying bear.

Stomargos, catching up with me at last, came pounding into the circular space and quickly splashed across the moat to stand beside me goggling at what lay on the dais. The schoolteacher pointed, goggled some more, and opened his mouth to begin an almost wordless cry for help. Then he turned and ran, and it was I who had to drop him with a desperate watery tackle in the moat.

"Theseus! Help me! We must keep this one quiet." And in a moment the Prince of Athens had taken charge. Stomargos's head was clamped down in the deepest part of the little channel, and presently the bubbles ceased to come up out of his mouth.

Then the two of us who were still alive climbed up out of the moat onto the dais. Theseus, still panting with the exertion of his struggle against the Bull, seemed to grow a little taller and straighter with every operation of his lungs, like some young tree freed suddenly of a deforming burden, reasserting its natural form.

He nodded toward the fallen Bull. "Does he still breathe, Daedalus?"

I was already crouching down, prodding and peering into gray fur, trying to find out. "I am not sure."

"Well, let him go on breathing, if he can. It no longer matters to me. I'm leaving Crete."

"But how?"

"My ship is still here—didn't you know? She can be made ready in an hour or two—if I can get my men rounded up out of the taverns by then—and I am going home. Or somewhere else, if my father will not have me in Athens now. But better a pirate's life, even, than this." And his eyes swept round, making a scan of the circular stone wall.

"You are right," I said after a moment's thought. "I think you should leave, must leave, if you can, before this is discovered."

Theseus looked at me and said: "Ariadne is going to come with me. I am sure of it."

"Gods of sea and sky! No! That would cause—"

"And Phaedra too."

I was stricken speechless for the moment.

"And you are welcome to come with us too, old friend," Theseus offered, almost as an afterthought, "though I can promise you no safe workshop, nor slaves, nor high place at any court but my own—if ever I have one."

"I want no place as high as a sun-dried pirate's, which I fear Minos might make for me here, as soon as he comes home. Comes home to find the Sacred Bull, the gift of Poseidon, dead. And you departed, with both his daughters who are his only heirs—come, you think they will really both go with you?"

"I'm sure they will."

He might not have been able to pass the tests of school, but in this I did not think he would be wrong. I said: "Then I must ask you as your friend if you have thought this through."

"What is there to think about, Daedalus? I could not stay here after attacking the Bull, even if he were still alive. And now I have killed this miserable teacher in the moat. And when the princesses tell me they are too frightened to stay and face their father, as I am sure they will, then I cannot very well refuse to take them with me."

"I suppose not," I said, and wondered if Theseus was having an affair with both princesses at the same time. "And if you go I certainly do not intend to stay and take all the blame. Very well, then, we must move swiftly, before this violence is discovered."

"Dae-dal-us." The unexpected voice was a mere thread of sound, stretched thin and about to break.

I bent down again, getting my ears closer to the furry head. "White Bull, how is it with you?"

"As with a man whose neck is bro-ken, Dae-dal-us. After to-day I teach no more."

"Would that I had been able to learn from you before today, White Bull. And would that you had learned from me."

The tall Athenian prince and I walked out of the Labyrinth together. No doubt both of us looked a little shaken, as would be only natural for two students who had probably just been expelled. Through the windows of the elementary school the usual voices came droning out, from classrooms in which the usual lessons were no doubt in progress. When a pair of teachers approached us, heading in a direction that suggested they might be bound for a conference with the Bull, Theseus—displaying, as I thought, excellent Tactical Skill—stopped them and informed them in a subdued voice that the Bull and Stomargos were talking together and did not want to be disturbed just now. The teachers accepted this unquestioningly, and walked off uncertainly in another direction.

The prince and I walked on, moving quickly but without hurrying. There was one more stop I had to make, within the precincts of the school. On doing so I was presented with more disturbing news—Icarus was truant yet again today, his teacher had no idea of where he might be found.

The prince and I hurried on to Ariadne. A minute after our arrival the princess had dispatched one of her most trusted servants to begin the job of rounding up Theseus's crew—his ship had been here for a month now, and apart from a few practice cruises little had been done to keep the men and gear in shape. Despite his evident faith in his men, I thought it highly problematical how soon he might be able to hoist sail.

A few minutes after the first servant left the royal quarters, a couple of others followed, detailed to help me look for my son.

The wild, rugged lands where boys were wont to go searching for birds' eggs and dreams swept up and up, one hour's walk after another, behind and above the House of the Double Axe.

The Prince of Athens said: "We can wait no longer for him, Daedalus. My men's lives are all in danger, and the lives of the two princesses too. As soon as those two bodies are discovered in the Labyrinth, some military man or sea captain is sure to take it upon himself to try to stop my sailing, no matter what the Princess Ariadne tells him. They know they'll stand responsible to the king when he gets back."

And Ariadne said: "Theseus must get away. You are welcome to come with us, Daedalus, but if you stay, I feel sure my father will not deal too grievously with you; he depends too much on you for that."

Only Phaedra, who had joined this hasty conference in the middle, had nothing at all to say

to me. For the most part she was silent, biting
her full lips. Her fingers, as if they moved without her awareness, had gone to caressing Theseus's
arm as the prince stood beside her. I saw this,
but Ariadne did not see.

I in my mind's eye saw more: the sun-dried
pirates on the dock. And his own workshop, and
the hidden room that held the hidden, unfin-
ished wings. All wrong; I would have to start
again from scratch. And I saw my living quarters nearby, and how the small, trusting shadow
would cross the threshold there, when Icarus
came running home . . .

Long, helmed shadows came across that threshold first, with the black triangles of shadow-
spearheads thrust ahead of them. This time the
soldiers grimly held their weapons as they
marched me, the king's chief engineer, deeper
into the House. Icarus, returning wearily from
another of his adventures, was only just in time
to see his father being arrested, and to be swept
up like a dropped crumb by tidy soldiery.

Grim military men, whose names and faces I
scarcely knew, were now in charge. Minos was
not due home for at least another month. The
de facto military government, taking over after
the defection of both royal princesses, did not
want to assume responsibility for judging me.
My son and I were both confined under strict
house arrest, our movements restricted to the
workshop and their living quarters.

All of the ordinary entrances and exits of this
small domain were promptly walled up—I tried
to comfort my son by pointing out that the

masonry was rough and temporary-looking. Icarus brightened somewhat after he had been convinced that this was not all some rather excessive punishment visited upon us both because he had played hooky once too often.

A continuous guard was also established. One servant only was allowed us, the maid Thorhild. No one else was allowed in or out of our quarters, and any conversation with the prisoners was forbidden. Food was slid in to us through a tiny door, and garbage slid out, and the water continued to flow through the plumbing I had designed.

Now at last I had plenty of time and privacy in which to work. Now at last I could let Icarus see what I was doing, and even set the lad to work helping me.

UNAUTHORIZED ABSENCE

What materials ought I to use, from which to sculpt the thousand channels in each wing? Offhand I could not have said. The names of the proper materials had not been included in the lesson seared into my brain; but the qualities those materials were required to possess had not been omitted. The substance at hand that most closely matched the requirements for the interior of the wings was wax, wax mixed with certain vegetable fibers, and sealed inside a sheathing of fine, thin leather. Fortunately for my project Minos had never been stingy; my workshop was well-stocked for a truly bizarre variety of projects, and by the favor of the gods everything I would need for this one was on hand.

I began by weighing and measuring both my son and myself. Then I cleared my workbench of the false start I had made on my own; then I

began to work hard, in sunlight by day, and
lamplight by night.

When I had the basic fabric of one large wing
completed, and had pierced it with a hundred
cunning perforations of the thousand that it must
ultimately have, I strapped it firmly onto my
left arm and shoulder and gave my arm a quick
push downward through the air, as if I were a
desperate bird. For just a moment my arm was
halted in mid-air by a responding pressure; for
just a moment it seemed to me as if the limb
had rested upon something solid and ready to
be climbed. In a state of considerable excitement I resumed my labors.

Days passed; how many, I did not notice.
One clouded night, when at last there were four
wings finished, with a thousand tiny channels
cut through each, I decided that we were ready
for a real trial. It was very difficult for one
person to put the wings on himself unaided, and
we had to assist each other. Then we climbed
up and out through the secret skylight above
the secret workshop, and stood upon the low
roof of the House. Ordering Icarus to wait, I
drew a deep breath and, encouraged by the
results of my limited indoor trials, launched
myself headlong from the edge of the roof out
over a ravine. Beating my wings, at first almost
in a panic, I mounted steadily into the sky.

There was a frantic initial awkwardness to be
overcome, the breathless feeling that at every
moment I was about to fall. But my confidence
increased with every wingbeat, every moment
of success, and before I had caused the lights of
the House to revolve three times below me, I

had started to learn to relax like a good swim-
mer. With each stroke the air beneath my wings
felt alternately as supportive as springy tree
branches, and as buoyant as sea water.

When I glided back to the roof and landed,
Icarus was waiting for me, clamoring as vocifer-
ously as he could in an enforced whisper for his
own chance to try. Next we plunged together
from the edge of the roof, and beat our way
completely around the palace at perhaps ten
times the height of a man, before I decided that
we had flown enough for one night, and that we
had better quit before we were seen.

The following night was cloudy too. Mounting
together once more into the air, we flew a greater
distance, going as far from the palace as Heraklion
and the edge of the ocean, rising as high as
birds, until what looked like a great part of the
northern shoreline of the island was vaguely
visible, picked out by the dots of fires in fishing
villages and isolated seashore camps and cottages.

It was so quiet in the air that we could talk to
each other almost in whispers.

"Father, we could just keep going, right now.
To anywhere we wanted."

"One night soon, Icarus, we'll do just that.
But there must be a few days left before the
earliest time when the king and queen could
possibly come back. And there are a few more
preparations we must make."

When after each flight we landed and crawled
back into the workshop through the secret skylight, I found that the wings had somehow been
warmed by their labor in the cool night air. And
strain my thought as I might at the problem, I

still had neither the words nor the ideas to make it clear to myself in my own mind just *how* they worked. That had not been part of the teaching.

Continued experiments indoors, in the daytime when the light was good, allowed us to see some puzzling things. A strong push down, with one completed wing, and you could sometimes see a vapor-puff as big as a pumpkin appear as if by magic in the beaten air, and fly off rearward, spinning gently. Icarus extending a hand into one of these puffs said that it felt quite cool.

Food and water and gold, in very small quantities, we were going to carry at our belts. We would wear a minimum of clothing, no more than loincloths, to save weight. My plan was to take wing just before dawn, and follow the northern coastline of Crete away from the onrushing sun, veering to the northwest when we came to the western end of the great island. The sun would be up by then, and the small island of Antikythera, and larger Kythera, must lie straight ahead of us. We ought to be able to reach Kythera in no more than a few hours' flight, if anything like the speed we had been able to attain at night could be sustained by day. I saw no reason why it should not be so.

We would be able to stop and rest, if necessary, somewhere on Antikythera or Kythera. After that, if all went well, the western coast of mainland Greece would serve as our guide, until we were far enough north and felt confident enough to strike out straight west over the Ionian Sea in the direction of southern Italy and Sicily.

On the island of Sicily ruled King Cocalus, who had long expressed his admiration of my work, and who had repeatedly invited me to come to work for him whenever I liked.

"Must we leave before dawn, father?"

"I think we must. Our servant will still be sleeping, and it will be safer. Now get some sleep."

. . . and I, the father, who cared more for my son than anything else I then possessed, dreamt of the flight before it happened.

I had not yet paid the price, but I knew that it would come. In my dream, squinting into the rising sun, feeling its touch already warm, I absently marked the dull sheen of its rays upon the wings of Icarus, and waited for the breath of wind that would come to help us rise among the gulls.

The real dawn overtook us just as I had planned, while we were passing westward over the northern coastline of Greece. It revealed to our eyes a beautiful daytime high-altitude world that we had never seen before.

For a brief period Icarus became very sportive with his wings, climbing and diving and trying to turn somersaults, urging his more cautious father to join in the fun. Momentarily tempted, I did an acrobatic twist or two. Then, after I had recovered from a temporary accidental plunge, I urged my son to greater caution.

We saw a few low-flying birds, who veered away from us crying in alarm.

We saw some people on the beach or in the water, fisherfolk up early, pointing at us and crying out in fear or admiration or perhaps both. Only the swifter runners below, racing on smooth sand, were able to keep up with the two flying figures in the sky.

One of those scampering figures had a bow slung on its back, and I, taking what I thought was prudent alarm, urged my son to a somewhat higher altitude. Now, being as I thought somewhat beyond bowshot, we resumed speed in a horizontal direction.

"Father, look there!"

A bronze-bright speck, glinting in the early sun, was darting toward us from the east, moving along the beach, outpacing running dogs with ease. Fisherfolk fell back as if in fear as the bright dot passed. In a few moments I was sure that the figure was that of Talus, coming at a run along the coast to overtake us. Perhaps someone had seen us rising on wings from the palace; perhaps the Bull still lived, to give his metallic servant orders, or perhaps the Bronze Man was capable of taking revenge upon his own initiative.

Though it seemed we must be safe from him at the distance we had attained, I did not in the least like the sight of that purposeful onrush, whatever authority had ordained it. "Higher, son. And we had better turn more out to sea."

Scarcely had we altered course in that direction when something, a missile of some kind flying too fast for me to see it, sang past us through the air.

"Faster, Icarus! Out to sea. And higher!"

Glancing back I saw the bronze arm, almost invisible with distance, draw back and then flash in a twinkling movement. A breath later, something, another invisible projectile, came whining straight between our airborne bodies.

"Hurry, Icarus! Twist and turn in flight!"

"Father—I—"

Then it was as if the Sun himself had stabbed us. The atmosphere around us wavered, and I think we both cried out in the intense heat. An almost invisible lance of power had struck at us. Something like a violet afterimage danced in the air between us and the Bronze Man. But the pain and the burning reached us only erratically. Our dodging in midair kept the weapon from being focused on us long enough to do real damage.

We labored on. The violet burning came again, but not quite as intense as before. I was beginning to think that we were safe, when, breaking the silence of mid-flight, there came a sound. In a moment I realized that this had been the muffled impact of some small missile tearing right through one of Icarus's wings, near the strapped root where it met the boy's shoulder.

I cried out my son's name, and he responded bravely. His own flesh was undamaged, and he could still fly, though now more slowly. Turning from right to left, trying to get my own wider pinions and larger body between my son and those deadly missiles, I did my best to urge Icarus on.

We continued to make steady headway out from shore. The next rock came more weakly, being visible through the upper portion of its trajectory and descending past us at an angle. The hurling machine, now standing up to its ankles in the waves, was working at the extreme limit of its range.

The wind, I thanked the gods, was in our favor, helping to carry us away from shore. The last rock thrown after us by Talus must have fallen into the sea some distance behind and below us, and I never heard its passage.

"Thank all the gods! You can still fly?"

"Yes, father." The boy sounded frightened but game.

"Then on, straight on. We dare not turn back."

I was concerned that Icarus with his damaged wing had some trouble in holding to a straight course, but I was reassured that my son was still able to maintain altitude.

Time passed. A grayish rock-speck of an island, uninhabited, waterless, useless except in the most immediate emergency, passed beneath us. We conferred in low, calm voices. If we were to stop upon that speck of land to rest, we would have to try to take off again from somewhere on its nearly level surface, scarcely above the level of the sea. And in my mind's eye I could visualize bronze Talus commandeering a boat, and rowing after us with inhuman speed and endurance. We decided that we should not stop.

The tiny island passed behind us.

From the look of the waves below, I thought that there might still be a mild breeze behind us, helping, pushing us toward our destination. But the only motion I could feel in the air was in the opposite direction, as we flew through it. When I thought upon the matter, I realized that this was logical.

Now a much larger island, one that could only be Antikythera, was coming clearly into our view ahead. There must, I thought, be Cretan settlements upon this isle; certainly there were patches of green, and some of them looked like cultivation.

Icarus now had to struggle continually to stay on course, as his right wing began to betray him more and more. Looking as carefully as possible at the constantly moving surface of the wing, I saw what turned my spirit dim within me. The hole made by Talus's missile was gradually tearing farther open, a little and a little more.

"Head this way, son. This way!"

"I can't, father—I—can't—fly straight—any more—" The child was laboring fiercely with his arms, running out of breath with which to talk. Panic was growing in his dark eyes, as he fiercely struggled to keep himself airborne.

In desperation I tried to fly close above my son, to help him somehow from above. But our hands were all but helpless, with our arms bound into wingstraps as they were. As I flew closer to my son I saw how the wax was starting to melt and run out of Icarus's right wing.

Next I flew underneath my son, and tried to offer support from that direction. But the necessary feat of balance appeared to be impossible to coordinate in midair. His feet that would have rested on my back slipped off, fell free, again and again.

Icarus's weakness was forcing him to fly lower and lower. Meanwhile another speck of land had appeared out of the sun-dazzling sea. It was closer than Antikythera, much closer. Now, tantalizingly, it was almost within reach.

"Father! Help! Help—"

My son's feet, that I had been trying to balance on my back in flight, slipped free one final time. Spinning out of control entirely, the boy's body plummeted away from me. Falling and falling. Shrinking and shrinking. By all the gods, and were we still so far above the water? Falling, like a bird struck in flight by a hurled stone, he splashed at last into the dark sea.

"Icarus. *Icarus!*"

But my cries went all unanswered by any gods of sea or sky. Only the raucous gulls flung back my shrieks of grief into the wind. The small splash made by the body of my son disappeared instantaneously amid the gentle waves.

I flew spiraling lower, my eyes still riveted upon the spot where he had vanished, my throat still screaming, hoarse and useless cries. I am sure that one or two tufts of feathers came to the surface, plumes that I in my pride had added to decorate my construction, and perhaps in hopes of some lingering effect of magic. Those feathers had pleased Icarus, the lad so interested in birds and egg-collecting.

I circled in the air. Nothing more came to the surface from below. Only the salt spray struck my face when I flew too low.

Wrenching myself free of the wave-crests, I flew on, borne by the freshening wind to the nearby beach of the tiny islet, where I landed hard, bruising and scraping myself on gravel and hard-packed sand. Not until much later was I aware that I had hurt myself.

One of my wings had been broken cleanly in the middle in the crash of my descent, and that fact made my movements a little easier when I began to try to tear the useless things completely from my arms.

Still the remnants of my wings impeded my progress as I raced into the mild surf, looking out to sea and screaming my child's name. The exact spot where Icarus had vanished was of course impossible to determine, yet in my madness I was sure that I knew just where it was. I believed that above the dulling roar of surf and wind I could somehow hear my son's voice as he cried continuously to me for help.

I do not remember retreating from the surf again. What I remember next is sitting on the sand or shingle, facing into a wind that carried the beginning of rain, a wind that streaked my graying beard across my face and out behind me.

How long I sat there staring madly out to sea I do not know. I was oblivious to the squall as it broke over me, and to the wind as it tore further at the fragments of my wings that were still strapped to my arms and shoulders.

At some point I lapsed into unconsciousness.

I awakened slowly, lying on my side, chilled and stiffened in the lighter, different breeze of another morning. Before full wakefulness arrived, there was one tolerable moment in which I thought that Kalliste and I were somehow together again, back in Athens. Then the moment of respite passed. Stirring slowly, I squinted my eyes in a new day's sun. Gulls were walking

on the sand nearby, prowling the littoral in
search of food, and it was their cries that had
dragged me out of slumber.

Then I sat with a groan. I could feel that my
lips were cracked; I was intensely thirsty.

The surf was never still. It mocked me. Somehow it seemed that I had been listening to those
mumbling, pounding waves for years.

My eyes were closed again. It may be that
once more I fainted. But presently new sounds
were demanding my attention. In time the realization penetrated my thoughts that some of the
cries I now heard were issuing from the throats
of men and not of birds.

Opening my eyes again, I saw that a ship was
standing only an arrow-flight offshore, her sails
furled and her oar-banks, twelve blades on a
side, all manned. Even as I shaded my eyes to
see, someone hailed me from the ship again.
Unable to answer, unable to think of what these
people might want of me or even to see them
clearly, I waited dumbly to see what would
happen next.

When those aboard her were sure that I was
alive, the ship—a Phoenician by the look of
her—turned her prow in to shore, and presently her oarsmen had driven her neatly upon
the beach. Figures leaped into the gentle surf.

"What have we here?" A man was saying in
accented Greek as he came close to me. Then I
was surrounded by men. I could hear their
voices, speaking Phoenician, as from a distance.
Presently someone was holding a skin of water
to my lips. I was helped to my feet.

The captain of the ship was a spare and wiry

man a few years younger than myself, with a
bold eye, and his dark hair tied up in a long
queue. He introduced himself as Kena'ani. The
captain and his crew were obviously impressed
by the remnants of my wings, though they hardly
knew what to make of them.

They kept asking me: "How did you come
here?"

I stirred myself at last, and answered them,
fearing that otherwise they might return me to
Crete. "I am a castaway, as you see," I said. We
were both speaking Greek by this time, as educated strangers encountering each other commonly do.

By now Kena'ani's men had pulled their lightly-
laden ship up halfway onto the beach, and, with
an eye to taking practical advantage of her situation, were looking at some spots of the hull that
I supposed must be starting to give them trouble. Out had come the calking pitch and fiber,
as well as the mallets and chisels with which to
force the stuff into the seams between her planks.

Then a cry was raised by one of the men,
who, posted as lookout, had walked some way
down the beach.

"A dead boy, drowned! And he still has wings
strapped onto him."

That roused me, and in my grief I rushed past
those startled men to reclaim what was left of
Icarus from where the waves had tossed him.
The traders watched, not without sympathy, and
waited to see what burial customs I would want
to follow. Presently I was able to regain some
control of myself, and went about doing what
had to be done. I placed a speck of gold in the

dead mouth, and hacked off my own gray hair and beard as a sign of mourning.

What remained of the tiny amount of gold Icarus had been carrying I gave to the ship-captain, in return for a live bird to kill over the grave in sacrifice, and some wine to pour on it. Though Kena'ani's ship was far from heavily laden, her cargo was able to afford these.

By this time I had so far regained my senses as to be able to thank the captain for his kindness to a strange castaway.

The captain had helped me gently remove the wings from the dead body of Icarus; and he asked me if I wanted them.

"I never want to see them again."

Quietly Kena'ani ordered one of his men to put them away on board the ship, though at the time I did not realize this, and thought the wings had simply been discarded.

"So you and your son were flying?" The captain's disbelief was plain in his tone. "Is that how you arrived here?"

"Yes. We were flying." I cared nothing whether I was believed or not.

"Where were you bound?"

"To Sicily—to anywhere but Crete."

"We have nothing better to do than go to Sicily," said Kena'ani. And again he had private conversation with some of his crew.

I started, at the sound of a wild cry from the sea, for I thought that again I had heard Icarus screaming. But this time it was only a gull.

FIELD TRIP

Since mainland Greece had dropped from sight astern we had made a long voyage. Struggling for many days, at times beset by unfavorable winds, we were at last able to effect a passage straight west across the Ionian Sea. This voyage gave me time to recover from the first raw grief attendant upon the death of Icarus. And thanks to my new friend the Phoenician captain, who insisted upon giving me gifts from the hodge-podge of freight with which his ship was laden, I was able to exchange my Cretan loincloth for garments more suitable for a man of wealth and substance to wear in Sicily. Not that I was wealthy, or wanted to appear so, but I had retained a morsel of gold, and so was not dependent upon charity.

The fact that I had never visited Sicily before rather surprised me, when I thought of it. Of course I knew that the land just below the toe of

Italy was a huge island, much larger even than
Crete; and my first sight of our destination, as
we approached the coastline near Siracusa, reminded me somewhat of my late place of exile.
The mountains of Sicily, like those Cretan peaks,
were impressive when seen from sea level; I
took particular note of the smoldering volcano
Etna, which was easily visible from the sea
though a considerable distance inland.

Then as now, Phoenician traders were generally welcome in any of the Sicilian ports, as they
were almost everywhere. Kena'ani said that he
had several good friends in the port of Siracusa,
where we put in.

The port at Siracusa could not compare with
Heraklion in the matter of size. But it was busy,
and on the docks one heard the same babel of
tongues as in the harbor beneath the castle of
Minos. No single sovereign had yet been able to
unite under his rule this oversized island, but
boundaries in general did not mean much to a
Phoenician trader.

Kena'ani's friends were helpful. Within a day
after we put into port, I was on my way inland,
headed in the direction of the territory gov-
erned by King Cocalus, which I was informed
compromised something less than a third of the
whole island. Kena'ani accompanied me, leaving his ship and crew in charge of his mate, a
countryman of his in whom he appeared to have
every confidence.

Our journey to the interior of the island was
fortunately uneventful. We traveled accompanied by a local guide, first by donkey and then
on foot. Scarcely two more days had passed

before we were standing in the presence of
Cocalus himself, whose palace, of which he was
quite proud, would have made a respectable
manor house in some suburb of Knossos. Our
meeting with the king took place in an audience
room that I at first glance took to be some
adjunct of Cocalus's stables, so great was the
contrast between what passed for grandeur in
this petty kingdom and what I had grown accustomed to while dwelling in the House of the
Double Axe.

Kena'ani was admitted first, while I waited in
an anteroom. Then it was my turn. The king
here sat on a great chair of black wood, somewhat larger than the Cretan throne though of
vastly less importance. Cocalus was a spare,
wizened man with a face like a dried fruit, very
much less impressive than Minos, and not only
because of the disparity in dress and personal
appearance.

This Sicilian monarch, twice widowed, had at
this time no visible queen, but was supported
on his throne and sometimes overwhelmed by
an entourage of three buxom daughters, named
Aglaia, Euphrosyne, and Thalia, after the Three
Graces of ancient legend. Aglaia and Euphrosyne,
the elder two, were certainly of an age to be
considered eligible for marriage. And assuredly
they were in no danger of being sent to school
in Crete, in view of the smoldering, long-standing
antagonism between Minos and their father.

The dress of all three Sicilian princesses would
have been unexceptional in Greece, but struck
me as startlingly modest, accustomed as I was to
the fashions of the Cretan court. Still, certain

hints of facial expression and behavior by the
princesses, even at that first meeting, gave me
to suspect that these young women might not
always be models of propriety.

From the suspicious way in which the king
gazed at me when I was presented to him, and
from the tenor of his first questions, I realized
at once that he had some doubts about my true
identity.

My benefactor the ship captain had had his
conversation with Cocalus first, and I, on entering the room, soon realized that one of the chief
topics of their talks must have been the wings
removed from the body of my son. Ever since
leaving the grave of Icarus I had assumed that
Kena'ani or his men had buried or discarded
those hateful devices somewhere, and indeed I
had no wish to see them ever again; but there
those poor relics were when I came in, spread
out on a table before his Majesty.

The pinions which had borne Icarus to his
doom had been completely ruined by their im-
mersion in the sea and violent return to land.
The fine pores of the leather surface were clogged
with sand, and all the slender stiffening members broken by the impact of sand and surf.
Indeed, those wings were so badly damaged
that no one looking at them would be likely to
suspect that they had ever functioned properly.

I stared at those crumpled pieces of leather
and wax, and was surprised at how little emotion I felt on beholding them; the weight of my
son's death was still with me, and those wings
could do nothing to bring back a burden that
had never lifted.

"Wings, hey?" said the king now, as if he had just noticed them. He reached out a jeweled hand and toyed with the frayed leather end of one poor pinion, making it flap back and forth. It looked very ineffectual indeed. "Daedalus, do you expect anyone to believe that you actually flew, with wings like these, from Crete to that nameless little island where you were picked up?"

"I do not expect anything, sire." Then I understood from the king's eyes that that was too blunt a reply. "Your pardon, Majesty. What I meant was that I am confident your royal wisdom will penetrate to the essential truth of the matter. The truth is that the wings were an experiment that had initial success, but ultimately failed. I am not anxious to repeat that effort, nor would I recommend it to anyone else."

There was a silence. King Cocalus, who had doubtless been prepared to deal with a slippery imposter pretending to have priceless secrets, or even a genuine inventor out to impress him with exaggerated claims, appeared not to know quite what to make of a man who was not out to convince him of anything.

His daughters however did have something to say at this point—a number of things, in fact—and all three of them began to speak at once. The older two in particular appeared to take my part, for which I was grateful, and they looked at my poor son's wings with interest and sympathy, and questioned me about him, and about any other close relatives that I might have. They

shook their heads in apparently genuine sadness
when I reported that there were none.

At last, when the princesses had for the moment satisfied their curiosity and their urge to
talk, the king looked at me closely once again.
In a more kindly voice he said: "Rest, then,
Daedalus. Rest and heal, if you can. I will send
my physicians to look at you, and I will talk to
you again when you have begun to expect things
once more."

I was somewhat annoyed with Kena'ani, for
preserving the wings without my knowledge and
then trying to sell them to this king, along with
my services as wingmaker. But when the captain and I were outside the audience room again
and I had a chance to speak to him privately, I
found that he was even more annoyed with me.
He had been in hopes of receiving a quick reward from the king, for bringing him such a
treasure as myself, but, in Kena'ani's view, my
behavior had spoiled this plan.

"So now," the captain complained, "he has
got it into his head that we are out to swindle
him somehow. He doesn't know whether to order you to begin making wings at once, or to
forbid it."

Shortly after we had left the audience chamber a message came to both of us from the king;
he was insisting that we both stay on indefinitely as his royal guests.

Kena'ani on hearing this brightened noticeably, while I did not know whether to be pleased
or not.

The next day I was summoned to talk to the king again, this time alone.

Another surprise awaited me at this second meeting with Cocalus, in the form of another exile from the court of Aegeus. I had known this man slightly at the court of King Aegeus, and despite my changed appearance—I was worn by grief, imprisonment, and danger, and my hair and beard had been cut crudely short in mourning—he was able to identify me as the almost legendary Daedalus, fellow exile from Athens.

Despite this positive identification, Cocalus was still skeptical of my credentials—or of something about me. Still, the king seemed to be trying sincerely to settle his persistent doubts; and in the course of this meeting it occurred to him that the best way to do so would be to set me a task and see if I fulfilled it in a truly Daedalian way.

By this time I thought I could see what was coming, and my suspicions were not wrong: it was to be plumbing again. I sometimes think that if my name is remembered at all by the inhabitants of the earth in the far future, it will be for my handiness with pipes and basins and running water, surely matters that require more diligence than inventiveness to master.

The king and I, as I say, began to discuss plumbing. And in the process of our tentative planning, the project, as projects are wont to do, became ever more grandiose. The king's three daughters intruded upon our meeting before it half over, and when they discovered what was under discussion, they adopted the idea unanimously and began to nag unmercifully to have new bathrooms finished for them at once. I think what most intrigued them about the project at that time was the possibility of having a luxurious bath without a single servant in attendance to overhear their intrigues and their gossip.

The next day a score of workers, some of them incompetent, many of them only indifferently skilled, and a very few quite worthy, were placed at my disposal. For my workshop I was assigned the main section of the abandoned stable that passed for the royal manufactory, and again my tasks commenced. Progress at the start was slow; I was quickly made to understand that this was no Crete, where all who pretended to be artisans were used to diligent and meaningful labor at the king's command. Still, the king seemed to find my early efforts satisfactory, another difference between himself and Minos.

I had been employed thus for some ten days, working with copper and lead, terra cotta and plans, and training my workers, when Kena'ani, who was growing ever more fretful and anxious to depart, was visited by a delegation from his crew. The men who had remained aboard ship had grown worried and uncertain by reason of our long absence from the port. Restlessly seeking information on the docks at Siracusa, they had heard confused reports of how their captain and I were being detained by King Cocalus. At length, not knowing what else to do, they had dispatched a few of their members into the interior of the island, in an effort to find out how matters actually stood with us.

We informed the worried sailors that while our situation was not exactly what we might have wished, yet still it could have been much worse. The king, as we assured ourselves and Kena'ani's crewmen, was not likely to detain a Phoenician sea-captain very long for no good reason, whatever His Highness might elect to do with a foreign artisan. Word of such abuse would get around, and the sea-trade was too important to risk for anyone who claimed to be a monarch, even of a domain so largely inland as this one.

The sailors who had come to ascertain our fate also brought us some news of the outside world. I was particularly interested to hear a story involving Theseus, Ariadne, and Phaedra. There were two versions of this tale; the first said that the older daughter of Minos had been abandoned on the island of Naxos by her faithless lover, who had then blithely sailed off with her younger sister. The second report was much more reasonable, and I was more inclined to believe it—it said only that the black-sailed ship of the Prince of Athens had been seen putting in at Naxos, with the two princesses on board.

Two of the sailors who came inland had heard other, possibly related news: that the strange phenomena involving gods and monsters, with which Thera had been infected for a generation or longer, were now reported to have spread to the somewhat larger island of Naxos to the north.

* * *

The delegation of seamen returned to their ship, somewhat reassured by our good spirits and the mild manner of the king who still insisted that we enjoy his hospitality. Another month passed at the court of Cocalus, while the king remained indecisive about me and the wings, his daughters yearned for their new baths, Kena'ani fretted, and I trained my staff of workers and labored at my task of plumbing. And then part of yet another month went by.

Here, in contrast to the situation on Crete, the best source of water was a mountain stream, a surface flow as opposed to springs. But the two places were alike in that the best source was at some distance from the king's chief residence, and a lengthy pipeline was required.

The royal daughters, Aglaia, Euphrosyne, and Thalia, all continued to take an interest in the work. The poor girls had little else to do; they were bored in their father's lonely kingdom, and could afford to invest their attention even in an itinerant plumber and a Phoenician sailor. I believe one of them at least took a notion to get me into her bed, probably out of sheer boredom; but I considered myself too wise to get into such an intrigue with any daughter of any king, and took such precautions as I could. I ignored temptation and stuck to my job. How Kena'ani fared I do not know, but he was wiser in the ways of the world, or some of them at least, than I.

There was another intrigue practiced upon me by the king's daughters, and on this one they were more insistent. It consisted in getting me to make wings for each of them, without their father hearing of the project. The princesses went to the trouble of arranging a secret place for me to work in. Teasingly they promised me great rewards, not all in gold, if I succeeded in providing them with what they wanted, and they more than hinted that they could make great trouble for me if I did not. I had doubts of the reward, but no doubts at all about the trouble, and reluctantly I began to comply with their wishes. I took care however, that the first pair of wings I made were constructed to my own measurements, so that if an emergency arose I might be able to use them to escape—naturally the princesses did not realize this, and each of them counted on being able to get the first pair for herself as soon as it was finished. Remembering how in my previous design the wax had overheated and softened with prolonged use in bright daylight, I painted the improved model a silvery white, the better to reflect the sun's heat.

Then to our small palace there came startling news, which Euphrosyne was first to tell me: that King Minos, or at least a man claiming to be that monarch, had arrived in Sicily with a small entourage, and was quoted as saying, among other things, that he was looking for me.

At first I was almost sure that the princesses were joking when they told me that King Minos of Crete was on their island, for one of their many developed skills was that of inventing wild stories. But when they had left me alone again and I had a chance to think the matter over, I was far from certain that they were not serious. Certainly Minos and his queen must have been back in Crete from their diplomatic tour for well over a month now, and certainly his reaction to the situation he found at home on his return must have been one of rage and a desire to be revenged on those he deemed responsible. Having known the king for some years, I thought he would be capable of going to great lengths to obtain revenge; his personal world must have been virtually destroyed, by the death of the Bull and the departure of both his daughters.

By this time also the first of the new baths, built as an addition at one corner of the modest palace, was approaching a state of readiness. I could assure King Cocalus that in a very short time a demonstration would be possible. Hot water would be provided from a rooftop tank headed by the sun. At night or on cool, cloudy days, a charcoal-burning brazier could do the job.

It was at about this time that another chance traveler arriving at Cocalus's court brought with him a story from Crete, a tale that had obviously grown as it traveled: it said that the craftsman Daedalus, who was still in residence upon that island, had constructed for Queen Pasiphaë a wooden cow, in which she had concealed herself, to receive in her lascivious body the lustful Bull; and that Minos on at last discovering the truth about the wooden cow, had slain his wife in a fit of rage. Daedalus had apparently been excused. It was rumored also that the White Bull had survived the attack by Theseus and was still alive. Though some said that the god was paralyzed, he was still capable of contriving to take vengeance upon others for his condition.

Among the people who retailed these stories at a distance, and those who enjoyed hearing them, none had ever come in close contact with the Bull, but to them it was obvious that such a being must be a god. So too, I thought, the case was likely to be with the strange creatures inhibiting Thera, whether or not they were of the same race as the Bull of Crete. It was quite possible, I thought, that there, too, the facts were much at variance with the rumors.

I sought out the traveler who had brought the most recent story of the visiting Minos, and talked to him alone, wishing to hear in detail all that he had to say. To my regret he could only repeat hearsay regarding the events on Crete; but fortunately he was able to give a firsthand account of some of the things Minos had actually been doing in Sicily.

It was probably true that the White Bull still lived, and there was no reason to think Queen Pasiphaë had really been murdered. But the ruler of Crete, punished by the desertion of his daughters and only heirs, had decided, or had somehow been compelled, to take to the sea in a penitential pilgrimage, trying to make amends to the gods for the attack upon their gift, the White Bull. Since the arrival in Sicily of King Minos—there was no doubt that it was really he—the king had acted and spoken as if he were at least half-crazy. Minos was reported as saying, among other things, that he wished to reward his former chief engineer, Daedalus, for all the marvelous work the artisan had performed for the king on Crete.

I went away from this interview frowning, not really understanding the behavior of Minos as it was reported, and certainly not liking it.

Within a few days of that first warning, other reports about King Minos reached my ears. It was now certain beyond doubt that he was actually in Sicily, by all reports traveling with only a small entourage, and showing little regard for his own security. All this was indeed unlike him. Those who had seen and talked with him did not know what to make of his behavior, and thought he must be indeed strongly under the influence of some god.

"What do you want me to do, Daedalus, when unfortunate Minos comes here?" King Cocalus asked me. "I felt that I could do no less than to forget our past difficulties and offer him entertainment when he is traveling so far from home." As Cocalus spoke his face wore the expression he was wont to use whenever he thought he had conceived a shrewd test by which to try the loyalty of someone. Cocalus was not the wisest nor the cleverest king that I have ever met—the pair of wings that I had built at the urging of his daughters were virtually complete at this time, lying in a workshop within a stone's throw of his bedroom, and I believe that he had no suspicion of their existence. Fortunately for him his clever daughters were all content to sustain him in his power.

I replied: "I am glad, my lord, to leave the matter in your hands. Certainly I have no wish to return to Crete with Minos, or to be anywhere but where I am. I do not particularly wish to see my former patron, but I am not afraid to do so." The simple truth has been known to cause problems on occasion, but not as often as its substitutes are wont to do.

Cocalus appeared to be pleased with my truthful answer, and sent me back to work. I pondered the invitation. It was common knowledge that for a long time my new patron had been no friend of the powerful sea-king.

And now I come to another of the sadder chapters in my story.

Until the last minute I continued to hope that Minos would bypass the court where I had found refuge; ordinary prudence ought to have kept him from putting himself virtually in the power of an old and unforgiven adversary. But what a man will do when he considers himself to be acting under a god's command—or when he is under the teaching influence of the White Bull— passes ordinary prudence.

A day came when my friend Kena'ani was at last allowed to take his departure from the court. We parted with some sadness on both sides, though the captain's regrets at parting were noticeably dimmed by his prospects for freedom.

Later in the same day on which Kena'ani took his departure, the royal visitor arrived. Minos was accompanied by a small entourage, which included only a few armed men. The members of this Cretan escort, while they smiled at their hosts, were nervous about the situation in which they now found themselves. But King Cocalus, seeming to have put all enmity aside, made the visitors welcome, and did his rather feeble best to provide a royal entertainment. That evening there was music, dancing girls, and feasting.

Through most of the day I, with my new patron's agreement, kept myself well out of the Cretan's sight. But I was told by one of the princesses that King Minos was asking after me, and did not seem angry. So a little later, during the course of that evening's festivities, I appeared in public.

My former patron, on being assured that I was present, soon found a chance to talk to me alone—I made no serious effort to avoid him, wanting to do my best to explain to him that I was guiltless in the matter of the downfall of his House.

The two of us encountered one another in near-darkness, with torches and naked dancers in the background. For the moment no one else was within hearing. Even in the darkness I could see that Minos had lost a considerable amount of weight, and that his face was haggard. His eyes gleamed with the sparks of the distant torches, and his clothing, that of an almost impoverished traveler, had been neglected.

"How is it with you, Daedalus?" King Minos's voice, far from being enraged, sounded uncharacteristically soft and almost wistful. There was nothing extreme in that voice—yet listening to it, I felt a chill, and understood why some who had talked to this man since he came to Sicily were certain that he was mad.

"It is well with me, great king." I bowed my head in fear, though here at Cocalus's court I felt—almost surely—that I was secure. "I have long feared the wrath of this great monarch of Crete."

"My wrath, Daedalus. No. No, all wrath has gone from me. Because I have listened to the teachings of the Bull, great is his wisdom. And the White Bull has told me that I must make peace with you, and with the king who has given you shelter." And here the King of Crete fell silent, gazing past me toward the firelight.

Having experienced the force of some of those teachings myself, I felt a shiver. But I said nothing.

"I have brought you a gift," King Minos went on at last, surprising me in no small measure. And he drew from inside his robe a small wooden chest, cunningly worked of several varieties of wood, inlaid and veneered together, and not much bigger than my two fists held together. He held the box out toward me, and made a gesture urging me to take it, and at last I did. The little chest was even lighter than I had somehow expected.

"Your Majesty is far too kind." I felt that was an appropriately logical reply to a completely mad speech.

"The gift is not only from me, but from my queen as well. And most especially it is from the White Bull, who sends his wishes that it may bring you the favor of all the gods of earth."

"I am glad to know that the Bull is still alive."

"Alive. Oh, yes. He is alive and teaching. He even told me to tell you that he regrets any harm that his bronze tool may have caused you or your son."

Muttering something that I cannot remember

now, some confused statement in the nature of
regrets or thanks, I ran my hands over the
surface of the gift, which was hard to see clearly
in the light of distant fires. The small coffer was
closed by a tightly fastened lid. It was possibly
of Egyptian workmanship, and I thought it must
be of some considerable value in itself. The king
had spoken of his gift in an almost reverent
tone, as if it might be of truly enormous value.
Certainly it was not nearly heavy enough to be
full of gold.

"What is it, sire?" I asked.

"It is a sacrifice. If you offer it up properly, to
the proper god, it will gain you—everything."
And again the eyes of Minos glittered.

Again I thought some kind of madness trembled in his voice, and I was afraid.

"Daedalus," the king whispered.

"Sire?"

"It will be better, perhaps, if you do not open
your gift before you offer it as sacrifice. Better if
you do not see what you are giving to the gods
of earth. I brought it here—I brought it here to
Crete . . ."

"Sire?"

Eventually the eyes of Minos came back to
me. ". . . Daedalus? . . . yes. I brought the
treasure here, to throw it with my own hands
into Etna, that the benefit of the sacrifice might
accrue to you, and to my brother Cocalus, and
all his people. But the Fates have set their
hands upon me, and my life is nearly finished."

I bowed my head.

"I owe you much, Daedalus. So now the gift,
the sacrifice, is yours to make. Before you do

so, you should first gather your friends about you. In particular your new patron and his daughters. It would be better if they were present too, that they may share more fully in the blessings of the goddess Gaea and the god Poseidon." The king's voice was growing stranger and stranger. "I shall tell Cocalus of the gift tonight."

"It shall be as you wish, Majesty," I murmured, feeling a great curiosity about the closed casket. At the same time I was in no great hurry to open it. I could wish that I had never accepted this particular gift, but the Fates had ordained otherwise, and now it was too late for such a wish.

The king was almost babbling. "I brought it here to Sicily to make sacrifice in my own interest. I was afraid that I would never see you again, Daedalus. But now I have seen you, and I have put the gift of the White Bull directly into your hands with my own." And then King Minos laughed; and presently, walking as if he were newly invigorated, he left me, and rejoined his host King Cocalus and the others who were watching the dancers.

For my part, I walked away in the other direction, with the small mysterious casket held in both my hands. Nothing moved inside the box when I shook it lightly, nothing made a sound. Sooner or later I would have to tell King Cocalus about it, but for the time being I took it to my lodgings and put it under my bed.

The visiting king was being lodged in the new wing of the modest palace, in the new apartment where only a few hours ago I had given the new plumbing its first complete test. From my own lodgings I went back to inspect the plumbing yet again. Everything, I thought, was in good working order; under the watchful care of a trusted servant, charcoal burned in the heater on the roof, keeping an ample supply of hot water in readiness.

Then I returned to the courtyard where the banquet was beginning. While it was in progress I failed somehow to find a good opportunity to revisit my own modest quarters and open the small chest. I ate moderately, and indulged only very lightly in wine. And as the hour grew late, before the King of Crete entered his guest quarters to retire, I returned yet again to his room to make a final inspection of the facilities. Something besides the gift was worrying me and I was not sure what.

The bath was as big as the bedroom, and contained a deep marble bathtub, almost an artificial pond, actually broad and deep enough for swimming. The tub was empty now, but it could be filled quickly, through the shower heads above it and the gold spouts and faucets at the side. All the newly designed fixtures were in readiness.

From somewhere out of sight I could hear a faint but steady drip of water; some imperfectly leaded pipe, I thought. Nothing worth bothering about tonight.

Yet I could not shake my restless mood. I tried my best to put away all thoughts of the secret gift of Minos and the Bull. Before retiring I took myself up to the roof once more, wanting to check yet again the new plumbing that had already been checked and tested a dozen times. I told myself that I feared some defect would show up, and that I would be blamed for it.

At the banquet Minos had spent a considerable time talking alone with Cocalus, and I worried about what the two kings might have decided in private, and if it had anything to do with me. Could their old enmity have been healed, and an alliance formed? Much would depend upon the attitude of the three Sicilian princesses toward their Cretan guest. They had attended the banquet too, of course, but I thought they might have been excluded from the discussions at the highest level.

The water tanks on the roof were not directly above the suite where Cocalus was lodging, but atop an adjoining wing of the palace, and the water from them went down through slanted pipes to the guest bathroom. Now I found an elderly slave tending the charcoal braziers that provided for hot water after sundown. The slave was doing a good job of keeping the fires up.

In fact it seemed to me that he was overdoing matters. I cautioned him: "No more fuel, or the water will start to boil and we'll have steam. That won't do at all."

The slave, like most of his class not afraid of me at all, stubbornly insisted that he had been ordered not to let the tank grow cool. But I persisted, and eventually persuaded him that some moderation in the fires was necessary.

From my vantage point on the roof beside the tanks, it was possible to see down at an angle through the roof-opening of a small atrium, directly into the very room where the visiting monarch was about to bathe.

Two or three other people were in the guest suite with Minos now. That would not have been surprising, but the people I observed were not the attendants who had been with him earlier. Nor were they concubines provided by his host. I experienced a chill near my heart when I saw that all three of the daughters of Cocalus had decided to pay Minos a nocturnal visit in his bath and bedroom.

I stood on the roof watching, wondering what this turn of events might portend for my future, while the princesses, who had come very informally dressed to begin with, delighted their royal guest by removing in turn certain items of their remaining clothing. Aglaia had come equipped with a set of pan-pipes, or had found them in the apartment, and piped a cheerful air with creditable skill. Meanwhile her sisters performed a teasing dance, that led their royal partner on a circuitous route through the room of the suite, ending in the new bath. At about this time I realized that the sisters had even persuaded Minos to send his personal bodyguards out of the room.

Now it appeared that the princesses were preparing to share with the befuddled king the inaugural bath of the new Daedalian plumbing. Some at least of the faucets had been opened, and a pond of steaming water was swelling up rapidly in the great tub. I wanted to leave my observation post—could they possibly discover that I was watching?—and at the same time I thought it vitally important to my own future that I know what was going on.

Meanwhile the hot water was still pouring heavily into the huge tub. From the way it steamed, it was easy to see that the admixture of cold water must be very small or nonexistent. I saw this, and yet in my simple artisan's innocence, I did not yet begin to understand.

Now Minos, himself naked, had been allowed to capture all three of his softly playful quarry. All were standing crowded together near the tub. With much laughter and energetic gestures the three girls, themselves in the last stages of disrobing, were assuring him that the bath facilities had already been tested. Suddenly for some reason I thought that they were talking about me. It was certainly not impossible that my name should have been mentioned, for the plumbing they were about to enjoy was mine, as was that which Minos was accustomed to using at home.

Only now did I fully realize that the sisters had managed to dismiss all of the slaves who would usually have been in attendance at a bath, their own as well as Minos's.

Minos was standing beside the sunken tub and fondling one of the sisters—I do not now remember which one—when the other two moved even closer to them, each of the two taking the monarch by one of his arms. In that moment, at last, I understood, too late to have done anything had there been anything for me to do. In the next moment, just after my shock of realization, the man had been tipped and pushed straight into the scalding water. A scream the like of which I have seldom heard tore out into the night.

Then, when Minos screamed again, and would have scrambled out of the burning tub, his three soft lovely killers shoved him fiercely back, with shrieks of laughter, so that the King of Crete, howling most pitiably, slid down the smooth and slippery side of the great tub, slid back helplessly into the steam and the murderous heat.

And now Euphrosyne was turning on yet another of the multiple shower heads, spouting yet more almost-boiling water in upon the helpless victim.

That was the last event inside the bath that I saw from the roof. In another moment I had broken free of my momentary paralysis and was scrambling down the nearest ladder, adding my own cries of alarm to the uproar Minos was still making. Charging into the nearest ground-level entrance of the palace, I turned toward the guest quarters. The door to Minos's private suite was latched, but Minos's Cretan bodyguards burst it open even as I arrived behind them.

I was next into the bathroom after them, and like them I was too late to be of the least help to the victim. By this time the three princesses had somehow disappeared.

Looping towels and sheets around the king's body where it floated, the Cretans and I dragged him from the still almost-boiling water. The soul of the victim had not yet quite departed, but he looked at us through eyes that seemed already to be peering from another world; it was obvious to me, from my first close look at the corpse-like whiteness of his steamed and parboiled body, that the King of Crete was already a dead man.

We laid him at full length on the tiles of the bathroom floor, and stood around him. There was nothing further we could do.

At the moment Minos did not seem to be in pain. He recognized me.

"Daedalus?"

"Sire, if there is anything that I—"

"Swear something to me, Daedalus." Word by word, the voice of Minos was sinking into a poisoned whisper.

"Anything, my lord." At such moments are rash words uttered that shock the gods.

"The gift I gave you . . ."

"Yes, Your Majesty."

"I want you to swear to me, Daedalus . . . that the gift I have brought you from myself, my queen, and the White Bull . . . swear by all you hold holy, that it will be sacrificed to the goddess and the god of earth, as I told you."

"I swear that it shall be as you say."

By now the three sisters, who had been nowhere in sight when the bodyguards and I burst in, had reappeared again. They were all wrapped in matrons' robes, as if they had retired decently for the night and then had been roused by the disturbance. And they were talking, sounding petulantly upset as at the spoiling of a party. They bustled about in the bathroom, giving irrelevant orders to the servants, who had also reappeared, and vaguely complaining that one of the slaves must be to blame for the tragic scalding.

Thalia met my eye, saw that I knew more

than she had thought, and drew me aside briefly.
To others it might have appeared that she was
questioning me on the tragedy, but in fact she
was imparting information.

"Know, Daedalus," she whispered, "that our
father was making plans, bad plans, with this
one who lies on the floor. You were to be sent
back to Crete as Minos's captive, in return for a
few maritime concessions. Our father has never
believed in your wings—but we know better."
And the princess smiled confidentially and left
me.

By this time it seemed that everyone in the
palace, drawn by the uproar, was trying to crowd
into the new bath. After uttering his last words
to me, Minos lay breathing lightly, staring
through an opening in the roof, as if he could
see death coming for him from the sky.

Meanwhile the members of the visiting king's
Cretan escort were hastily gathering in the apartment where their lord had been fatally scalded.
Some high-ranking folk among them demanded
explanations, but I thought that their demands
were half-hearted. From their first look at their
master they must have known that he could not
possibly survive, and it was now time to see to
their own welfare as best they could.

The three princesses departed, some time before Cocalus at last appeared. The king, doubtless coming from a conference with his daughters,
coolly offered his royal sympathies to the members of the Minoan entourage. He assured the
Cretans in a calm voice that there would be a
complete investigation of the accident, and that

whichever slaves were found to bear responsibility would certainly be executed.

Then Cocalus asked the Cretans if they wanted to take the body of their king with them when they left. This was even a few moments before the Cretan king had actually breathed his last.

The handful of high-ranking folk of Crete who had accompanied Minos to this place were frightened, and at the same time I thought they were in some sense relieved. Several of them now admitted to me in whispers that the king had been mad during the last month or two of his life. None of them mentioned the plan to return me to Crete, or the gift Minos had handed me—perhaps none of them knew their king had been carrying it.

One of the Cretan nobles did utter some sober words, for my ears only, about the dangers of anyone's returning to Crete. Observing these people, I felt sure that even among themselves there was now widespread doubt as to whether they wanted to go back.

Now that they were freed of the constraint of Minos's presence, some of them had some new stories to relate about the Bull and the queen.

And another member of the delegation hinted that Minos had planned to see to it that I died horribly, if ever he were able to get me into his power again.

A process of ritual mourning was outlined, to begin at dawn. Meanwhile I spent most of the hour after the king's death talking quietly with the visitors, wanting to know if they would converse more freely now that their master was dead. But there was little that the visiting Cretans were able to tell me about Theseus, or about the royal princesses of Crete, who were still said to be living abroad somewhere. Some stories still put the princesses on Naxos, and by some Prince Theseus was thought to be still there as well.

I thought with some sadness of Ariadne at least, who had considered me a trusted adviser, almost, as I thought, an uncle.

Despite the death of my would-be persecutor, I did not retire that night to my usual room to sleep. I had collaborated only indirectly in the death of Minos, and that death in itself was not greatly displeasing to Cocalus. With the ruling house of Crete in such disarray, he probably feared no military retaliation. But I knew that whatever King Cocalus might say to me now, and however he might congratulate himself upon the elimination of a rival, he would someday begin to look upon me as a regicide. Nor would he himself ever, I suppose, dare to take a shower in any plumbing of my construction, whatever precautions I might build in against a repetition of the "accident."

I thought that my Phoenician friend Kena'ani, having departed just before the arrival of Minos, must still be on his way overland to the port where his ship lay. It seemed to me that with my wings I ought to be able to overtake him easily before he reached it.

I felt a deep reluctance to fly again for any purpose. But I could foresee only trouble for myself if I remained—trouble that would be multiplied whether I actually made wings for the princesses to fly with, or finally refused to do so.

I put on my secret wings, and leaped into the air from the roof of that shabby palace, and soared into the night. I did not forget to carry with me the secret, sacred gift of Minos. Whatever it was, whatever power for good or evil it might contain, it was now my responsibility.

GRADUATE STUDY

Realizing that to locate my traveling friend by night would be virtually impossible, I decided to find some secure tree and roost in it until dawn. To manage this in darkness proved more difficult than I had thought, but at last I was successful. My final choice was a tall pine, leaning inward from an almost inaccessible rocky ledge. With my wings unbuckled I slept curled at its foot—not in its branches, which proved impractical.

Taking to the air again as soon as dawn gave light enough to see, I found little difficulty in identifying the particular series of roads by which my friend the captain and I had ascended to King Cocalus's domain. Skimming downhill close above these sinuous thoroughfares, I began in earnest my search for Kena'ani. My appearance in the sky created some wild confusion among some slaves and peasants who were early in beginning their day's labors, and also in a party of hunters who had spent the night in camp.

But with the speed of a bird I soon left these perturbed folk behind me. My flight was much faster than the progress of any man who was forced to follow the switchbacked roads on foot, and I caught up with Kena'ani long before he had reached the harbor.

My friend was traveling alone, hiking along briskly with staff in hand. Recognizing him at a distance and from behind, I flew low over some trees to get ahead of him, and landed in the road so that as he rounded the next turn he came upon me as I stood waiting for him.

Kena'ani stopped in his tracks, staring as if I were a ghost. "Daedalus. How did you get here?"

I was standing with my wings down at my sides, so that the fringes of soft leather that imitated great feathers trailed in the dust, and the effect must have been of a silvery cape rather than wings. For a moment or two more I might have deceived my companion. But, I reflected, I would hardly be able to do so any longer than that.

"With these," I answered, and spread my pinions wide.

The eyes of the Phoenician trader widened; I had concealed from Kena'ani my secret project for the Sicilian princesses, and he had never before seen any wings of my making in an unbroken state.

"Then it is true—but let me see you fly!"

Considering that I owed him my life, I could hardly refuse this modest request. But almost as soon as I was airborne, my friend became fearful that I would be seen by someone else, and that the secret of my invention would somehow be lost for nothing. So after completing one brief flight, up to treetop level and back, I landed in response to his urgent gestures.

"Then it is true," he muttered when I once more stood beside him on the ground. "Really true."

"You still had doubts?" I did not know whether to feel amused or wounded.

"I had—but never mind. My friend, can you begin to realize what an invention like this is worth?"

I sighed. "I suppose not—I only know what it has cost me."

"You will need help—of course you cannot begin to manage it yourself."

Then, following the good captain's almost frantic urgings, I immediately unstrapped my pinions from my waist and shoulders, rolled them up carefully—the improved model allowed this—and stowed them neatly out of sight in my friend's backpack. While doing this I told him what had happened to Minos.

He frowned and agreed that I had been wise to flee.

Realizing that I would probably have to do so sooner or later, since we would be traveling together, I told Kena'ani next about the gift of Minos, and showed him the small mysterious box.

For once, staring at the small coffer in my hands, my friend was silent. At last he asked me: "Have you opened it?"

"I pulled on the lid once when it was first

given to me; but the lid stayed closed. It is somehow locked or sealed, though no fastening is visible. No, I have made no serious attempt to get it open. Nor do I intend to do so, for the time being."

Again Kena'ani was silent for a time, staring at the box, though making no attempt to take it into his own hands. "You are probably right," he sighed at last, caution winning out for the time being over curiosity. "Let us get to my ship while we can."

Whether I was going to be pursued or not we did not know, but it seemed a reasonable assumption that my absence was unlikely to have been discovered until morning, and that therefore we had a substantial start on any possible pursuit. Flight in the literal sense should not be necessary. Making the best speed on foot we could, we reached the harbor late that afternoon. My friend was welcomed tumultuously by the men of his crew, who had once more been on the point of giving us both up for dead. We wasted no time in putting out to sea.

We had a fair breeze to carry us to the northeast. Only after Sicily was well astern did we inform the crew of the startling events at the court of King Cocalus, leading to the death of the visiting King of Crete. The seamen were impressed to hear of my involvement in such great affairs, and thankful that we had been able to depart without further trouble.

We were well and safely away from Sicily, but my friend the captain was at first undecided as to where to go next. I had my own ideas on the subject, and by next morning I was working hard to convince Kena'ani and his crew that we ought to sail to Naxos, where we had good hopes of catching up with my old friend Prince Theseus, or at least of learning where he had gone. Though Kena'ani had been but poorly rewarded by King Cocalus for bringing me and my wings to Sicily, the captain was still determined to sell the idea of human flight to some wealthy potentate, and Theseus seemed the most logical choice. I suppose that the indefatigable merchant had plans also to dispose of the gift of Minos at a profit, but he was wise enough not to mention them to me.

Kena'ani prayed to his Phoenician gods, and observed the flight of sea birds, seeking an omen. To my relief these oracular efforts confirmed that my advice was good, and trying to find Prince Theseus would be our wisest course.

The voyage to Naxos was quite a long one, I suppose five thousand stadia as the winged creature flies, and it occupied us for nearly a month. This time included several short stops for supplies of food and water, and a small amount of trading—and the whole of this time I kept my new wings carefully rolled up, concealed from everyone but Kena'ani. He was assuming an ever more openly proprietary interest in my invention, until I sometimes wondered silently which of us was the inventor. Constantly he reminded me that the wings must not be revealed to anyone but a person of immense wealth, someone who would have the power to suitably reward the proprietors.

During our voyage to Naxos we traversed a great part of the coast of mainland Greece, following the shoreline closely as a rule, doing a little merchant business here and there at the small ports. There came a day when I realized that we were in the vicinity of Kythera, and that we must therefore be passing close to the small and nameless islet where my son lay buried, and from which Kena'ani had originally taken me aboard his ship.

I mentioned to my friend the possibility of stopping to try to find the grave of Icarus, that I might mourn and offer sacrifice anew; but he convinced me that the shape of the islet would most likely have altered by now, as the sand was moved about under the influence of wind and wave and current. The chances were, Kena'ani thought, that we would no longer be able to recognize the spot where poor Icarus lay; and in the black mood that came upon me then it seemed to me unlikely that my son's unhappy shade would know the difference anyway.

As we were now so near Kythera, Crete itself must lie at no great distance to our south and east. But we were determined to steer clear of it. Who ruled upon that island now in Minos's absence, and who would control his lands and fleets when his death became known, were mysteries that neither of us had any wish to investigate personally.

We even sailed at night, to minimize as much as possible the chance of an encounter with the Cretan navy. But our precautions were perhaps unnecessary. These waters, once so heavily patrolled by Minos's navy, were now all but empty of his ships. Kena'ani frowned upon realizing this state of affairs, and predicted that such a situation could not endure for long without bringing on a recrudescence of pirates, who for generations had been virtually nonexistent in this area.

Enjoying a fair wind again, we passed north of Crete, I think just out of sight of her tallest peaks, and were on a course for Naxos that would have brought us very close to Thera, had not many of the crew complained, causing the captain to alter his heading somewhat. No one, to Kena'ani's knowledge, had traded on Thera for a generation.

Twice taking the opportunity to hail a passing merchant ship, we received information on both occasions regarding the situation on Naxos and on Thera now—but the information we received from the two ships was confusing and contradictory. I also found it disquieting. One of our informants assured us that Theseus was still on Naxos; the other, that he was not. The gods were swarming over Naxos now, said one; no, said the other, they had all departed for Thera months ago.

Only on the single occasion when one of the Cretan navy's war vessels came over the horizon and came in our direction as if meaning to hail us, did I prudently descend into the small below-decks compartment of our ship. I did not want the Cretans to have any idea that the famed artisan Daedalus was on board this particular Phoenician. But the navy craft changed course and ignored us, and I was soon topside again.

At last the lovely isle of Naxos lay before our prow, looking calm and peaceful in the sunlight.

There was a range of mountains, their slopes generally forested, running north and south upon this island—these were really more like great hills, in comparison with the much higher mountains on the much larger land masses of Sicily and Crete. Kena'ani pointed out the highest peak on Naxos to me as Mt. Drios, saying that was its ancient name.

When our small ship had made her way into the one small harbor that Naxos possessed, we found the quays and docks there ominously deserted, totally empty of ships except for a couple of unseaworthy hulks. Trade, as on Thera, must have come to a halt here some time ago. Screaming sea birds, already unaccustomed to disturbance, rose up from nests already established on what must have been, only a few months past, a busy mole. No one, not a single person, appeared to greet or challenge us when we tied up at a dock.

This situation was worse than we had expected. With a squad of half a dozen volunteers from among the crew, the captain and I at once began a cautious search of the waterfront area. Very quickly we discovered that all of the buildings we entered had been for some time abandoned.

When we reported this discovery to the rest of the crew, there was strong muttering among the men, many of whom openly refused to go anywhere inland.

The captain accepted their decision. This was not a situation at sea, where tradition would have allowed Kena'ani to enforce his captain's orders by death if need be; instead, as he assured the men several times, this was more a matter of trading, in which all the crew traditionally were allowed a say.

There was a minor uproar when one of the crew, while drawing fresh water from a well on the hill above the abandoned town, discovered in the muddy soil what he claimed were the footprints of some Bull-like creature, walking on two legs. I had seen the tracks of the Cretan Bull on the rare occasions when he had ventured off pavement, and I could have attested that these were very similar. But I kept silent, not wishing to spoil my chance of meeting Theseus or Ariadne, if either were still here.

We continued for a time to look around among the empty buildings of the town; then Kena'ani, frowning, announced that he saw in this situation a rare opportunity for trade.

"I think you see such golden chances everywhere, my friend. Tell me, how do you plan to engage in commerce with empty buildings?"

"But don't you see? If only we can find out where the people who lived here a few months ago have fled, our chance will come then. Of course they will have taken their most precious valuables with them—and they will be in sore need of many things as well, and ready to pay dearly."

I sighed and gave up the argument. We persisted in our search, enlarging its area until at last we were able to locate a few of the local people, who were eking out a wretched existence in a cluster of dilapidated huts—these were a mere handful of old folk, too feeble, or too indifferent to life, to have got away with the

rest of the townsfolk when they believed themselves threatened by disaster.

When we appeared before these elders most
of them looked at us fearfully, and were as silent
as the rocks in the harbor. But one toothless
crone was more than ready to talk with any
visitor who would listen. From her we were
able to confirm that the gods, or at least one of
them, had been active on the island for several
months, from about the time the black-sailed
ship arrived until it left again. Further details
were hard to come by.

The crone's speech encouraged some of the
other ancient ones, who in exchange for honey
and mead brought from our ship's stores began
to tell us stories of the Bull-like creatures from
Thera, who had recently started coming here to
Naxos, evidently in search of something. No
one had dared to try to speak to those august
visitors, so no one had a clue as to what they
might be seeking.

"How do they travel?" my friend the captain
demanded. "In what kind of ship?"

One old man, whispering hoarsely, reported
having seen with his own eyes the god Dionysus,
traveling here from Thera in a kind of flying
chariot, which he had caused to land on a ridge
above the town. After getting out of his machine
and looking about him for a while, the god had
remounted and flown away again. He had not
looked at all like a Bull, but had appeared in the
guise of a handsome young man.

"How do you know it was Dionysus, father?"
Kena'ani asked, with tolerant skepticism.

"It was he, no doubt about it." The elder,

looking frightened, dropped his voice to a hoarse whisper. "The one all the women have lately taken to worshipping."

The captain and I exchanged glances, both of us being puzzled by this description. All our lives we had heard of Dionysus as an ancient and kindly god of vegetation. So had the rest of the world until that time. Kena'ani looked back to the crone who had spoken to us first. "What does he mean, 'the women?'"

The old woman cackled, as if at some delicious joke. "Not me, I'm too old for that kind of worship. The young ones do it."

"Do what?"

But she would only repeat the name of Dionysus to me, over and over, the one word interspersed with her cackling. Eventually I said that I thought that particular god concerned himself only with harvests and the like.

The talkative old woman only laughed.

One of the old men who had so far been silent now spoke up in unsmiling warning to us: "Watch out for the women."

"What women?" I was as puzzled as my friend. "What is all this about 'the women?' Are the females on this island more dangerous than those elsewhere? Why?"

But the ancient and feeble ones had been imbibing our mead as steadily as they could, and by now the great majority of them were nodding off to sleep. The talkative woman, having had her share of drink as well, would only sing in a cracked voice.

Returning to the ship again, we informed the rest of the crew of these latest mysterious developments. Before the captain and I could ascertain how many of the men might still be willing to explore the interior of the island with us, a sailor we had posted as sentinel raised an alarm.

A savage-looking group of half a dozen men, all crudely armed though none of them were dressed like soldiers, were approaching the town and port from inland. Cautiously Kena'ani and I, with half the crew beside us, went a short distance to meet them. We identified ourselves to these men as traders, and they said in reasonable tones that they were citizens of the island who had seen our ship and had come to give us warning. Also one or two of them pleaded to be allowed to sail away with us, and urged us to leave while there was yet time.

Talking with the members of this savage-looking band, we learned that they were in fact the formerly peaceful natives of this town and island; but for the past several months they had lived effectively cut off from the equally wild and savage women, who were formerly their wives, sisters, and daughters.

The men told us that ever since the arrival of the new Dionysus on the island, most of the women of Naxos—almost all of them except the very old—had abandoned their homes and families in favor of being the cult-worshippers of this new, mysterious, and decidedly fleshly god who bore an old god's name. As for the men of the island, as represented by this band, they almost never had contact any longer with the women, except for occasional armed clashes. Men who were caught alone by the roaming packs of predatory females were kidnapped and carried away to be used as sacrifices in the strange new rites. I gathered that these men in return now routinely engaged in ambushes of the females, kidnapping, raping, and usually murdering women whom they accused of already having murdered their own menfolk.

It sounded utter madness to me. As we talked, I saw movement in a thicket on the hillside above the town; small heads appeared there, with dark feral eyes gazing down at us. I was told by the native men that here and there the surviving children of this island still existed, running like their elders in wild packs divided by sexes, armed and carrying out a war of mutual destruction on their own level.

Our crew of traders had now heard more than enough to satisfy them about the local situation. All but a very few of the Phoenician sailors now gave up completely on the idea of trading here, or conducting any further exploration. The Phoenicians were men accustomed to danger, but still very prudent about sticking their heads into it when there was no immediate prospect of profit.

But Kena'ani himself, along with one or two of his crew, were able to accept this situation, as he did all other situations, as a challenge. He was determined to be able to extract a profit anywhere, and if he had been sentenced to hang he would probably have managed to sell the rights to his freshly-executed body to a wizard first. At least we were not going to cut and run from the harbor immediately.

Some of the more sober of the gang of island men informed us of something that, in contrast to all the loose talk of gods, was easy to believe. Some months ago the ship of Prince Theseus had been in this harbor for a few days. But then one morning the black-sailed vessel had been gone. However, one of the princesses who had arrived with the Athenian was still here—indeed, she had become the leader of the worst cult-group of women—and now lived up in the hills.

Another of the men confirmed that the princess who had come with Theseus—or one of the two princesses at least—was still here. Yes, our informants were very sure of that. The taller princess—that would certainly be Ariadne, I thought—was up in the hills, at the center of the council of the most dangerous women.

Presently the band of men went back into the woods, except for a couple of their number who were determined to take passage on our ship, being willing to risk anything rather than stay on this island any longer. These two sat down on the dock beside our ship, until we should be ready to depart.

Both Kena'ani and myself were somewhat encouraged by that last relatively credible report. Neither of us entirely believed the stories of packs of cannibal women seizing men and killing them in strange rites; but obviously, at best, a dangerous situation obtained here, and something we did not understand was going on.

In the end it was decided in a conference with our crew that the captain and I would do all the exploration from here on. Leaving the entire crew aboard ship, the two of us went inland a very little way, until we were just out of sight of the harbor village. There I put on my wings, being determined to undertake some further explorations on my own, in what seemed the least dangerous way possible.

Leaving Kena'ani, who said he intended to conduct some explorations of his own on foot, I rose into the air and flew, dodging away among the treetops so that none of our crew were able to see me on the wing. The captain and I were both uncertain of what effect the sight of a flying man might have on them.

My course took me at but a slight altitude around some low hills, and carried me completely out of sight of the harbor. It was still broad daylight, and the land below me lay open for discovery.

In less than an hour I had surveyed most of the lower regions of the island, everywhere observing neglected fields, abandoned cottages, and uncared-for vineyards—though I saw evidence that some of these latter, at least, were still being cultivated.

In one woody glade a band of naked female children, armed with bows and slings, went scrambling away in fright as I soared overhead. I turned the other way, not wishing to provoke a shower of missiles.

Gradually I rose higher over the mountain's increasing slopes. As far as I could tell, it was possible that a dozen bands of feral men, and of separated women maddened by their strange new god, might be concealing themselves in the trees below me. If the men of the island had told us the truth, the Princess of Crete might be attached to any one of those bands. But from what I knew of Ariadne, I thought that, mad or not, if she had a choice she would choose no ordinary setting in which to live.

Higher and higher I flew, continuing my search as best I could. Eventually, in another glade high on the mountain's shoulder, and almost inaccessible by land, I saw the princess, recognizing her at once.

To all appearances Ariadne was alone. I beheld her sitting, apparently at ease, in a small natural hollow between two mossy' rocks. She did not look up when I passed almost directly overhead at a low elevation, but remained busy with some fabric work, sewing or knitting, that she held in her lap. Though her face was turned down to her work, her gown looked royal, and I felt certain that it was she.

I landed lightly upon an exposed crag nearby, and without loosening my wings walked back into the woods along a little path, cautiously observing to see if anyone else was about. But at first I was able to see no one.

As I approached the princess looked up, recognized me at once, and in a calm voice bade me welcome.

"Daedalus—but those are wings that you are wearing. Are they real? Can you fly?"

I thought she was accepting the invention with unwarranted calm. "They are real enough, Your Highness."

"How very clever!" She might have been complimenting me on a new design for a wooden toy.

I knelt briefly before her, as of old. "Not entirely a result of my own cleverness, Princess, but partly a gift of the White Bull."

A small frown creased Ariadne's lovely forehead, and she was silent for a moment, as if she might be trying to recall who the White Bull might be.

"How clever of him, then," she said at last, dismissing the matter with a small sigh. It was as if her mind, her real attention, was somewhere else. Then the Princess brightened again. "But in any case I bid you welcome, Daedalus." And now her welcome sounded almost as if she had actually been expecting me. There was a sweet, dreamy expression upon her lovely face as she put down her knitting, and clapped her hands to summon an attendant—certainly there was no sign in her demeanor of the raving cultist who had been described so luridly by the frightened men below.

Looking around to see who might answer the princess's summons, I heard a liquid murmuring, and saw how a pretty little spring emerged from between rocks, and went trickling away downhill. A pair of human figures now caught my attention, as two female attendants emerged from a poor hut, the only building in sight, tucked away among the nearby trees. Somehow I had missed seeing the hut when I flew over. Whatever this encampment might be exactly, it did not meet the usual standards of a royal lodging. And here in her sylvan dwelling the princess appeared to be attended by only a few ragged, uncivilized-looking, rather ugly young women.

After having been warned by the men below, I took careful note of the two attendants as they approached. But they were unarmed, and did not look particularly dangerous. Ignoring my wings entirely, they gazed at me with evident dislike, until their mistress chided them into some semblance of hospitality.

Soon, as if in a parody of palatial entertainment, the Princess and I were brought poor drinking vessels—mine was only a cracked clay cup—and furnished what I was assured was wine; but when I tasted the clear liquid poured by one of the scowling attendants into my cracked cup, I was sure that I was drinking the water of the nearby spring.

"Is it not delightful, Daedalus?" Ariadne asked me as her own cup was refilled by one of her attendants. Indeed, as water it was not bad. But evidently my hostess sincerely believed our drink to be the finest wine, for now at last her voice took on some animation, and a slight flush touched her sunburnt cheeks.

I muttered something in the way of agreement.

"Are not all things here the most beautiful of their kind that you have ever seen?" And she made a graceful gesture with her tanned arms, inviting me to study our surroundings. I studied her instead, and only now did I notice that Ariadne's hair was somewhat unclean and matted, her full Cretan skirt was slightly torn, and that the bodice that upheld her lovely breasts was soiled.

"Yourself the most beautiful of all, Highness." That I could still say with but little damage to the truth.

She accepted the compliment as complacently as a princess ought to acknowledge such things; then, with another sharp little clap of her hands, she ordered food to be set before herself and her guest. My hopes rose for just a moment; but then, on seeing what gristly scraps presently appeared before me on a wooden plate, I could only protest that I was not hungry.

That was fine with the princess, whose own food appeared no better than what had been brought to me; whatever pleased her visitor pleased her. "But how do you like our wine, Daedalus? Tell me truly, now." Ariadne smiled at me serenely, the hostess never doubting that she was about to receive another compliment.

I shifted from foot to foot uncomfortably, wondering if all this could possibly be some monstrous jest. No, not on the part of Ariadne. No.

All I could say was: "Seldom or never have I tasted its like, Princess."

She nodded complacently, and took another sip herself. And now I was aware of a most painful duty that I could not postpone any longer. I had to tell the princess that her father was dead. Somehow I stumbled through the announcement.

She thought the news over for a moment or two, and then she wept one slow tear. "Oh, Daedalus, sometimes I am so—so—"

In a moment I was kneeling before her again, offering her my help. But I could not get her to complete that statement. She insisted there was nothing wrong.

I had dreaded having to inform the princess of the horrible details of her father's passing, but to my amazement she never asked to hear them, even though I told her the tragic event had taken place in Sicily. And in a frighteningly

few moments she had resumed her air of gaiety
and laughter, to all appearances completely
delighted with her rural poverty. Next, in all
apparent seriousness she was inviting me to ad-
mire the beauty of her servitors, who, the gods
knew, had little enough of that commodity to
share among them.

Was Ariadne's strange behavior the result of
some great enchantment? I had never put much
stock in magic, but still I could not imagine any
other cause save madness. At last I mentioned
to the princess the strange band of men we had
encountered in the harbor town, and the even
stranger warnings those men had given us.

Ariadne's face grew troubled, and she ordered
me to silence, saying that it pained her to think
or talk about such things.

It was with a strong feeling of foreboding that
I at last asked her to tell me what had become
of Theseus and Phaedra. The princess had volunteered no information about them, or indeed
about anything except the water she called wine,
and the beauty with which she thought we were
surrounded.

An expression of fear grew on Ariadne's countenance as soon as I mentioned her sister and the
Prince of Athens, so that I regretted my question. But it was too late.

"They are gone," she cried. "They left me
here and sailed away together. I can only hope
that they are as happy as I am." And saying
that, Ariadne burst into tears.

I did what little I could, as a man and a mere
commoner, to soothe her royal self. To my own
surprise, my clumsy efforts were immediately

successful. Then, as soon as the princess was composed again and beginning to smile, I asked her why she stayed here.

Ariadne's eyes lighted up, and she began to tell me about one whom she called her master.

These were strange words from a princess, stranger than any I had heard yet. I could not understand her at all, and was trying to think of how to express this fact diplomatically, when she was interrupted and rebuked in an incredibly rude way.

"Ha! Little you know of our master!" This startling outburst came from one of Ariadne's attendant women—this particular one so ugly that I thought even Phoenician sailors would have shown little interest in raping her.

To my astonishment Ariadne ignored the woman completely and went on with her description of the mysterious master. At this point I became firmly convinced that at least one, and probably both, of the women before me must be mad.

While I was wondering what to do next, a large shadow passed silently over us. A whispering sound ran through the air above us, too steady, I thought, to be made by wings. Looking up with some half-formed idea that I was going to see another man who had been taught by the White Bull how to fly, I beheld an even stranger sight. What looked like a closed chariot, its surface half bright glass, half of metal that was almost as bright, and drawn through the air by invisible horses, passed above us at a leisurely speed. A moment later the vehicle had landed easily in the small glade, fitting itself precisely down among the trees.

The shape of this peculiar craft was roughly that of a wide, short cylinder, with most of its glass on top. As soon as the cylinder had come to rest, a door slid open in its curved side. I stood gaping, half in wonder, half in envy, at the art and strength that must have gone into the creation of such a device.

At first I was more fascinated by the machine than by the man, or rather youth, who now came climbing out of it, followed promptly by first one and then a second giggling female. But that state of affairs did not last long. The head of the youth who had just arrived was wreathed with ivy, but he wore almost nothing else, as if he were coming fresh from winning a prize at wrestling or bull-dancing. His body had once been that of an athlete, but it was already going soft with evident dissipation and lack of exercise.

First one of the newly-arrived young women and then the other, both of them as scantily clad as the god himself, and obviously much under his spell, joined him standing in front of the marvelous machine in which they had arrived. All three were laughing.

I stood uncertain as to whether to try to flee, but the princess, laughing happily, urged me to remain. The new arrivals came walking through the trees to join us. The youth, completely ignoring me at first, greeted Ariadne carelessly, but still with respect. The impression I received was of a returning king being reunited with a favorite concubine, or perhaps his morganatic wife.

And Ariadne, humbling herself before the youth in a manner ill-befitting a princess in any company, addressed him as her divine lord and true god Dionysus, and presented me to him under that name.

Cautiously I genuflected as if to royalty. I was puzzled and wary; my first glimpse of the Bull on the shoreline of Crete had told me that I was in the presence of something other than a human. But this person, at first sight, was not obviously anything but a man. Certainly a young and handsome man, if not a completely healthy one—but I had seen others his equal in youth and beauty.

Like most of those others, who were surely only mortal, this self-proclaimed deity had a certain haughtiness about him. But on the whole this Dionysus impressed me as a mild-mannered chap, almost diffident, though dressed rather indecently in only a couple of very small animal skins and a few leaves. A god? I really had grave doubts about that, even though he had arrived in a chariot that might have been borrowed or stolen from some divinity. This Dionysus looked very human indeed, a radiant, amiable, though perhaps not strictly handsome youth with grape-leaves in his hair, a sniffle, and the beginnings of a paunch resulting from too much easy living.

After a brief exchange of greetings, I retired a step or two into the background and stood listening. The more I overheard of the conversation of this strange person with the princess, the more I became convinced that these two were indeed, in some sense, man—or god—and wife.

Moreover, this strange god had somehow convinced Ariadne that he was faithful to her, though I saw no possibility of that actually being the case; the two girls or young women who had arrived in the metal chariot with our new Dionysus clung to him sleepily during the conversation, and he, in a kind of divine arrogance, took shameless liberties with them in the very presence of Ariadne; his hands fondled their voluptuous bodies in an absent fashion, even as he spoke to the woman he had styled his queen. And meanwhile she, gazing at her lord with every appearance of adoration, did not appear to notice.

At least this Dionysus had certainly convinced her that his unfaithfulness did not matter in the least.

From the position to which I had retreated, a few paces from the others, I examined the supposed god Dionysus as objectively as I could. He in turn threw a bored glance my way now and then, and eventually began to take something of an interest in me.

This interest, to begin with at least, had little to do with the wings I was still wearing—at first I think he was hardly aware of those artificial attachments, and when he noticed them he was even less surprised than Ariadne had been. When at last he did take full notice of my wings, he for a time assumed, for some reason, that I had just come from Thera. At this Dionysus began to talk to me, almost as to an equal, about what events might be occurring upon that island now. I understood hardly a word of this effort on his part to make conversation.

I assured the supposed divinity that I knew nothing of what might be happening on Thera, and that in fact I had never been there. With what I hoped was acceptable humility I informed him that I was only a poor artisan.

Now at last the one who called himself Dionysus blinked and scowled at me. It was only at this point, I think, that he realized that he had never seen me before.

For a moment I feared his anger, but I need not have worried about that; he was seldom angry, as I learned later, and never violently or for long. Nor was he very intelligent. But my fear was well-founded all the same.

How shall I describe what happened to me next? When it began, and for some minutes thereafter, I did not realize that what was happening had anything directly to do with Dionysus.

Once that most extraordinary being—whether he, deity, or mere man—had smiled upon me, and decided to employ his powers, there was nothing I could do about it.

As I say, I was at first not even aware that the one who smiled and talked with me was doing anything else.

The effect began with a warm, glowing feeling of well-being, which I attributed at first to the wine I had drunk—how could I ever have thought this clear and sparkling stuff was only water?—and with which Ariadne's cup-bearers were plying me again. Then, just when the effect was reaching its full force, the youth who had been talking to me changed his expression, giving a little lift to his eyebrows as if he would have said: There! How do you like that?

A moment later he had turned away from me again. At very nearly the same moment I was dimly aware that Ariadne had arisen from her cushions among the rocks, and with her own hands, was bringing her master red wine. The wine that she brought to him was genuine; I could see the true color of it, and I could smell it faintly in the sparkling air, even as it was being poured several paces from where I stood.

Dionysus gulped down the wine and seated himself, lounging on pillows softer than those used by the princess, which had been brought for him by one of Ariadne's ugly attendants. One of his own pretty traveling companions came to seat herself in his lap; from somewhere this young girl produced a bunch of fresh grapes, which she proceeded to pop one by one into her god's laughing mouth. Only now did I notice how badly stained were the teeth of Dionysus.

But now such trivialities as stained teeth or odd behavior could not matter. Dionysus had ordained a celebration, and no one within reach of his will could wish for or think about anything else.

I was indeed fortunate that during my personal encounter with this god, or pseudo-god, he chose to treat me kindly. He was not unkind even after he must have realized that I was truly only a mere mortal, an ordinary man, a rude stranger engaged in close conversation with his queen. Fortunately Dionysus was not jealous. I must have seemed to him a poor, weak-willed, ugly man, hardly a rival for the affections of the princess or even the other women—what mere man could have been a real rival to him? Like the other humans with whom he came in contact, I was only a toy, no more—a toy, perhaps, with good potential for amusement, and so he chose to treat me gently. Also he must have been able to see that I was really an old friend of his beloved queen, and that a visit from me might be good for her. Ariadne still suffered moments of sadness despite all that he could do for her—or all that he cared to take the time to do. But I am getting somewhat ahead of my story.

I can remember vaguely how, during that sunny afternoon on Naxos, the mighty Dionysus told me in a wistful voice at least some of his concerns for his queen. But he could never turn his own thoughts very far from revelry. Even when he spoke of Ariadne's suffering, it was as if he were remembering something from long ago, something that no longer mattered very much to him at all.

It must have been a very peculiar conversation that the two of us, that god and I, enjoyed that day. At one point, as I remember, Dionysus expressed the wish that I might someday fashion a pair of wings for him. Of course I assured my powerful companion that I would, and at the time I undoubtedly meant it. And when he heard me mention my skill in plumbing, he spoke wistfully on that topic as well. He hoped, he said, to have a truly magnificent palace of his own one day, and it would be wonderful if he could have plumbing in it too. Thus are the gods—at least the ones that I have met—subject to the same indignities as the rest of us.

The personal wings would be useful, Dionysus told me, because his own flying machine had lately been giving him trouble. To begin with, some months ago, it had always carried him immediately to the exact place where he wanted to go, but lately it had shown signs of becoming unreliable. And there was no longer anyone on Thera capable of repairing the flying chariot for him, restoring its full proper magic. None of the Bull-people were any longer on that island. And besides, my kind of man-made wings just looked like more fun.

I drained my water-cup with delight, as if indeed it had contained some nectar of the gods.

None of the Bull-people. My companion had spoken those words so calmly that at first I almost missed them. Besides, I was too dazed by the Dionysian powers employed to make me think of nothing but debauchery to take much conscious note of exactly what he said. But I had certainly heard those words, and I was not going to forget them. *None of the Bull-people.* Then the White Bull had not lied to me, on that point anyway; there were certainly more of the Bull's race in the world.

As Dionysus and I continued our conversation, some demon of foolishness urged me to volunteer to repair this young god's flying machine for him—I wanted to do so mainly because I was so curious about the strange device that I wanted to examine it closely. But fortunately I realized there was a strong possibility that my skills would prove inadequate to the task; and so I bit my tongue and with some effort remained silent.

At about this time Dionysus said: "There are still those living on Thera who want me to come back there. And stay."

"Those? Do you speak of other gods, Divine Leader?"

"Gods? What are gods?" It was as if he really wanted an answer to the question, though he did not really expect to get one. And for the moment he seemed scarcely more than human.

Then the moment passed. "No, the gods are all gone from that island," Dionysus told me, almost frowning. Then he brightened quickly. "Thera is the place, my friend," he said. "Where the real gods once decided to make their home— and where they proved not to be so godlike after all." And Dionysus laughed, enjoying some private joke.

I puzzled over everything he said, trying to understand it. Meanwhile about a dozen more women had begun to emerge from the forest, singly and in couples, and to gather around us. These women were all of them healthier and better-looking than Ariadne's ill-favored attendants, and to my vision, distorted now by the influence of Dionysus, they appeared as nothing less than visions of divine beauty. They bore slings and bows, the weapons of hunters, and most of them were carrying fresh-killed game. It was as if these women had sensed the presence of their master here; or, more likely, they had simply observed the arrival of his flying machine, and were gathering from the surrounding woods, coming to adore their god. These newcomers cast looks that would have frightened me under ordinary circumstances; even

under the influence of the god as I was, I found
them vaguely disturbing. But none of those
women would do anything to molest a man who
was engaged in such friendly conversation with
their master.

Prostrating themselves before Dionysus, they
offered him their fowls and rabbits. He accepted
these gifts in a kindly, indolent way, and indi-
cated that it was time for someone to get busy
cooking.

Now one of the older women was beating on
a drum, and another was blowing on the pipes
of Pan. Additional female voices were singing,
chanting, in the distance, coming closer. Somehow I had seated myself on a patch of grass, and
had become an audience; and now one of the
two girls who had arrived in the magical chariot
of Dionysus had cast aside her last scraps of
clothing, and was moving before me in an abandoned dance. The young dancer smiled at me
invitingly. There seemed to be nothing in the
whole world beyond the craving of my flesh,
and when she threw herself down on the grass
beside me, I without thinking enfolded her in
my arms and wings. Around us the music continued, amid screams of laughter.

Some little time later I disentangled myself
from the dancer, who immediately arose to dance
again. I noticed now that the smell of food was
beginning to arise from cookfires. And when I
looked toward Dionysus, I saw with mixed feelings that this god was obviously beginning to
overindulge in wine. His laughter was louder
than before; his eyes looked glazed, and he

swayed lightly upon his Arcadian throne of grass
and pillows.

Ariadne kept repeatedly refilling her master's
golden cup, and his control over the minds and
souls of others was starting to become erratic.
By now I had dimly realized that I too had been
brought at least partially under that control.
There were moments of confusion, when fear
tried to establish itself in my mind, and could
not; and then I would wonder what I was doing
in this strange glade, and why I should feel such
overwhelming excitement and devotion whenever I looked at the young god.

The women around me were affected even
more intensely, to the point of madness. From
time to time one of them would suddenly turn
aside from her cooking, or her more personal
service to her lord, and weep.

But for the most part we all existed in an
atmosphere of pleasure and excitement. No one
but myself was even faintly shocked when at last
Ariadne, Princess of Crete, lost all shame and in
the presence of all threw herself wantonly upon
her young lord, moaning and wrapping all her
limbs around him. Grinning, he rolled over on
his couch and began to try to know her; but it
appeared that the excess of wine he had drunk,
or his earlier frolicking with one of his hand-
maidens, might prevent his achieving what he
wanted now.

Turning my gaze away from this embarrassing
sight, I stared at the other women. A number of
them were beginning to embrace each other in
an unnatural way.

The realization struck me belatedly that, besides the god himself, I was the only male in sight. Also some vague echo of the warnings I had received from the lowland people now awoke in my memory: the most terrible of the rites attributed to these groups of Dionysian worshippers required a male victim.

By now all of the women had joined the orgy, in one way or another, and there was no one left to serve as cupbearer. The god, when he had finished with Ariadne for the moment—or else had temporarily abandoned his attempt—lurched to his feet and stumbled behind the hut, where, as he seemed to know, the supply of red wine, real wine, was kept concealed. I heard the sound of divine retching; then a moment later the god reappeared, raising to his lips a rare glass flask, in the apparent act of polishing off the last of the good stuff.

I had long since dropped my own poor, cracked cup and had seen no reason to pick it up again.

For a few moments the idea of getting away had labored to establish itself in my mind, but for the time being that thought was gone again. My mind struggled to attain coherence. My mood, under the varying influence of the god's power, was changing with the swiftness of a summer storm at sea.

Two drums were sounding now, along with a stringed instrument and the ancient pipes of Pan.

The dancing girl was back before me, and had once again thrown herself down in the grass where she lay moaning lustfully. She was trying to entice me to lie with her again. But instead, with a growing sense of terrible danger, I staggered to my feet. Slowly and with a feeling of growing horror I realized that when I had lain with the woman earlier I had taken off my wings, being frantic to free my arms for other matters. And now the pinions were missing.

I questioned the dancing girl, and shook her as she lay moaning in the grass, but she only laughed, and clutched at my arms and refused to let me go. Desperately I struggled free, the skin of my arms torn by her nails. As in a nightmare, I ran in circles, searching.

Fortunately for me, the other women were all distracted by their own sensations. The god, as powerfully affected by drink as any mere mortal might have been, had now begun to sing; Dionysus had a truly inferior voice, as I look back on it, yet at the time, of course, I thought it of surpassing beauty. Several times I paused in my search for the wings, forgetting the deadly peril in which I stood, to listen to the song.

The song was interrupted, began again, broke off once more. And as Dionysus nodded in the midst of song, with his own consciousness swaying in its sovereignty over his body, so did his control over me waver also. I suppose that the women, too, may have been released at this time, but as I remember nothing in their behavior changed. It may have been that they had been so long and so willingly his slaves, and were now so caught up in their orgy, that no effect of freedom was apparent in them.

Unless it were that cruelty now began to take

a place in the festivities. Or perhaps it was only when my mind grew relatively clear that I began to notice it. I saw two of the women pinning down a third, burning her deliberately with a hot brand from a cooking-fire—and as the screams of pain and laughter of this trio went up into the sunny sky I felt an urgent need to get away while I was still able to do so. But I could not find my wings.

At last I found them. The young dancer had recovered them from somewhere, and was trying to put them on her own shoulders, meaning, I suppose, to dance in them. But it was impossible for her to put them on, for in her ignorance she had them reversed right to left. I had to struggle briefly with her to get my wings away, but when I had them in my hands again, to my unspeakable relief they appeared to be essentially undamaged.

Immediately I began to edge my way toward the trees, carrying my wings rolled up under my arm. I thought I now had a better understanding of what might have happened to Theseus and Phaedra, if they had left the island only after the arrival of Dionysus. I understood now that if this god, in full possession of his faculties, had ordered them to leave, refusal would have been impossible, even for a hero. And in the circumstances, if Ariadne were already under the god's spell, it would have been impossible to persuade her to come with them.

I was still edging my way toward the trees when at last Dionysus drained the last of the red wine from the last glass flask, and passed

out completely. He fell unconscious to the turf,
his handsome face raised to the sky in blank
stupidity.

Moments later the Princess Ariadne, lost in
her own trance of ecstasy, her clothing torn and
in a shameful state of disarray, sprawled unconscious beside him. But the frenzy that had been
growing among the other women showed no
signs of diminishing, and they continued their
orgy, complete with pounding music. The screams
of the victim who had been selected for burning
torture went up and up. The celebration gave
promise of degenerating rapidly into something
truly horrible.

As for myself, I had to struggle at every step
to somehow retain enough wit to recall the warnings given me by the native men below, warnings that no longer sounded at all foolish or
exaggerated. The revel had not yet attained its
climax. Someone else was going to be required
as the next victim, and I managed to realize
how eminently I, as a man and an outsider, met
the qualifications.

The dancer, her face bloodied where I had
struck her to get the wings away, still beckoned
with her arms and body to get me to return.
But step by step I moved away.

With a total disregard for the glory a true
hero might have gained by enduring these circumstances and somehow overcoming them, I
sneaked off into the woods, while the women
who were still conscious were momentarily engaged in trying to arouse their master. And
from the rocky crag where I had landed I

sprang into the air and climbed on my wings to safety.

Flying once more around the low hills, retracing my aerial course back down to the harbor, I lurched through the air somewhat unsteadily, feeling the aftereffects of my experience, as much or more than if I had been drinking real wine.

Topping the last hill, I knew a shock of horror at seeing that the Phoenician ship and its crew were gone from the harbor.

But by this time fear, and the rush of cool sea air, had restored me almost to sobriety. In a moment more I was able to get a grip on myself, and realized that the absence of the ship presented no insuperable problem to an active man with wings. It was the work of only a few minutes to fly high enough to see where they had gone, and of only a few minutes more to overtake them, cruising as they were a couple of stadia offshore. I assumed that Kena'ani had felt confident that I would be able to rejoin them at sea, if I had survived at all.

I landed on the trader's deck—much to my friend's delight, and to the consternation of his crew, none of whom had ever before seen me fly. Immediately I began to give my friend an explanation—it must have been somewhat incoherent—of what I had discovered on the island.

But I had not been able to proceed very far

with my account before we were interrupted by a cry from a man in the stern.

Turning, we saw that a pirate ship had emerged from concealment amid a cluster of tiny islets nearby. Her prow was set in our direction, and she was quickly overtaking us.

FACULTY OUTING

The ship had appeared with great suddenness, popping out of concealment amid a cluster of brush-grown islets so closely grouped that they might have been designed as a place of ambush. She had her white sail already hoisted and was rapidly overhauling us. No one aboard our vessel had any doubt that our pursuer was a pirate—who else would chase a Phoenician merchant in such a fashion? The men on the stranger's deck, already almost within the range of voice, were yelling something to us across the water, but with the wind and the crash of waves against our prow, we could not hear. In any case it could hardly be anything but a demand for surrender.

Squinting into the sun, I was able to make out that the lines of our pursuer's hull, and of her sail, strongly resembled those of an Athenian warship. In the circumstances I did not find that reassuring.

Meanwhile our own crew, experienced sailors and fighters all, were no trembling cowards in this situation. In obedience to Kena'ani's shouted commands, they were preparing as best they could to fight, and at the same time trying to get more speed out of our own vessel.

The time elapsed since my landing on the deck of the merchant had been so brief that I had not even started to remove my wings. Now, as our pursuers drew nearer still, I tightened my shoulder straps—again blessing the improved design which made this maneuver possible without assistance—and made ready to leap into the air. My intention was to fly toward our pursuers and try to frighten them away. But a moment later, taking one last look over the stern before I leaped, I cried out in joy. I had recognized Prince Theseus, standing on the deck of the Athenian ship and giving orders.

Kena'ani, oblivious to my repeated cries that all was well, was swearing mighty oaths, invoking gods or devils whose names I had never heard before, and urging his men to make some adjustment of the sail they were trying to hoist. At this point our ship plowed into a large wave, and the sail, old and weathered canvas, suddenly ripped free of the lashings that secured it. What little hope we might have had of getting away from the onrush of the ship astern was abruptly dashed.

I continued to cry out the good news, that the commander of the other ship was my good friend, and eventually my cries were heeded. In another moment our men had ceased to row. Some gawked at the approaching Athenian, while others concentrated their efforts on disentangling the wreckage of our sail and its lines. Very soon after that the other ship caught up with us.

Meanwhile I had sprung onto the rail, and leaped from there into the air above, ignoring Kena'ani's stifled oath of protest behind me. Unhurriedly I flew in the direction of the other ship. It was now going to be impossible for me to keep my wings a secret from Theseus in any case, and so I wanted to reveal them as impressively as possible.

My princely friend and his crew were indeed astounded to behold a flying man, and in fact a general panic ensued upon the Athhenian deck. As the crew had nowhere to flee, they made ready to defend themselves. Fortunately their captain recognized me, and kept them from trying to riddle me with arrows or slung stones. Soon, at the invitation of the prince, I landed on his deck, where he greeted me warmly, and in the same breath demanded an explanation of my wings.

This I was able to provide, and the prince in his practical way quickly accepted my answer. In turn he explained to me that the black sail formerly adorning his mast had worn out; the ordinary white replacement had prevented my identifying his ship at first sight. Then he returned to the subject of the wings.

"You never cease to amaze me, Daedalus," Theseus muttered, the finest compliment I think that I had ever had from him. Gripping one of my pinions gently but firmly in each of his huge hands, he spread them out curiously and made them delicately flap, a warrior intrigued by a new weapon, and instantly visualizing possibilities for its use. "I have always thought that if anyone could make wings for a man to fly with, it would be you."

I suspected that the prince was not really capable of thinking about inventions, not until they appeared before him in concrete form. But all I said was: "I thank you humbly, sir."

He nodded. All trace of the harried student and the frantic rebel had disappeared from the man before me. Once he had filed away the idea of my wings as a new practical possibility, he let go of them and went on. "You and that clumsy trader have just come from Naxos."

"Indeed we have."

"What word of the Princess Ariadne there?"

"She is still there," I said unwillingly. "I have just seen her and spoken with her."

"What said she about me?"

"Alas, sire! Nothing at all."

Theseus nodded, as if he had expected to hear that bad news. "She abandoned me, Daedalus," he informed me, sounding and looking as sad as Ariadne herself when I had tried to talk to her about whatever had happened between them on the island. Obviously Theseus did not want to discuss the subject either, but he appeared to have no choice in the matter. "Abandoned me. But I am sure that she was under an enchantment when she did so."

"I am sorry, sire." I ventured a question of my own: "And where is the Princess Phaedra now?" I was hoping to get all unpleasant revelations over with as soon as possible.

"She is in Athens." My young friend stood a

little taller, and looked proud. "And she is more than a princess now. She is my queen."

I needed a moment to take in the full implications of that statement. "By all the gods . . . then you are king." I genuflected hastily. "That means your noble father is no more?"

A momentary shadow passed across the face of Theseus. "Some months ago, just before I came home, King Aegeus plunged from a clifftop into the sea. I am told, Daedalus, that the illnesses of old age had begun to—look there!"

I spun around, which is no easy maneuver when one is wearing wings of a god's design. My arms, in trying to move swiftly, had to grapple with the air as if it were a heavy thicket of bushes.

What I saw was a small and distant object moving in midair. Only a bright speck at the distance, but it was easy enough for me to recognize, having recently seen it at close range. It was the flying, gleaming chariot of Dionysus, looking almost sunlike with reflected sun as it rose from somewhere in the highlands of Naxos, and then accelerated across the sky. Traveling at a speed I considered worthy of divinity, it soon disappeared in the direction of Thera, to the south.

"I am told he rides in that," Theseus growled. He sounded anything but awed.

"Dionysus? True enough, for I have seen him disembarking from it." I did not mention that Ariadne had now become that sky-rider's erotic slave.

The young king slammed his fist down on the

rail. "Then how is a man ever supposed to come to grips with him?"

I reflected that this self-confident young man who now stood before me had already broken the neck of one supposed god, and therefore was not likely to stand in too much awe of another. Still I thought that it would be inadvisable for Theseus—or any other mortal—to attempt to come to grips with the Dionysus I had encountered. Nor did I hesitate to say as much. "Sire, whether he is a god or something less—I think that there would be no glory in such an effort. He is not a warrior."

Theseus smiled tolerantly and took me by the shoulder—by the wing-root, rather, shaking my whole body gently. "You are a good man, Daedalus, and in some matters you are a good adviser. But I think I will not follow your advice in this."

Meanwhile the Athenian crew were pulling closer to the trader, where the crew were still trying to untangle themselves from the fallen sail. Theseus and I continued our talk. The new king explained to me how he had come to leave his new queen behind in Athens, and why he and his crew had been patrolling off the coast of Thera, rather than landing on the island boldly.

"The two of us, your man-god Dionysus and myself, had a strange encounter on the island some two months ago." Theseus was reluctant to tell me the details of the story now. Perhaps he could not remember what he had said and done on that occasion, when his mind must have been clouded and his feelings controlled by his rival. But as Theseus now remembered and described the encounter, Ariadne herself had ordered him to depart, if he loved her; and he had taken an oath at Ariadne's urging never to land on Thera again unless she summoned him back.

Having myself experienced the influence of Dionysus at first hand, I could well believe that even Theseus would be unable to overcome it. But knowing Theseus the hero, I doubted that he would ever admit or accept such a defeat.

"You say you saw her just now, Daedalus. Tell me, try to remember, had she any message for me. Am I to land on Naxos again, and rescue her?" Here my young friend was almost pleading for the answer that would release him from his solemn oath.

I was unable to give him what he wanted. "No, Your Majesty. She said nothing of the kind." I suppose that would have been my answer whether it was true or not, but of course it was true enough. I tried again to remember anything that the Princess Ariadne might have said about this man who only a few months ago had been her lover; but I could not recall a word.

"Then what *did* she say?"

"She spoke of—of women's matters. And of neutral things." I gestured vaguely, thinking that it would do no good, but probably great harm to tell Theseus how the woman he loved— even if unfaithfully—had doted on the god of intoxication. The vanity of the young hero before me would certainly not be able to stand hearing that, and I feared what the consequences might be.

Even as matters stood Theseus was greatly upset. "Ah, Daedalus! Women! How by all the gods can a man ever hope to understand them or cope with them?"

I could only shake my head in response to a question which no counselor however sage has ever been able to answer in a wholly satisfactory way.

The king continued to talk to me—I think he was hungry for a chance to talk—and gradually a little more of the story came out, of what must have been a memorable encounter. I could visualize the three of them: First, Ariadne, already under the spell of her new master. Second, the young man before me, who had not yet known that he was king, his hero's pride hurt deeply. (What had Phaedra urged him then?) And third, the being called Dionysus, who, as I was beginning to realize, must be more powerful in some ways than any king on earth.

Theseus, thinking back now over the circumstances in which he had been persuaded to take such an oath and sail away, was more puzzled than ever as to how such a thing had come about.

"By all the gods, Daedalus, what I did then seems now like—like a base thing. And yet at the time . . ." He gave up in bafflement, knowing himself to be no coward.

I did what I could to reassure him. "I too have talked with Dionysus, sire. I can appreciate what you must have experienced. It is a matter that will bear much thinking about."

"Then do you think about it, counselor. I rely on you for that." And my friend sounded much relieved, at having someone who might do that kind of thinking for him.

By this time our two ships, the Phoenician and the Athenian, were standing close alongside each other, and the two crews, understanding that they were to be in some way allied, had begun to exchange greetings. The Athenian crew were a hard-bitten, experienced lot, unimaginative for the most part, though superstitious like all sailors. I learned later that these men were all picked volunteers, come willingly on this voyage to help their new king win glory in whatever manner seemed to him most fitting.

Of course by now my friend Kena'ani had come aboard the ship of Theseus, to be presented to the new King of Athens. The merchant outdid himself in obsequious obeisance on this occasion; I got the impression that no one in the long line of his trading ancestors had ever had such an opportunity to ingratiate himself with royalty.

Theseus was sure that the flying god, whose departure from Naxos we had just witnessed, had gone to Thera. It seemed to all of us a likely goal. Beyond that island to the south, the direction in which the flying chariot had vanished, there was only Crete, where the gods were not commonly known to be visitors, and beyond Crete only Africa.

And so the King of Athens informed us all that, since Ariadne still declined to release him from his oath regarding Naxos, he planned to set his course for Thera. Turning his most commanding gaze on me directly, he insisted that I accompany him there—bringing my wings, of course, and standing ready to use them in his service as well as my wits and skill.

I was wary of this king's impetuous youth, but still, having long been intrigued by the mystery of Thera, I had no wish to refuse him, even had a refusal been possible. I had to transfer my few belongings, including the mysterious gift of Minos, to the Athenian ship.

As far as Theseus was concerned, what Kena'ani and his crew might want to do was up to them. The Phoenician captain, on the other hand, continued in his determination to sell this king—or some other presumably wealthy potentate—on wings. But Theseus had already seen the wings, and cheerfully assumed they were already at his disposal. Kena'ani did drop a hint or two regarding payment, which Theseus ignored. Wisely the merchant forbore to press the matter now. The best he could do for the time being was to involve himself in the process of explaining possible uses for the invention, and he began to urge me to provide the king with a fuller demonstration.

But Theseus had always a habit of wanting to organize his own plan of learning, and, having already seen me fly, nothing would now satisfy him but that he make a trial of the wings himself. He insisted on doing this immediately, despite my protests that the wings I had made for myself would never fit him, being constructed for a smaller, considerably lighter man than he.

The straps could barely be made to fit upon the royal shoulders. Then the new king's effort on leaping over the side of the ship could hardly be described as a success, though by heroic effort he could just manage to keep himself aloft for the space of a few breaths, and at least avoided falling unheroically into the sea.

Carefully we unbuckled the straps from his shoulders and his waist as Theseus sat panting on the deck. When he had breath enough to speak again, he said: "You must make a set that will fit me, Daedalus."

"Gladly, sire. Of course. But to undertake such a project I must be provided with a workshop, well equipped with tools and well stocked with the necessary materials."

He smiled boyishly. "That was one of the things, as you recall, that I said on Crete I could not promise you."

"In Athens, sir, where you are now the king, I am sure we could find—"

"But we are not going to Athens. Not just yet. I suppose my wings will have to wait."

Kena'ani decided to accompany us to Thera, being advised to do so by the same oracular methods he had used before. These never seemed to give him any advice erring on the side of caution, or opposed to the spirit of the entrepreneur. His first mate stood ready to take over command of the Phoenician ship and crew, and of the remainder of their trading voyage. The mate said that he hoped to see his captain at home again one day. He also said that his first act as captain of the merchant ship would be to put her ashore for repairs on one of the dozen or more smaller islands nearby.

All was soon in readiness for the separation of our two ships, and not much time was wasted in farewells. Thera lay about forty miles almost due south, and we aboard the Athenian vessel sailed in that direction, interrupting our voyage only once to put into a cove on another small island, where we looked for fresh water and tried to replenish our food supplies.

Two of our men went off foraging on land, while others fished. None of the native population appeared. We dined well that evening, the shore party having returned with a few domestic geese, which the King of Athens accepted as his due from whatever inhabitants this island might possess. The wine was passed around the fire that night, and the bawdy jokes went with it. My friend the Phoenician and the pair of adventurers who had come with him from his crew were soon convinced that this king was not the stuffy type.

It was early the next day when Thera rose over the horizon ahead of us, and late afternoon when we drew close to it. This supposed abode of the gods was not quite so big an island as Naxos, but at a distance there was a certain resemblance. Thera looked like little more than a single mountain rising from the sea, double-peaked and surrounded by a thick platform of lowlands that gradually came into view as we sailed closer. Here, as on Sicily, one of the first features to become visible during an approach by sea was a volcano, from which a faint thread of smoke ascended to heaven. None of us knew what this fiery mountain might be named.

There was no visible evidence of any intelligent activity, either human or divine, as we surveyed the island from the sea. Darkness was approaching and we postponed our exploration until tomorrow. The weather was so calm that night that we could lie at anchor on a shoal. The stars as always wheeled overhead, and we picked out the eternal figures of gods and monsters in their majestic posings, and wondered as men will wonder about their influence on humanity.

At dawn we raised our anchor and set sail again; in a matter of half a day we were able to circumnavigate the island entirely, despite some unfavorable winds.

There was only one harbor on Thera, a small one, with no traffic at all to be seen at its mouth.

By now murmurs had begun among the crew that it would be good to have a man with wings scout ahead on approaching such an ominous place as this abode of gods, innocent and peaceful though the island looked in the full sunshine. There was no hint as yet among the sailors of any real refusal to obey their king and captain; they still loved and feared Theseus more than they could fear any mere stories and rumors.

For my part, I needed no muttered hints. If we were really going to put into the harbor of Thera—and I had no doubt that we were—then I preferred making my first approach from aloft, where my own chances of escape, at least, ought to be much better. The truth was that I had the choice of doing this myself, or loaning my wings to whichever crew member might happen to be approximately my size. Under the circumstances I preferred to take the lead.

Anyway, none of my shipmates were rushing forward to volunteer. And I had another reason for preferring to use the wings myself, thinking that a clumsy neophyte would almost certainly damage them. Surely some powerful gods had been on my side on Naxos, that I had managed to bring away my wings unhurt from that orgy.

Still it was with considerable misgivings that I strapped my wax-and-leather pinions once more to my shoulders, and leaped overboard, this time launching myself from the small elevation of the prow. As before, I had to beat the air smartly to keep my feet from dragging in the water. But once launched, I easily attained a good altitude and set my course for the center of the island, while a small and rather nervous cheer went up behind me.

Soon I decided to deviate somewhat from the direct course toward the central mountains, thinking that it would be wiser and more productive to survey the whole extent of the island from a moderate altitude before approaching the peaks.

It was soon evident to me, from the appearance of some scattered habitations and cultivated fields, that a few humans at least still remained on Thera. When presently I caught a glimpse of some of these people, they did indeed look somewhat more civilized than the current residents of Naxos.

Some of these Therans showed so little curiosity at seeing me fly overhead that my own curiosity was aroused by them in turn. I landed near a small village, in an effort to discover how great their familiarity might be with flying men in general.

The villagers eyed me timidly when I approached them on foot, yet held their ground. Thus encouraged, I questioned them, and learned

that they had adapted well to what they described as the almost continuous presence, for
many years now, of gods and goddesses upon
their island. At least the situation had left them
virtually free of any worry about merely human
brigands and oppressors, as none of those had
dared to come near for more than a decade.

These commonplace inhabitants of Thera spoke
what was evidently their own dialect, with which
I had some difficulty. They were vague in their
replies to my questions, and reluctant to give
me any information. When at last I tried to
reassure them that, despite my wings, I was
only a human being like themselves, this rather
than easing their minds seemed only to upset
them all the more.

When I tried to convey to these people my
intention of exploring some of the higher portions of their island, they reacted with alarm,
and some tried to warn me against any such
effort. They themselves were all determined to
stay clear of those upper regions, where, they
swore, the caves and meadows had for years
been occupied by the gods, or beings claiming
that distinction.

Looking up at the looming volcanic peaks, I
could see, as I had on the previous day, a trace
of rising smoke. I asked about eruptions, but
that was not what bothered the natives. They
assured me that the volcanos had not been really active within living memory, and indeed I
could observe no evidence of fresh lava upon
the higher slopes.

I leaped into the air and flew, then circled
uncertainly for a time. But presently I made up

my mind, deciding to return to the ship and report to Theseus before exploring any further.

I reached the ship without further incident. When my royal companion had heard my report, he remained, as I had feared, utterly unshaken in his determination to search the island thoroughly for Dionysus, and if possible to try conclusions with the god. The young king fretted and fumed that he could not fly as I could, and come to grips with his rival that way. But at the moment there was no way to remedy that.

Only now, at last, did a general murmur of protest arise among the crew. Theseus quieted this incipient grumbling by telling them that all who wished to do so could remain aboard the ship, while he led a small party of volunteers inland. He told the men, and we all believed him, that he was perfectly willing, if need be, to attempt the expedition without the help of any of his Athenian volunteers.

This shamed a couple of the Athenians into agreeing to come with him. And Kena'ani insisted on going ashore too. "Why else have I come to Thera, if not to land on it?"

And as before, I volunteered without fuss to go along, knowing there would have to be a flying scout, and not wishing to trust my precious wings to anyone else.

We never did put into the harbor, but rowed into the shallows near a beach on the other side of the island. From there I fluttered ashore, while Theseus, Kena'ani, and the two members of the crew who were to accompany us leaped into shallow surf and waded. Once inland past

the beach, we climbed a trail, or rather Theseus
and the others climbed it, while I flew on in
advance to reconnoiter. Generally I kept a few
score paces ahead of my comrades, scouting out
the best route upward and looking out as best I
could for any surprises.

Before we had made half the distance to the
top there was no longer any real trail to find. No
one, or very few people, had climbed this way
on foot for a long time. I sweated and labored,
seeking out the most practical route; flying, in
fits and starts is hard work, especially when
done only a short distance above the ground.

I still remember that day, and the discoveries
we made then, as if it were only yesterday.

To begin with, I recall very plainly how we
came without warning upon the first of the
strange dwellings. This happened only a little
way below the rim of the broad plateau that
roughly encircled the twin peaks just below the
feet of their barren upper cones.

Not that we immediately recognized that first
strange find of ours as a dwelling, or as something constructed by the gods. It was more like
a great inverted wine-bowl, the size of a respectable house, and broken as any common
wine-bowl might be broken, so that most of its
substance lay in shards. It had been constructed
almost entirely of some material resembling dark
glass, or Baltic amber, and when we first gazed
on it, its purpose was as much a mystery to us
as its construction. Yes, I too was mystified,
even though I at least had seen glass many
times before, glass of Egyptian and other ori-

gins, and had even worked with it in my Athenian workshop.

The five of us stood in a circle around this shattered structure for some time, trying to decide what it had been before it was destroyed. That destruction was unmistakably deliberate, as if it had been accomplished by the repeated blows of some giant armed with a hammer. I think none of us suggested that this glass bowl might ever have been a house. But the truth was, as we later came to understand, that if one of us had mentioned a prison cell, he would not have been far wrong.

Before our party moved to ascend the trail again—from here on up a thin path was indeed visible once more—I went scouting ahead again on my wings.

When I had flown high enough to be able to peer above the level of the uppermost meadow, or plateau, that more or less surrounded the high peaks, I beheld a grassy expanse studded with boulders, and marked here and there with small streams, some of them issuing from springs that must have been near the extreme heights.

Here and there this broad, extensive meadow bore clusters of broken dwellings similar to the one we had already discovered. All of these buildings, or ruins, appeared to be completely deserted. I hastened back to my companions and reported this discovery.

When I rejoined the young king and his companions they were climbing steadily, toiling back and forth among the rocks, and they of course paused to hear what I might have to say. Theseus listened without surprise or excitement to my report of what awaited us above—his only reaction was one of disappointment, that the god Dionysus did not appear to be there now.

Now I used my legs instead of my wings, though I kept the pinions strapped on and was ready at every instant to leap into the air. After climbing on foot the remaining distance to the high meadow, we peered into one after another of these great mysterious inverted wine-bowls. Everything we saw confirmed that no one dwelt in any of the structures now, though there were suggestions—animal bones gnawed and discarded, footprints and trails too vague and old to read—that once, not too long ago, someone had.

Some of the structures were larger and more complicated than others, and one, I recall, was at least as big as the Temple of Athena in Athens itself, rising three or four stories above the meadow. Some of these buildings had been constructed in part of other and even stranger materials than glass or amber. But all of them now looked deserted.

And it seemed to me that everything in them, or almost everything, was broken. It was as if some ritually thorough policy of destruction had been enforced.

Then, while we were in the midst of exploring these ruins, there came for me another of those moments that will never be possible to forget.

I was standing in front of a shattered wall, made of one of the mysterious opaque substances used in so much of the construction here; and this wall was very much like all the other shattered walls around me, except that I realized abruptly that a human face was peering at me through one of its many holes.

It was no ordinary face. On my second glance at this apparition, with my previous experience with the Bull and Dionysus never far from my awareness, I was not entirely sure that the countenance now confronting me was wholly human.

Not that there was any gross disparity in shape or feature. My first logical impression of the man behind the wall was only that he must be of no more than ordinary height, and young, so that his brown beard, bleached somewhat by the sun, still grew patchily. His brown eyes were large and round with astonishment as he stared at me through the hole, and the expression on his face suggested that he had never seen anything quite like me before. But somehow, before I had seen anything of this man but the central features of his face, I knew that he was extraordinary. This person was somehow of a kind with Dionysus—which meant that to me he was, perhaps, more than a mere human being after all.

I called out in a low voice to my four companions, who were moving about at no great distance behind me. And at the same time the stranger and I, as if by common though unspoken consent, both began to move toward the place where the wall separating us ended in a broken opening. When we reached that point we would be able to confront each other fully, at scarcely more than arm's-length distance.

The man I had discovered was clothed only in a lion-skin, I saw when we had both moved beyond the corner of the wall. But even this bizarre garment was not the first nor most remarkable thing that any of us noticed about him.

As greatly as Theseus had excelled the clerk Stomargos in strength and bulk of muscular development, even so, it seemed to me, this stranger excelled the King of Athens, or any other mortal man that I had ever seen. And yet the massive body poised in front of me looked neither fat nor slow; and the muscles under the tanned skin were not only extraordinarily large, but appeared to have a different *quality* about them as well, as if, despite their natural flow and movement, they might be formed of some material harder than human flesh. This peculiarity is something hard to put into words. I was reminded of the Bronze Man patrolling the shore of Crete; not that I thought the figure in front of me was rigid metal, or had the least doubt that it was fully alive.

Of course the sole garment worn by the stranger, the lion-skin, was remarkable enough in itself. Lions were not native to any of the other Greek islands, and could scarcely be commonplace here on Thera. But still here was an undoubtedly genuine skin—I had seen one of the great cats alive, caged in Athens, and some of their pelts in Crete, and I could not be mistaken. In confirmation, there were the skull and gaping jaws, from which fanged bones our new acquaintance had fashioned himself a kind of crude helmet.

The man who stood facing me, thus adorned, was carrying a club, a tapering length of splintered log. The log was deeply dented in several places, and most of the bark was worn away by some kind of heavy use. I am not usually considered a weak man, yet I would have used two hands to lift that club, and would have found it much too ponderous to serve as a practical weapon. Yet this fellow waved it lightly in one fist, so that I thought at first it might be of some kind of peculiarly light wood. I discovered soon enough that it was not.

Still, with Theseus and several others standing armed and ready at my back, I was able to remain calm in the face of this apparition. And as no one else was in any hurry to speak, I took it upon myself to open conversation.

"Greetings, sir. I am Daedalus, an artisan, lately of Athens and of Crete. May I ask your name?"

There was a pause, as if my interlocutor found it necessary to think for a moment to be sure of the question.

"I am Heracles," he said at last. The young man spoke as good Greek as any of us, and in educated tones, not in the local dialect. His voice, though not unpleasant, was high-pitched, not nearly as deep as might have been expected from the possessor of such a body, so that at first it struck me as incongruous.

Heracles—the glory of the goddess Hera. It was an unusual name, though not unheard of, and I wondered silently how this remarkable-looking youth might have come by it.

Haltingly, somewhat uncertain as to protocol, I did my best to introduce this somehow godlike person to the new King of Athens. I thought that Theseus looked jealously upon this strange man's massive muscles—as would any man who prided himself on his own strength—and I was sure the king was calculating in his own mind how soon he could honorably issue a challenge to a wrestling match.

Trying to fill a somewhat awkward silence, I questioned our new acquaintance about his dress.

Heracles answered simply that he had killed the lion and taken its skin.

"You killed the beast in Africa?" Theseus asked him.

"No. No, sir—I should say 'Your Majesty.' I killed the lion here. I have never been to Africa. I may not leave this island."

Theseus blinked at him, not understanding.

"You mean that you are not allowed to leave, good Heracles?" I asked. "Why not?"

"I have taken a vow," the strong man answered solemnly. "I am trying to make up for the grievous harm that I have done."

The rest of us looked at one another in puzzlement; and Theseus, also the victim of a self-inflicted vow, showed sympathy.

Somewhat haltingly, with the air of a man who needs encouragement to be sure that his audience is really interested, Heracles began to tell us something of his history—though many a day was to pass before I heard very much of it.

He also spoke of a race of Bullheads, as he called them, who until recently had occupied the highlands of this island, but who were now departed. These Bullheads were two-legged beings who nevertheless looked something like cattle, and who spoke the languages of men in a slow and halting way. From the way that Heracles described them, they were definitely not men; whether he thought they were gods or not was not easy to tell. And either our new acquaintance did not understand the reason for their leaving, or he was having trouble in communicating that information to us.

Theseus and I, who had known the White Bull on Crete, looked at each other. And I understood that Heracles was confirming—as had Dionysus, on Naxos—what the Bull himself had told me of a whole race of such creatures.

Kena'ani, who could have no patience with a race of beings who were already gone beyond the range of trading, asked: "Will you show us where the lion came from?"

"If you wish."

So saying, Heracles led us to a different kind of shelter, a huge, compound structure now broken in all its parts. Within its various yards and cells, he said, a number of specimen animals, including snakes and at least one lion, had been confined as far back as he could remember. Some of these beasts had managed to escape during the confusion attendant upon the general flight or failure of the Bullheaded gods. Heracles related how he, with only the kindest of intentions, had then hunted some of the more deadly creatures down and killed them after they escaped. His intention, as he said, had been to protect the weaker people, the villagers and fisherfolk who were still living on the lower levels of the island.

I objected: "Then killing those animals cannot

be the 'grievous harm' you say that you have done."

"No. No. After that, I grew angry at the gods, you see. Because it seemed they had deserted me, and others who lived here." Here the strong man gestured vaguely toward the sky. "So I began to destroy their buildings." He gestured at what was left of the structure in front of us, whose ruin I had thought perhaps an earthquake had accomplished. "I smashed the nest where the flying chariot had always rested. And the places where the Bullheads themselves had slept and lived, before they decided to depart."

"Where did they go?" I asked.

"I saw them get into a greater flying chariot, one big enough to hold them all, and one of them told me they were returning home; they sounded very sad, and talked of conflict among themselves, and failure. Among themselves they said much that I could not understand. And I grew . . . worried. So I hid myself for a time, until after they were gone. Then when they were gone I grew sad and angry too, and I broke all the fine things that I could reach."

Heracles gestured with his great club; then he hung his head and mumbled: "After that I was sorry for what I had done. So I made a vow to stay here always, and protect people. And every day, or almost every day, I climb to the lip of the crater above, and sacrifice something I like."

"Sacrifice it?" Kena'ani asked.

"I throw it into the volcano. Some of the people who live below in the village taught me to do that."

"But are there any other people here now?"

The strong man raised his head and sighed. "No, not up here where I live. People still live down in the villages, and they visit me sometimes, and bring me something to eat. Some of them are women." He brightened slightly. "There are no longer any people besides me living up here on the meadow. You may live here if you like. But if you intend to stay here, I wish that some of you were women."

"I do not think that we will stay," said Theseus slowly. Obviously he did not quite know what to make of this strange man. The rest of us looked at one another, but no one else had any immediate comment. We continued to explore the ruins, with Heracles now in attendance on us as a willing guide.

There were many buildings scattered about the meadow, and we did not visit all of them. Some that we entered contained underground sections, and in general these basements had suffered less damage from the club of Heracles than had the upper floors. Heracles himself provided no further details on the subject. Perhaps there was simply less room underground to swing a club, or perhaps his rage had begun to fade by the time he reached the cellars.

Here, below the surface level of one structure, we found a frieze, marvelously carved in stone, and some other artwork as well, showing some of the Bullheaded people in the act of bringing light to the poor human people of earth. Most of these in the picture stretched up their carven arms in gratitude. I supposed that this must have been carved by the Bullheads themselves.

At some point during this tour our guide informed us that he had been born in one of these broken dwellings—just which one he was not certain—and had spent his entire childhood and youth here in these buildings and on this meadow, under the tutelage of the Gods-Who-Had-Come-From-Afar. This was another name of his for the Bullheads, as he more often called them.

Theseus and I both questioned him about the youth who called himself Dionysus, and traveled about in a marvelous flying chariot.

Heracles nodded calmly. He knew Dionysus, who had grown up here too. And he, Heracles, had seen that smaller chariot many times at close range—the Bullheads had left it behind, perhaps by mistake, when they departed—but he had never ridden in it. And the dissipated youth I described was indeed Dionysus—at least the strong man had never known him by any other name. He had been one of Heracles's siblings—or at least one of his childhood playmates, he was not sure whether a blood relationship existed between them.

"Yes, that's Dionysus, of course. A difficult young man to get along with. But he and I came to an agreement finally." Heracles did not sound at all like a man talking about a god.

Theseus was uneasy, displaying the chronic uncertainty that I myself felt upon this subject. "But how can he be really *Dionysus*? I've seen him and talked to him. He's not the true and ancient god of vegetation that our fathers and mothers worshipped now and then."

Heracles made an impatient gesture; probably it was only accidental that he gestured with the hand in which he was still absently carrying his club, and that the club smashed into a wall and cracked out fragments. Then he frowned at the wall, as if it might have deliberately got in his way. "Why not let him be called that if he wants? We were all of us allowed to choose our own names."

My curiosity was straining. "Then you had other brothers, other playmates as well? Perhaps you had sisters too?"

"Yes, I did. But they're all gone now." The powerful man's frown deepened. "I don't really know where they are."

"Did they depart from Thera with the gods? The Bullheads?"

"No, I think not." Heracles did not want to discuss the matter further.

"Anyway, the one in which we are especially interested," the King of Athens persisted, "is he who now calls himself Dionysus. You say you know him. Where can he be found now?"

Heracles answered that question readily enough; more and more he sounded as if he did not particularly like his former playfellow. "Dionysus paid a visit here only recently, traveling in his flying chariot as usual. We talked together for a time. He has gone on now to a place called Crete, about which I have heard some marvelous stories. He asked me to forget my vow of service and go with him, saying that vows meant nothing, and mine were more foolish than most."

Theseus swore at such a scoundrel, who could take the attitude that vows and glory meant nothing. Naturally the rest of us contributed some indignation.

"Dionysus," I said, "can be very persuasive, when he asks a man—or a woman—to do something."

"True," said Heracles. "But he and I came to an agreement long ago. He will not try to persuade me, in that special way of his, to do anything. And I will not get angry at him."

The King of Athens and I both asked Heracles for more details about his earlier life with Dionysus, but he seemed to want to avoid the subject now, and we did not press him.

By this time Theseus was unable to restrain himself any longer, and challenged our new friend to a wrestling match. Heracles accepted indifferently.

A ring was quickly arranged, and the two powerful men stripped and grappled. Heracles seemed to understand the rules and traditional procedures quite well.

The signal was given for the bout to begin, and in a moment the King of Athens had been defeated. Not only defeated, but picked up and tossed down as if he were a child; it gave me a strange feeling, of mixed anger and satisfaction, to see this result, which the winner appeared to accept as a matter of course. From the expressions on the other onlookers' faces, I could see that they shared my feelings.

As for Theseus, he sat motionless for a long moment in the middle of the ring, where he had been thrown down, his face white with a

combination of what I supposed must be surprise and shame. It must have been his first
defeat in years.

Heracles began to look gloomy when he observed the reaction of his opponent. Then the
victor expressed a wish that he had done the
great king of Athens no harm.

Color flowed into the face of Theseus again,
and he sprang to his feet and immediately renewed his challenge. "Let's make it two falls out
of three!"

His shorter adversary shrugged. "If you wish."

The second trial lasted no longer than the
first, and had the same result, except that Theseus
sprang at his opponent even more fiercely, and
hit the ground somewhat harder a moment afterward. After lying stunned for a moment he
bravely bounced up again, though I could see
that his head must still be spinning. Two of
three falls had already been decided, and all the
young king could do was offer the winner his
hand, and assure him that he was still perfectly
all right.

Then Theseus offered his conqueror a place at
his side in the great adventure upon which we
were embarked, explaining that he, Theseus,
wanted to try conclusions with Dionysus.

Heracles, who was neither sweating nor breathing hard, looked somewhat relieved that the
king was still uninjured. Then he expressed some
doubt about the wisdom of attacking Dionysus,
and said that anyway he, Heracles, was bound
to stay here, as he had already explained.

Before the strong man had ceased altogether
to feel some apprehension over the king's wel-

fare, Kena'ani stepped in to play cleverly on his incipient sense of guilt over this victory. The Phoenician tried to persuade Heracles to give up his self-imposed vow to remain on Thera. Seeing Kena'ani doing his best to ingratiate himself with the royal house of Athens, I considered the cause a good one and put in a word or two for it myself.

Between us we eventually achieved our objective, but our success was some time in coming, because an objection had occurred to Heracles that made him unhappy and delayed matters. It seemed to Heracles that a special sacrifice, something beyond the daily effort—say a live lion—would be required to free him entirely from the burden of his vow, and he had no suitable animals available at the moment. There were none left aboard our ship either.

But at this point I was visited by what I considered a happy inspiration. Remembering the mysterious gift of Minos, that still-unopened box, I explained where it had come from and under what circumstances. All save my friend Kena'ani agreed with me that the enigmatic little casket ought to make a more than adequate substitute for a live animal; and I, for my part, was glad at the chance to be rid of it. In truth I would have felt uneasy about any other method of disposal. Kena'ani was not altogether happy about my suggestion, but by now he had come to share some at least of my misgivings about the gift of Minos.

Heracles was impressed to hear that our potential sacrifice had come from the King of Crete himself, who seemed to him an almost legendary figure. Whatever Heracles knew of Minos had evidently come from the vanished Bullheads of Thera, who had been somehow at odds with their compatriot the White Bull of Crete. So Heracles saw Minos as something of an evil or at least a misguided figure, who had dealt with the outcast Bullhead who had taken refuge upon that island and begun a course of interference with the natives that most of the other Bullheads had thought completely unwarranted.

I flew down to the ship to get the casket, and labored back with it by air to the high plateau. Kena'ani cast one more glance of longing at the small wooden box, but he did not attempt to interfere.

Heracles showed us the way to the highest crater, along a thin path worn in recent months by his own feet.

He also expressed a wish to try my wings sometime, but he did not press the point when I explained the need for correct sizing. Anyway, the straps of my wings could never have been made to fit his shoulders.

We had to climb another difficult stretch, this one of sharp and barren rock, to reach the lip of the crater. Or at least everyone but myself was required to climb.

We climbed, or flew, and then looked down into a fiery scene of smoke, scorched rock, and blackened lava. Even in daylight, a faint reddish glow could be perceived in the depths of the crater. If this volcano was asleep, its sleep was restless; below us molten rock, in places barely crusted with dark ash, bubbled heavily and stirred thickly as if some unimaginable monster could be in restless motion beneath its surface.

After appropriate prayers—Kena'ani was always good at extemporizing these invocations as required—I handed the precious chest to Heracles, who without further ceremony hurled it still unopened into one of the high volcanic vents. The actual vent aperture was small and distant, but his arm was very strong and his aim accurate. The box bounced once, without bursting open, and disappeared into what seemed the very heart of earth.

At this the rest of us sent up a small cheer, assuring Heracles that this gesture had completed his release from his ill-considered vow, freeing him to enter the service of Theseus.

Heracles now formally swore an oath, on the bones of his father and his mother—though as he said he did not know where they were—to serve the King of Athens faithfully, and to accompany us on our expedition to Crete.

A few minutes later, when we were all on our way down to the meadow once more, there were strange rumblings behind us, sounding as if they came from deep within the crater, and a puff of thicker smoke went up. Perhaps this demonstration was a result of the sacrifice, perhaps not, but I at least was happier the farther we retreated from the overhanging lip of rock.

"Now let us go to our ship," said Theseus, a man never willing to waste any time. The King of Athens was more determined than ever to go on to Crete, now that the presence there of his chief enemy seemed to be confirmed.

Heracles delayed briefly to enter one of the

broken dwellings on the meadow, there to pick up what he said was his favorite bow—it was almost as thick as his club—and some arrows. Then he pronounced himself ready for anything.

Filled suddenly with a presentiment of evil, I protested once more to the king that I would never be able to build him wings unless we first returned to Athens to rest and refit. But, as I had feared and expected, my protests did no good.

HOMECOMING

If the way Heracles handled his club had not been enough in itself to convince me that he was far stronger than any other man on earth, the outcome of the wrestling match would certainly have brought me to that conclusion. I did not doubt for a moment that our new recruit might have slain a lion in equal combat. I remained convinced that he was—in some way that I could not get perfectly clear in my own mind—in a class with Dionysus. Whether those two were fully human, or whether they were something greater than mankind, was a question on which I could not yet make up my mind. But they certainly fell into a special category. How much their special category differed from that of the White Bull was yet another difficult question.

Assuredly our new shipmate was a moody and dangerous man, the possessor of a quick and violent temper. If ever someone on our small ship jostled him accidentally, or sat in the place on deck where he had decided to sit, he would frown and mutter ominously. On the other hand, his mood calmed as quickly as it became disturbed, and when he was calm again he was ever anxious to make amends for any offense his display of temper might have given. Utterly lacking in guile, he was not in the least ambitious, and in his heart thought himself to be a good man. I could not help but concur with him in this last opinion, dangerous though his companionship could sometimes be.

We had no more than completed our high sacrifice upon the crater's rim, and were starting down together from the high plateau, when the talk among us turned, as men's talk will, to the subject of women. Somewhat to my surprise, given his claim to have lived his entire life in relative isolation, young Heracles considered himself something of an expert on the matter. He had lain with his first woman, he informed us, many years ago, at a truly precocious age. Though he was reticent on details, in this as in other matters pertaining to his personal background, I gathered that there had been females among his siblings and playfellows on the island; and also that a fair number of the girls and women of the villages below had not been at all reluctant to visit him in his high meadow. In earlier days, we were informed, before the Bullheads had all gone, Dionysus had organized some truly memorable parties. But celebrations shared with Dionysus always left a man with a terrible hangover.

Heracles showed a greater willingness to discuss the sport provided him by the female islanders during their visits to the high plateau, after the departure of the mysterious Bullheads. To hear our newest hero recount his amorous exploits—which he did in a calm, matter-of-fact way—he was as far superior to all other men in male potency as he was in sheer muscular strength. We all listened to him noncommitally; no one was going to lightly suggest that this man was a liar, even in good-humored jest.

I had been somewhat apprehensive that Theseus and he would no more be able to get along on one small ship than two young bulls in a single pasture; yet, as I should have realized, men are frequently more than animals. Despite their natural rivalry, the two heroes quickly began to evolve a strong friendship in a way that I had not foreseen. But that developed gradually, and its full maturity came later.

Again, while we were still making our way on foot down to the ship, before we had descended half the distance to the harbor, Heracles spoke to us of a pair of giant snakes that had been sent to kill him in his cradle. We let this incredible tale pass at the time, but a little later, when we were all aboard ship and had some time to spare, we questioned him curiously about this incident. To no avail, for by then he had decided—or so he pretended—that it would be wise to say no more.

The strong man was very vague about the role of his human parents in his upbringing; he could remember his father and mother, he said, but they seemed to have faded totally from his life long years ago.

He was sure, he said, that he had been born on Thera. And he had actually never set foot off the island until now, except for a couple of brief boat rides, which he had of course enjoyed in the days when the Bullheads were still in residence, long before making his ill-considered vow never to leave.

Coming aboard the Athenian ship, therefore, was really a new experience for him. And yet he knew the function of oars, and sails, and weapons, as soon as he saw them. He even, as we realized later, understood something of the sailor's art, enough to help in managing the ship; in one way or another this strange man garbed in a lion's skin had already managed to learn a good deal about the world. I wondered privately if he had been subject to the strong, strange, teaching that can only be imparted by those who belong to the race of the White Bull.

On his catching sight of our modest shipboard stores, the eyes of Heracles brightened, and he began to tear open skins and boxes of food and devour the contents. Then he stopped suddenly, on realizing that he really ought to have waited for an invitation. This was promptly offered by the king, and the newest member of our crew promptly resumed his feasting, which he topped off by a draught of wine so prodigious that the rest of us gazed at one another in wonder. Any ordinary mortal would have collapsed shortly after such a drink; but Heracles only belched, blinked, wiped his beard with the back of his hand, and pronounced himself satisfied for the moment. Since we were now saddled with the Heraclean appetite, we thought it fortunate that there were other islands nearby where we should have little difficulty in replenishing our supplies.

As we sailed out of the silent Theran harbor, Heracles—speaking as clearly as if he had never tasted wine—began to tell us a little about some of the other companions of his childhood and early youth, people who like himself and Dionysus had grown up from infancy on Thera under the tutelage of the Bullheads. These included one called Orpheus, who like Dionysus seemed to be a skilled hypnotist; Tiphys, also called the Helmsman, who had an unerring sense of direction; and Idmon, a soothsayer to whom the veils of chance and time were frequently transparent. Where any of these people might be now, Heracles did not know, or so he said. There had been other companions, too, he concluded vaguely; but he was not minded to talk of them just now. I remember the names of Calais and Zetes, Castor and Polydeuces.

All went smoothly on our voyage to Crete, despite a few minor difficulties with supplies, until we came near the halfway point, where we had an encounter with real pirates.

There were two large ships full of these buccaneers, else our sturdy-looking Athenian vessel would probably not have been attacked. Altogether our attackers must have numbered at least fifty or sixty men, as each of their vessels boasted about thirty oars—it seemed likely that one of their objectives in pursuing us was to capture another seaworthy vessel and thereby expand their enterprise.

Surely many poets more eloquent than I have already sung the glory of the Athenian arms upon that day. The pirates had picked the wrong victims this time, though they outnumbered us by about four to one.

Hastily extracting my wings from their place of concealment, and putting them on again, I armed myself lightly with a few stones, and took off from the rail, ready to drop missiles upon the heads of our attackers if I were unable to frighten them away.

Better for them if they had been willing to be frightened. Some indeed displayed fear when they saw me hovering birdlike in the air, but by the time I got well into action, the pirate commanders had already committed both of their ships to attacking us.

It was a sorry parody of a battle, with Heracles and Theseus arrayed against a mere two pirate ships, whose crews were disheartened from the start by the sight of a winged man flying above their heads.

Apart from a certain amount of fear and confusion I undoubtedly caused among the enemy, my effect on the outcome was actually quite small. The pair of stones I dropped had little effect. But while soaring and hovering above the three ships, I had the ideal position from which to view the progress of the fight.

As soon as one of the enemy ships had come within bowshot, Heracles plunged into the sea, swam with incredible speed to the attacker and climbed its nearest bank of oars; while clutching

six or eight of the long shafts together in his two
arms, he succeeded in breaking some of them,
and terrorizing a whole bank of rowers, thereby
effectively immobilizing the whole ship.

But only when Heracles was able actually to
set foot upon the pirate deck did he reach his
full effectiveness in combat. And that was truly
a marvel to behold. I saw some arrows actually
bounce back from his skin, while others penetrated only a finger's width. Slung stones that
would have crushed ordinary flesh and broken
normal human bones rebounded from his hide;
after the battle he had no worse than pinpricks
and bruises to display as wounds.

Theseus, on the other hand, retained his royal
dignity even as he fought. Made of humanly
vulnerable flesh inside his bronze armor, he
remained aboard his own ship, a commanding
figure with sword in hand, bravely defying the
enemy, who were so greatly superior in numbers, to try to cross onto our decks. Thus, de-
fending skillfully with his shield, he drew to
himself much of the storm of stones and arrows
that would otherwise have fallen on our men
who were less well-protected than their king.
He sustained several wounds, fortunately light.
Meanwhile his sturdy Athenian crew were free
to man their oars, which they did admirably,
pulling their smaller, lighter vessel out from
between its two attackers. And still the crew
had some time to fire their own missiles back at
the foe.

Meanwhile I, flying above, had little to do
but dodge a few arrows and slung stones that

were launched at me in midair. None of our shaken adversaries came close to hitting me.

Within moments after Heracles had gained the deck of the first of the enemy ships, the carnage there amongst the pirates became truly frightful. Putting his god-like strength to effective use, the strong man bestrode their deck with one of their own long oars in hand, making it do the work of scythe and spear and lance. Pirates swarmed toward him at first, and then those few who survived the first passages at arms fell back. In the end, of course, the enemy's rout was total.

Before the commander of the remaining pirate vessel could begin to comprehend what sort of foe he faced today, his ship too had been boarded by the superhuman attacker, in the same amazing way, and the slaughter had recommenced. Now Theseus gave orders to his oarsmen to close with the remaining enemy, and he and several of his fellow Athenians boarded the foe and were fighting on the pirate's deck when the end came.

I landed on the second pirate ship at about the time that enemy resistance ceased. Heracles appeared before me, moving through the carnage at the end of the fight as a figure from the underworld, a broken oar in hand, his lionskin torn and hanging from him, his hair and beard and body all smeared and caked with blood, only a very little of which was his own.

At first our inhumanly powerful recruit was smiling, but that did not last long. Already his chronic tendency to remorse and guilt was showing itself. We had some small difficulty in con-

vincing Heracles that there was really nothing
wrong in exterminating pirates to the last man.
The crippled survivors who lay about their gory
deck we dispatched efficiently, and hurled into
the sea. Incredible as it seems, the casualties on
our side had consisted of no more than a few
light wounds.

The unequal battle had occupied no very
lengthy period of time. And when it was over,
we found ourselves in possession of three ships,
though with hardly more crew than was required to man the smallest of them adequately.
After some discussion, Theseus decided to sacrifice the two larger vessels to Poseidon, setting
fire to them after removing from them such
piratical stores as we thought might prove valuable. These included not only food and water
and wine, but a spare sail that we thought could
be made to fit our Athenian mast, and a good
selection of abandoned weapons. As to gold and
other treasure, we searched both of the enemy
hulls thoroughly but were disappointed.

Then we sailed on.

As our royal ship drew near to Crete, and
even when we came in sight of the chief harbor,
we saw surprisingly little maritime activity.
Things here were not quite as lifeless as they
had been on Thera, but certainly the volume of
shipping and of naval activity was considerably
down from what it had been when I escaped by
wing some months before.

Flying close to shore to reconnoiter, I was
recognized at a distance of two stadia or more
by the Bronze Man, and promptly greeted by a

series of hurled rocks, the first of which howled past me before I had any indication that my inanimate enemy was anywhere near. It was as if Talus had been waiting for me during all the months of my absence, and was ready to resume hostilities just where he had left off.

As had been the case on my departure, some of the rocks he hurled missed me only narrowly. I remembered the searing heat-ray, and feared it would be the next weapon turned against me. Obviously it would be suicidal for me to try to approach the island now, and so I turned sharply in midair, deciding to return to the ship.

This was a natural enough decision, but as I soon realized, it might have been a mistake. It informed our enemy that I was no longer alone, but had returned with a shipful of allies. But where else was I to go?

Once Talus had made sure that I was connected with this particular ship, he hurled more stones, and larger ones and to a greater range, that threatened to cripple our vessel, or even sink us well offshore.

We were still at a distance from shore that made it hard for any of us to see the Bronze Man at all, and I remember wishing that at least one of our heroes might be gifted with exceptional eyesight.

Heracles was not so gifted. But at last, squinting into the distance, he made out the Bronze Man, and said that he had never seen the like of him before, but that a metal man surprised him no more and no less than some of the other wonders of the world.

Soon, when Heracles realized how hard Talus

could hurl rocks, our shipmate began to view
the situation as a serious challenge. Searching
aboard our ship, he soon found some small rocks
and a sling with which to respond in kind.

Regrettably, this hero's efforts with the sling
proved to be more of a danger to his shipmates
than to our enemy. Several men actually leaped
or fell overboard, trying to get out of the immediate danger posed by their own formidable ally.
The leather thongs in the mighty hands of
Heracles sang through their airy circle with an
awesome power, and each rock on his releasing
it went shrieking through the air toward the
shore faster than any arrow, indeed faster than I
could well follow with my sight.

But all this heroic effort went for naught,
because the strong man's accuracy with the sling
was very poor.

Still, a few of the many missiles he hurled
came quite close to Talus—I could see a distant
splash or two, and puffs of rock-dust bursting on
the rocky shore. But the chief result was that
our opponent on shore, taking a cue from
Heracles, switched to using smaller missiles,
and attained better accuracy as a result.

The duel went on, while the rest of us, even
Theseus, could only watch, keeping ourselves
low in relative safety, trying to dodge when
necessary, and holding our breath. A few of the
stones launched by the Bronze Man now began
to strike the ship, splintering wood even with a
grazing touch, and puncturing sails, so that at
last we were forced to put out away from land
again.

Heracles, who had been running out of rocks

anyway—his only supply on board was of course the miscellaneous gravel left lying about by other slingers after the encounter with the pirates— was not discouraged. Next he assured us all that he was quite skilled with the bow, which had been available to him for practice during his boyhood on Thera. He had not tried to use the bow to begin with, he said, because he feared there were no suitable arrows on the ship.

But when we looked for the bow he had brought with him from Thera, we found it had been unaccountably lost during the struggle with the pirates. Of course we had aboard no replacement weapon that was worthy of his strength. He broke several bows, as well as several borrowed strings, before he gave up in frustration at their weakness, and sat down in a black mood to sulk. The owners of the ruined weapons did not quite dare to protest openly.

Naturally I had already begun to speculate on the best way, if I could be given the necessary materials, tools, and time, to create a weapon worthy of this warrior's power. But lacking a workshop aboard our ship there was nothing I could do to solve the problem.

One look at the face of Theseus convinced me that there was no hope of convincing him to abandon his hunt for Dionysus. He remained determined to go ashore on Crete, and so we faced the immediate problem of how to get ourselves ashore alive.

Heracles, as usual, was no help at all in planning. He continued to sulk, grumbling and mumbling that he had to find some way of coming to grips with his own most challenging enemy ashore, while remaining faithful to his new oath of obedience to our king. Theseus had already forbidden the strong man to simply swim ashore and hurl himself at the foe.

Theseus shared Heracles's impatient attitude, but approached the problem somewhat more constructively, as befitted his position as a military commander, his royal standing, his much greater experience in the world—his formal education in the school of the Bull may have had something to do with it, but I am not sure.

Before long the well-schooled King of Athens was able to come up with a plan that at least satisfied himself. Theseus decided that we should stand well away from the land until darkness fell. Then I would fly ashore by night, coming to earth at some spot well inland, where he intended to meet me later.

Meanwhile our ship, under command of the Athenian mate, would sail round the island, while Theseus, Heracles, and anyone who wanted to join them dropped off one at a time and swam ashore under cover of darkness. The mate and whatever crew remained aboard would keep the ship in Cretan waters, and try the shore again and again at various landing-places around the island.

No one voiced objections to this scheme—chiefly I suppose because none of us could suggest a better one—and we began to put the royal design into effect. But just before I took off from the rail, while the ship was coming close to shore, we were at last struck directly by a sizable missile from the hands of the Bronze Man. It was a large rock that stove in two of our deck planks, though luckily it did not penetrate the hull. Our simple assumption that the darkness of night would offer us protection from his bombardment was shown to be a fallacy.

But our heroes were not men who could be so easily forced into retreat. Heracles vowed that nothing was going to keep him from eventually coming to grips with his terrible opponent. Yet the strong man was still under his vow of obedience to Theseus, which prevented him from immediately leaping into the water and charging the enemy.

He was soon in action, though. Shortly after my departure on wings (as I learned later) Heracles, sitting on one plank and paddling with another, was able to make such speed through the water that he managed to get ashore without encountering Talus directly—this may have been due largely to the fact that Talus was coming after me instead, as I flew inland. Fortunately for me some formidable cliffs stood in the Bronze Man's way, and one thing he could not do was fly.

Theseus meanwhile also came safely ashore by swimming, though in the process he had to leave his armor either in the ship or on the bottom of the sea. But he counted on being able to acquire more weapons once he had the chance.

Knowing nothing of what might be happening behind me, but trusting in the Fates, I flew inland, over the firesparks of cottages and camps, and came down, as my king had planned, somewhere in the hills.

FINAL EXAMS

I had come back to Crete, back to the soil in
which I had buried Kalliste, whom I loved.
Crete was also the land where I had watched
our son grow up as far as he would ever grow.
And yet my thoughts on returning were not
chiefly of grief and loss, or even of danger; this
coming back felt in a strange way like coming
home.

As I winged my way inland over the firesparks
of that darkened coastline, I found that I was
leaving most of my fear behind me. Somehow,
during the long journeying from Sicily, my awe
of the Bronze Man and the other dangerous
powers that might now rule in this island had
diminished. By degrees, especially during the
last stages of the journey, something of the fury
and determination of King Theseus had caught
in my heart and brain, and now I found I had
abandoned my timid wish to flee immediately to

the safety of a snug workshop somewhere in Athens.

You must understand that I make no claim that I was free of fear entirely.

There were mountains ahead of me now, and little enough moonlight by which to see their gray and ghostly shapes. I spent another hour or more in dark loneliness aloft, seeking a good place to come down. I wanted a place not too far from my ultimate goal, the arranged rendezvous which was not far from the House of the Axe. At the same time I thought it vitally important that I not be seen on landing. At length I chose a hillside that appeared in darkness to be uninhabited, in a region that I thought would be within a day's walk of the rendezvous.

It was not without some trepidation that I managed my landing in the dead of night. Getting my feet safely on the earth was a difficult task, and I was forced to abort my first landing attempt when a darkened shepherd's hut loomed up in front of me at the last moment. But I switched my attentions to another hillside nearby, and at last I accomplished my goal successfully, my sandals crunching and sliding on gravel as I stumbled to a stop.

Once I had attained solid footing, I looked around me as best I could in the faint moonlight, then cautiously removed my wings and rolled them up. I was unable to see much, but I smelled familiar Cretan vegetation, and heard the cry of a nightbird that I had often heard from my window in the palace when my beloved Kalliste and Icarus were with me.

All seemed peaceful; apparently my arrival

had caused no alarm. But somewhere, a few hours away at most, Talus had sought to find and kill me. And if half of the stories that I had heard since my departure were true—and I knew of no reason to disbelieve them all—then somewhere on this island now, probably at the center of the Labyrinth that I had built, the White Bull was still alive. If the Bull was still alive he was almost certainly my mortal enemy, despite all the soft words and the worrisome gift I had had from Minos. And I considered the Bull, being intelligent, a vastly more dangerous enemy than Talus. I knew that the Bronze Man had no thoughts, no plans, no desires of his own; if he had sought to kill me and had killed my son, it was only because the doctor of education had ordered him to attack us.

Shortly after I came to earth, the moon went down behind the mountain to my west, and the darkness of the night intensified. I sat waiting on the hillside till nearly sunrise, when something like a path became visible on the slope beneath me. Then I began to walk downhill.

The point of rendezvous where I was to meet Theseus and Heracles was near the summit of one of the lower hills in the vicinity of the palace at Knossos, and I thought I now knew exactly the best way to reach it from my present location without encountering unnecessarily large numbers of people, or drawing undue attention to myself. Theseus, who had selected the place, had given me the impression that he knew it well. Perhaps, I thought, that resulted from his having held secret rendezvous there with Ariadne or Phaedra. Or perhaps with both of them.

*   *   *

As the light increased, I found myself making
my way among familiar-looking Cretan farm-
steads, orchards, and vineyards. Of course I was
now carrying my wings concealed in a small
pack on my back. When I came to a handy
thicket, I paused, and with a bronze knife I had
borrowed from one of the sailors on the Athenian
ship, cut myself a traveler's staff. Then I pressed
on.

As soon as full daylight overtook me on the
road I began to encounter small numbers of
people. They were peasants and bird-catchers,
women fetching water, and young priests climbing to a mountain shrine. No one appeared surprised to see me, and I had no reason to think
that I was recognized. Each time I met someone, we exchanged nods or gestures of greeting.
Once or twice, when I thought some useful
information might be obtained, I approached
the other party boldly and spoke to them; each
time we exchanged a few words. And I learned
what I considered valuable facts, along with the
usual hearsay and rumor.

The news of the death of Minos had come as a
serious shock to the entire population, but now
conditions appeared peaceful, on the surface at
least. Queen Pasiphaë ruled Crete at the moment, but with the princesses both gone, the
future looked uncertain to everyone. At least
civil war had not yet broken out upon the island, though as I was soon to find out, it was
already threatening.

My first real clue as to how things stood in
this regard came when I ran into some of the

potential combatants, a small group of off-duty soldiers. They were returning to their garrison from a visit to the farm where the family of one of them was living. When I asked them how things were going in Heraklion, and in the palace, they gave me two different answers, and immediately began to quarrel among themselves.

Gradually the political picture became clear: A large faction of the people, including the army and navy, were ready to rebel against a queen who secretly claimed an alien consort as her lover, and conducted a bestial relationship with him, though she pretended to deny the fact.

I pretended to be astonished to hear such accusations. My informants asked me where I had been; I replied that I was a scholar recently arrived from Greece, and had been hiking from palace to palace on the island, in search of my old compatriot Daedalus.

At this the soldiers began to wrangle again among themselves, some claiming that Daedalus had flown away from the island to Sicily on wings of his own invention, while others dismissed that tale as a preposterous invention. The White Bull, they were quite sure, had had the inventor murdered months ago. I bade them goodbye and slipped away almost unnoticed while they continued their argument.

Half an hour later, during a conversation with certain milkmaids who were engaged in rounding up their goats, I at last heard some word of Dionysus. When I first mentioned the god's name, the young women exchanged sly glances among themselves and tittered. But then they were not altogether unwilling to talk. It was plain to see that they found Dionysus very intriguing. Yes, they told me, that restless god was even now reported to be visiting the island once again, as he had at intervals during the last few months, ever since the reported death of mad Minos somewhere in the petty kingdom of a foreign enemy.

On this latest trip to Crete, Dionysus had once again arrived in his wondrous chariot, which he had landed more than once during the last few months inside the Labyrinth itself. Some of my informants thought that he was there now, visiting the White Bull; others giggled and refused to speculate. But one of the girls said that she was looking forward to a chance to attend one of the Dionysian parties. Then she burst into laughter and would say no more.

Soon I walked on, wondering if the presence of that god would destroy the rest of human life on Crete, as it had appeared to come close to doing on Naxos. But no one else I talked to that morning volunteered any information about Dionysus, and when I cautiously mentioned his name I had blank stares for an answer. Probably, I thought, that god (if in fact he was a god) did not really care anything about ruling Crete or any other land. Most likely his primary reason for visiting here was to restock his wine supply from the almost bottomless cellars of the late king. Probably the new divinity of wine and madness was not averse either to recruiting a few attractive Cretan goat-maids for his orgies.

Around midday a small coin from my light purse bought me a satisfactory dinner from a farm-wife. While munching on my bread and cheese I pondered what I had learned so far, and came to the conclusion, or at least allowed myself to hope, that I need not worry too much about Dionysus—at least not unless Theseus actually succeeded in catching up with him and challenging him directly. On vastly smaller Naxos, where there were not nearly so many people, the more or less steady influence of Dionysus had triggered a vast change in the general behavior of the population. But here on Crete the divine comings and goings tended to be unnoticed by most of the inhabitants. With public attention focused on the strange events taking place in the House of the Axe, one orgy more or less somewhere else caused little excitement. And it occurred to me to wonder whether, if Dionysus ever attempted to control too many people at one time, he became distracted and found it impossible to get them to do anything in particular.

As for the chance of Theseus bringing this convivial monster (or god) to bay, it seemed unlikely, as long as Dionysus wished to avoid him. The King of Athens could travel from island to island no faster than a sailing ship, while his great antagonist soared overhead and out of reach in what might have been the chariot of the sun. Small wonder that Theseus wanted wings of his own; but fortunately—as I thought—no wings that I could build could ever match the speed of the vehicle borrowed from the departed Bullheads.

I hiked all the remainder of that day, with brief rest stops, realizing that I was somewhat farther from my goal then I had originally thought. By the time darkness had fallen again, I thought I knew almost exactly where I was in relation to the House of the Axe, and to our planned place of rendezvous. Once it was dark, with the thin moon behind some friendly clouds, I dared to fly again. And as soon as I had risen above some small nearby hills, the distant lights of the great palace and the adjoining town were unmistakable. Thus, with no very great difficulty, I had in the course of a day and a night arrived at a position very near the appointed place of meeting.

The exact place of meeting, which I managed to reach during that night, was a small cave on a rugged hillside. This cave had been frequented from time immemorial by the local peasants, who considered it a minor shrine to some local god so ancient that I suspect his very name had been forgotten. From the mouth of the cave it was possible to see anyone approaching along the ascending path some time before the visitor actually grew near; thus I suppose Theseus thought it made an excellent place for clandestine meetings.

A light rain had begun to fall when I established myself snugly just inside the cavern's mouth, and went to sleep. Near dawn I was aroused from a light slumber by the sound of someone climbing quietly along the path below. Arming myself with my staff I waited, ready to fight or retreat along the rough terrain of the hillside behind me, which was marked by innumerable places of concealment. Presently I could be sure that only one person was coming up the path; and a few moments after that, straining

my eyes in near-darkness, I determined to my
joy that my visitor was Theseus.

The young king, bareheaded now and wrapped
in a long Cretan cloak, with his short sword
ready underneath it, was pleased to find me
already in place and undetected by the Cretan
authorities. He told me with cheerful excitement of the considerable difficulties, including
the necessity of abandoning most of his armor,
that he had experienced in getting ashore without being destroyed by Talus. But by dint of
swimming, wading, and running, he had managed the feat at last.

I thought, but did not say, that Theseus never
would have managed to do so unless Talus had
been distracted from pursuing him by some other
perceived duty. That duty might well have been
the pursuit of me. Of course I too had been
fortunate to survive; and I supposed that I could
attribute my good fortune to the fact that I had
placed enough steep-sided ravines and cliffs between myself and the Bronze Man to keep him
from keeping track of me.

The king asked me: "Have you had any word
yet from Heracles?"

"Not a word, sire." And now it occurred to
me to wonder if the strong man had unwittingly
sacrificed his life to provide the distraction necessary to save both the king and myself. "Did
anyone else volunteer to come ashore?"

"I think not." The king did not seem in the
least perturbed, of course, by this lack of heroism in his crew. What use would one or two
more ordinary mortals be in this situation?

Theseus graciously heard the story of my ad-

ventures since we had separated, then modestly
told me something of his own. He too, on his
journey incognito overland to this place, had
seen and heard things suggesting that the land
of Crete now faced increasing anarchy and strife,
perhaps intense enough to threaten civil war.

He had also heard the same stories I had
heard regarding the god of wine and celebration. With the tension among the people growing closer and closer to an open outbreak, King
Theseus hoped we might be able to count on
some support from strong factions among them
if we entered the Labyrinth to try conclusions
with Dionysus if he were there as reported, and
with the White Bull as well, if necessary.

This struck me as a truly heroic plan. I have
said that my fears were much diminished, but I
had not grown suicidal. The idea that two of us
might be able to defy our enemies in such a way
seemed so to me.

I expressed my doubts that any great number
of the Cretan people would support a foreign
prince, and my companion had to agree that my
objections had some force. Theseus wished aloud
that he could have manned one of the captured
pirate ships and sent her to Athens for help, so
that he might have the prospect of assistance
from something of an invading force. But there
was no use wishing. In any event, he had been
unable to spare the men to work even the smaller
of those captured pirate ships.

The day was now well advanced, and still we
had seen no sign of Heracles. The question now
was how long we ought to wait for him. Theseus

was anxious to reach the Labyrinth as soon as possible.

"There is one thing that concerns me, though."

"Yes sir?" I waited, hoping for reasonableness.

"It is this, Daedalus. Are you going to be able to guide me through that place when we get into it?"

"Of course, sire." There had been just a hint of a momentary change in my young friend's voice when he spoke of the Labyrinth. I thought to myself that he was doubtless going to need all of his heroic nerve to make himself enter that place again for any reason. But still I had little doubt that his nerve would be equal to the task; and of course I had full confidence in my own ability as guide. It was the other problems, including the Metal Man and an army of human enemies, about which I did not feel so confident.

Remaining in or near the cave, we waited for Heracles through the rest of that day, and the early part of the following night, meanwhile sharing between us the small amounts of food we had each brought. But the strong man did not appear, and at last Theseus made up his mind to do the best he could without that formidable helper. About two hours after sunset the king and I started down the path from the cave.

"Sir, what are we to do when we actually reach the Labyrinth? As you know, it is heavily guarded."

"We'll find a way to get in. Trust me, Daedalus. As long as you can guide me once we are inside."

Our plan, which I had been waiting to hear elaborated, apparently did not exist except in the most rudimentary form. And the skeleton

was going to be fleshed out by the King of
Athens at the last moment, using whatever men-
tal materials he might then find ready at hand.
At about this point I became better acquainted
with despair than I had been for some time.
Then a happy thought struck me.

"There may be one person living near the
palace, sire, who would be willing to help us."

"So? Who's that?"

I told my lord of the devoted slave Thorhild.
Many months had passed since I had seen her,
but I believed her devotion had been genuine,
and it seemed at least possible that she might
still be dwelling outside the palace proper. Al-
ternatively some loyal relative or close friend
might be there, available to carry a message to
her.

We determined to do what we could to seek
out Thorhild, I suppose simply because we had
no better hope. Theseus, once an even faintly
better hope was offered, admitted freely that it
would be sheer madness to simply try to sneak
into the Labyrinth on our own. He questioned
me several times on all its entrances and exits,
and I told him of all I knew—of all but one.
That portal was a secret one, that might conceivably be of benefit to us if we were trying to
get out of the Labyrinth—but it would, I thought,
be of no real use to adventurers insanely bent
on getting in, two mice approaching a huge
trap. Of course, as the king and I both realized,
it was possible that there had been extensive
reconstruction of maze or palace, or additional
building since our hurried departure from the

island. In that case even I might prove inadequate as a guide.

Having walked until near midnight, we decided to rest until morning before trying to locate Thorhild, and turned off the road into a thicket where a murmuring stream promised water. Theseus, ever the hearty warrior, thought nothing of spending a night in the open. And in his company I felt considerably easier about it myself.

We slept soundly enough, wrapped in our cloaks, and next morning were up at the first light and on our way. When we reached the top of the next hill, the House of the Axe and the Labyrinth were in sight before us, with Heraklion and the sea visible beyond them.

As I recalled, Thorhild had lived not far outside the walls of House and Labyrinth proper, in a quarter of the adjoining town that was largely given over to housing the more dependable slaves and servants of the crown. These chattels lived in a state of freedom actually greater than was enjoyed by many who were not called slaves; Minos had believed in rewarding competence.

"My Lord Theseus?"

"Yes?"

"I will be much less recognizable in the eyes of most people here than you will. At the same time, Thorhild is much more likely to recognize me than you." That young woman would also, I thought, be more likely to trust me than to trust a king, but I did not say that to the king's face. "Therefore I should be the one to go to her door. It will be better if you remain out of sight somewhere nearby, while I try to establish contact."

At first Theseus would hear nothing of any plan that put him in a position of lesser danger. But eventually he was so far persuaded by the force of my arguments that he consented to remain standing across the street, face muffled in his cloak, while I knocked at the humble portal that I thought must be Thorhild's door. No one answered my repeated knocking, which was hardly surprising since at that hour most of the able-bodied servants were at work within the palace.

There was nothing for the two of us to do but seek shelter somewhere for the day, and return at night. Accordingly we retreated toward the hills again. No one hailed us or questioned us as we passed, but I was sure that a good many people turned their heads to look after us as we walked through the town.

Theseus and I spent the remainder of the day hiding in a hedge that formed the border between two olive groves. This time our conversation lagged. No doubt the king would have preferred trying to enter the Labyrinth without the aid of any local person, but our brief sojourn in the town had shown us that there were plainly too many guards about, not to mention other people, to allow any rational hope that such an attempt would succeed.

As soon as darkness was completely fallen we made our way back to the servants' quarter of the town and tried again to contact Thorhild. This time the door burst open at once when I tapped on it, and a host of armed men in palace livery came pouring out. I was roughly seized, and then abruptly released, as my captors lost a hand or two to the sword of Theseus. My companion had needed no more than the space of a heartbeat to cross the street and fall upon them.

The skirmish was a brisk one, and I did the best I could with my simple staff to aid my sovereign; but the few blows I could deal out were not enough. The odds against us were far too great. I saw a circle of spearmen closing in, and someone with a net in the act of entangling the king's swordarm; and then I was struck from behind upon the head, and for the time being I knew no more.

STUDY HALL

When my senses at last returned to me, I found myself lying on the stone floor of a small cell, enshrouded in almost total darkness. A chain of bronze hobbled my ankles, leaving little scope for movement, while another chain pinned my wrists even more closely in front of me. The cell was cool and dank, the sound of running water reached me from some distant source, and I knew in my first moments of consciousness that I was somewhere in the Labyrinth.

Slowly stretching forth my linked hands, I touched a wall. From the rough texture of the stone I knew that I was in one of the regions of the great maze from which sunlight was perpetually excluded; whether day or night ruled outside at the moment was something that I could not immediately determine, nor could I guess how long I might have been unconscious. There being nothing else to do, I sat up, prayed to such gods as might be conceivably interested in hearing from me, and took stock of my injuries. Fortunately, aside from a small swelling on the back of my aching head, it seemed that little damage had been done. My clothing, except for a loincloth, had been taken from me. My other belongings, weapons and the small pack that had contained my wings, were of course gone as well.

A jug and a small slab of bread had been left on the stone floor beside me, a discovery that I found heartening as far as it went. I lifted and swirled the jug and found it full of liquid. I sniffed at these offerings, and then decided that it would be foolish to worry about my captors drugging or poisoning me when it was in their power to murder me at any moment. Finding myself extremely thirsty, I raised the jug to my lips and drank deeply of the water it contained.

Then, with minor difficulty because of the ankle-chain, I got to my feet. The next job was to explore my cell. My only hope in this effort, such as it was, lay in discovering or reminding myself of some peculiarity in the construction that would offer me a chance of getting out—so far this thought, this hoped-for hope, was so dim and remote that it scarcely attained conscious form.

But the exploration was trivial and futile. Everything that came within range of my groping hands and straining vision only tended to confirm my first impression of the place in which I had been confined. The walls were of heavy stones, mortared closely together, and arching together overhead at twice a man's height from the floor. The floor was of stone and wood, with several small openings in it, too small to permit me to think of squeezing my body through one of them. Besides, having designed the drains, I knew that they offered no way out. Water, I knew, was running underneath my floor, moving too slowly for me to hear it even in the general silence; the running water I could hear intermittently was at some considerable distance. Perhaps my finely designed plumbing was now poorly maintained, and had recently begun to leak.

Shuffling slowly between the walls, I reached my cell's door and stood in front of it. This door was a wooden slab, armored with metal plates in the vicinity of the lock, and pierced only with a small metal eye. The corridor outside was not quite so dark as the chamber in which I was confined, and now I could confirm my location precisely and beyond all possibility of a mistake. From certain clues that were visible in the corridor, I knew that my cell was the second in a row of six, occupying one side of a perpetually gloomy passage. This small portion of the Labyrinth had indeed been designed as a place of confinement.

I listened carefully, but at the moment all was quiet except for that faint, continual, and distant splash. Was it possible that my king and comrade Theseus was even now locked up in the next cell? Possible, of course, but I feared he had been slain.

I was about to call out in a low voice, when a

new sound, very faint, reached my ears from
somewhere nearby. It was a faint and hopeless
weeping, that certainly could not come from the
King of Athens.

"Ssst! Who's there?" I tried to pitch my voice
to reach the next cell, or cells, without unnecessarily disturbing any guards who might be doz-
ing at some greater distance down the corridor.

The almost silent sobbing broke off in a faint
intake of breath. Moments later words reached
me in soft but joyful whisper: "Master Daedalus?"

"Is that Thorhild, then? Thank the gods that
you are still alive, at least. Where is Theseus?"

"Theseus, sir?" There was a pause. "But I
know nothing of the Lord Theseus. Men came
and arrested me at work—I suppose it was yesterday afternoon—and I have been here in this
dark place since then. But are you really Master
Daedalus? Oh sir, I would be very glad to
have you here, more or less with me, except—
except—"

"Yes, yes, of course. Well, we could both of
us be worse off than we are." I thought I could
understand, now, the full extent of my master's
royal foolishness in coming here, and of mine in
following him, with no better suggestion to make
than trying to make contact with Thorhild. Of
course one or both of us must have been recognized, knocking in daylight at her door—servants
are not ordinarily blind or stupid, unless they
choose to be. And so the queen's loyal soldiers,
or the Bull's, had been waiting for us there
when we came back in the evening.

Soon footsteps echoed in the corridor, and a
pair of bronze-helmeted guards appeared to un-

lock the door of my cell. They removed the
chain from my ankles, though they left in place
the one that bound my wrists. Then they led me
away.

We were headed in the general direction of
the Bull's quarters, and once my escort hesitated, as if they were on the verge of getting
lost. Twice we came within sight of a small
window, as I had known we must sooner or
later, and I was able to see that it was indeed
daylight outside. We turned aside before coming near the Bull's private chambers. The room
that was our destination was as windowless as
my little cell, though several times as large.

I trembled as I entered, because I saw that
Queen Pasiphaë herself was waiting there for
me, looking no different than when I had seen
her last before she left with Minos on their royal
tour of diplomacy. The queen was dressed in
formal robes, and seated on a high chair, behind
a high table of Egyptian make.

My escorts cast themselves down before her,
and hurled me to the floor with them, of course.

The queen's voice sounded neither angry nor
excited. "Arise, Daedalus. And tell me why you
have come back to Crete."

I got to my feet slowly. "Majesty, I mean
neither you nor your people any harm." Which
was true enough. "I have come here in search of
the being who is called Dionysus."

The queen considered that claim for a moment. She sat on her high chair almost in formal
state, with a thin diadem on her natural-looking
black hair, that must be, I thought, subtly dyed.

Then she demanded in a sharper tone: "What have you to do with the invader Theseus of Athens?"

"As you know, madam, he has been my friend for a long time. I am now in his service, and it is at his command that I seek Dionysus." I drew breath, emboldened at the queen's evident lack of anger. "As for his being an invader of Crete, I am sure that the king has never—"

"Never mind. Tell me what you have seen of my daughters since you fled this island."

As truthfully as I could, I related to the queen my experience on Naxos, including my encounter with her older daughter there, but omitting all details of Ariadne's part in the orgy. I mentioned having heard that Phaedra now ruled as queen in Athens, and to Phaedra's mother I expressed my regrets that I had not seen her royal daughter since before my flight from Crete.

Before I had to deal with another question there was a stir at the doorway behind me, as of people arriving, and the queen unceremoniously motioned me to stand aside. Turning as I did so, I beheld to my vast relief King Theseus, walking unaided and apparently not seriously hurt. The king was undoubtedly a prisoner, for golden fetters manacled his wrists together in front of him, and he still wore the simple traveler's clothing as he had been wearing when we were taken. He was of course not thrown to the floor by his accompanying guards. Nor did they grip his arms, but rather followed, watchfully but respectfully, a step behind him as he strode into the chamber.

For a moment neither of the monarchs spoke. Theseus, though he must have been aware of my presence, did not take his eyes from the queen.

She boldly returned his stare, running her eyes lasciviously over the stalwart frame of the young king. At last Pasiphaë said: "You may be sure of one thing, Athenian. Never will I allow my torturers to do anything that might spoil such a body."

"I had never thought you would." Theseus sounded quite unperturbed.

Slowly the queen's gaze turned to me. "As for you, Daedalus, I am inclined to believe your story. But I have not made up my mind about your fate."

Inwardly I trembled, but I said nothing. Theseus beside me was silent too; no doubt both of us realized that for him to try to speak on my behalf might well be counterproductive.

Queen Pasiphaë turned her gaze once more on him. "I hear that my daughter rules this day in Athens."

"That's right. Phaedra rules till I return, and I am sure that she rules loyally."

"Well, well. My husband and I were once sure of her loyalty too . . . all in all, I do not regret her going. Of course I have a mother's feeling for her all the same—and for her sister too. But it is interesting that now Athens has a foreign queen. A very young queen too, and newly installed . . . tell me, King Theseus, how much control do you believe your bride will have over the generals and admirals who are accustomed to taking their orders from your late great father, or yourself?"

Theseus said nothing. But I thought that he did not appear unduly worried.

The queen went on: "I think that my next step must be to send an embassy to Athens. To explain to your dear bride, and to those admirals and generals, that circumstances here prevent your leaving as soon as you might wish to leave. That we, you and I, are in the process of negotiating a treaty—yes, a treaty that will be of benefit to—well, to both our houses. There are matters of trade and tribute to be discussed."

Leaving the silent Theseus with much to think about, Pasiphaë swung her gaze to me again. "Artisan, we have your wings, you know. Are they the ones you wore when you flew out of the Labyrinth before?"

"No, Majesty. These are an improved model."

"Someday, soon, I think I shall want to see you fly. With a long chain, of course, around your ankle . . . but for the moment I believe you. Your life is safe—for the moment."

I bowed, feeling unheroic relief.

"Talus is no longer commanded to kill you on sight. But you will remain in prison for a time—no house arrest. When the greatest artisan in the world has built for me a perfect prison, why should I not employ it? Soon, Daedalus, we will speak of building wings."

I would have liked to know whether the Bronze Man accepted orders directly from the queen, or from any other human being. But I was in no position to ask questions.

The queen was standing now, and everyone

else in the room save Theseus, knelt down. Then in a moment, in a swirl of golden robes, Pasiphaë had swept out of the room.

I now expected that Theseus and I would be quickly returned to our respective cells, and I was hoping to have a chance to speak with the king before this happened. But before the guards could escort either of us away, there was another approach in the corridor outside, and the White Bull himself appeared.

It was a startling appearance. The Bull was being carried on a crude-looking litter by six strong students, and they had some trouble in maneuvering this awkward conveyance through the corridor, and the doorway into the room.

The occupant of the litter was sitting upright, as royalty customarily do when carried, but this inhuman body was strapped into its chair, and it was plain at second glance that he had little power of movement.

At first the White Bull largely ignored Theseus, which may have surprised the King of Athens, but did not really surprise me, who had a better understanding of the great educator. After all, in the eyes of the Bull, Theseus was no more than a failed, delinquent student without any notable potential.

The litter had to be maneuvered slowly into the room, then parked wedged into such space as was left when the student bearers had moved the high chair and table out of the way as far as possible. Seated in this position, the Bull had to turn his head to look at us directly.

"Dae-dal-us. It sad-dens me to see you so."

"I suppose you have the power to order my release."

He shook his massive head. "I can-not release you from your own will-ful ig-nor-ance."

"White Bull!" This challenge came, of course, from the young and royal hero, who was not going to submit to being overlooked.

His former teacher turned on him a slow and patient gaze of inquiry. If there was in that look any desire for revenge, it was well masked.

"White Bull, I demand that you tell me where the one who calls himself Dionysus can be found!"

The Bull looked at the guards, and pointed at the king, with the one arm in which he seemed to have free movement. "Re-move this one to his cell."

Theseus, dumbfounded at such treatment, had nothing more to say as he was escorted away.

When the two of us were alone—except for my own pair of guards—the White Bull informed me that the time had finally come to press on with Project Two, the plan for interspecies reproduction.

I said that I was sorry to hear it.

Ignoring that, the Bull told me that he would see to it that my life was spared if I constructed the necessary wooden cow. Looking down at his own damaged body, he said, in words even more stilted than usual, that a considerable amount of artificial aid would be necessary if he were going to couple directly with a human female.

The guards, their faces expressionless, stared straight ahead. I wondered if they might have been chosen for deafness, or an inability to comprehend anything but the simplest orders.

Apparently the stories about Bull and queen were not, at least not yet, founded on fact. I was wondering what to say about Project Two, when the Bull interrupted himself. "There is an-o-ther prob-lem, e-ven more ur-gent."

"And what is that?"

"If I give you a new teach-ing, Dae-dal-us—a teach-ing like that which en-a-bled you to make the wings— will you make for me a bet-ter ve-hi-cle than this?" And in a sudden uncharacter-istic display of violence, the Bull smote with his one good hand at the side of the clumsy wooden conveyance into which he was bound.

"Sir, I am sorry for your crippling, as I have said before, and I never intended it to happen. If given my freedom and a workshop, I promise that I will make you a much better vehicle than that—or several of them, different kinds for different occasions. I can promise that even without the benefit of any more of your special teaching."

"I can pro-vide the work-shop. Free-dom will have to wait."

"I accept."

"And in the mat-ter of what your peo-ple call the wood-en cow?"

I was still hesitating, wondering whether or not his intended partner was really Queen Pasiphaë, when he cut me off again. "That can wait." Again he pounded at the armrest of his litter with his hoof-nailed hand. "I must have some-thing bet-ter than this, I must. The discom-fort is too great. What type of con-vey-ance would you build me now?"

I considered the problem quickly. "As I said, more than one type, for different situations. One at least with wheels. First I would consider in which position your wounded body is most comfortable, and then—"

"I would like to be ab-le to change pos-i-tions with-out help. I have the par-tial use of one arm and one leg."

"Then in my construction I would be sure to allow for that."

But it turned out that I could not possibly be allowed to return to my old workshop; not just yet. The best compromise I could obtain was that I should immediately be given a cell with good lighting, and that small tools and whatever modeling materials I wanted should be provided, along with a workbench. I could create models of several vehicles for the handicapped for the Bull's approval before making a full-sized version.

Our agreement was completed for the moment, and I was ready to be taken away; but the Bull delayed me at the last moment.

"Dae-dal-us, I have heard that you were present at the death of King Min-os."

"That is true."

"Be-fore he left Crete for the last time, he said that he wished to be re-con-ciled with you."

"Yes, White Bull. He told me that also."

"It was his plan and mine that he pre-sent you with a gift."

On hearing this I hesitated. But so far, I thought, the truth had served me well. "I did receive a gift from the king before he died, and

he said that gift was partly from you too. You
have my gratitude, for what it may be worth."

"And the gift was—?"

"A small box of wood, carven and richly inlaid. Yes, King Minos brought it to Sicily with
him. He said it was meant to be used as a
sacrifice—"

"Ah!"

"Yes. Intended as a sacrifice to the gods and
goddesses of earth. And I saw it go into a
volcano."

"Ah." And the White Bull sounded satisfied.
"Then I hope that King Co-cal-us may de-rive
great ben-e-fit from it. And the earth-gods of
Si-ci-ly as well."

It was plain to me that this creature before
me did not have any idea as yet that Theseus
and I had visited Thera, disposed of his gift
there, and also brought away with us Heracles,
who might have been the most enigmatic of that
island's remarkable inhabitants. Sometimes a par-
tial truth serves better than the whole, and I
said nothing to enlighten the White Bull upon
this point.

But the Bull was growing more thoughtful
anyway, as if he were aware that there was
much about the situation that he did not know.
"And where did you join for-ces with the new
King of Ath-ens?"

"That came about as the result of an encounter at sea."

"Ah. Where?"

"Some distance to the north."

"Ah. Near Ther-a, perhaps?"

"It was closer to Naxos, sir."

The White Bull was silent for a time. "And have you been to Ther-a, Dae-dal-us?"

"Indeed, sir, we put in for a brief visit."

The Bull waited, as if he expected me to say more; but now I was silent too. At last he asked me directly: "Were an-y of my peo-ple there?"

"No, sir. Not when we were there. On Thera we found strange buildings, all ruined . . . where they had once lived. Theseus had thought to find Dionysus there, but he was gone."

The Bull was silent for a time, nodding, a human trait of communication that he had picked up sometime during his years on Crete. Then at last he said: "It does not sur-prise me. My peo-ple must have a-ban-doned their mis-sion and gone home. Lea-ving me. A ter-ri-ble pun-ish-ment for me. A-mong my kind, the most ter-ri-ble that can be met-ed out. I am now more ut-ter-ly an ex-ile than any of your kind can i-ma-gine." Then he glared at me fiercely. "But it does not mat-ter! The teach-ing is all that mat-ters to me now!"

Shortly after that I was escorted away by the guards, this time to a different cell, much more spacious and livable. It should have been called a room, save that the door could be locked only from the outside, and the windows were too high and narrow and heavily barred to allow any thoughts of escape. Here my clothing was re-stored to me.

This chamber was furnished with a bed, a table that would serve as workbench, and two chairs. It had its own supply of water, which ran in through a pipe at one corner of the ceiling and gurgled away through a hole in the floor that also served for waste disposal. I remembered carrying out some of my earlier experiments in plumbing while constructing this small row of rooms; I was surprised to see that the water was turned on here now when, as I recalled, the supply to the palace was not always adequate. Then I understood—it was very likely that Theseus was being kept in the even more luxurious room next to this one, and naturally a king, even in prison, must have fresh water.

If Theseus were really my neighbor, then I must find a way to speak to him. It might of course be possible to communicate between the cells by shouting through the corridor, but there could be no privacy in such a conversation. Tapping on the wall between the cells would also serve to send a message, but only if some kind of code had been arranged in advance.

But between these two particular cells yet another connection existed, in the form of a curving and recurving passage, built carefully within the thickness of the wall. The tunnel was narrower than a man's arm, and in its windings resembled a kind of miniature Labyrinth. The small opening to this passage was set high in the wall, so difficult to see that I might well have missed it had I not known that it was there. I had to stand on my table to bring my head close to the inconspicuous opening. This small labyrinthine passage, too small for any creature bigger than a mouse to attempt to use, was the result of another experiment in construction, carried on at the request of King Minos. The king had been thinking of having facilities for eavesdropping built into his palace. As in the matter of the plumbing, I had thought to test my techniques in the dungeon portion of the Labyrinth before putting them into construction within the House of the Axe itself.

The minature labyrinth had proved to offer no advantage, for purposes of espionage, over a simple opening; but with cooperation on both sides of the wall, it ought to serve, I thought, to carry a few whispers back and forth.

I hissed and whispered. To my joy, I was able almost at once to catch the attention of the neighboring inmate, who proved indeed to be my comrade Theseus. In another moment the two of us were engaged in quiet but urgent conversation.

"I must escape, Daedalus. I cannot endure being long confined like this."

I shuddered inwardly for my young king, remembering his terror of being closed in during his earlier adventures in the Labyrinth. "I built these cells myself, Majesty. Short of bribing the guards, I know of no way you can get out quickly. Of course we must not despair."

"If it were not for the windows, I would be mad already. Even with them—" Theseus let his words trail off, but I thought I understood what strain there must be behind them. Alas, for the time being there was nothing I could do.

Within a matter of hours the modeling materials and small tools I had requested were delivered to me in my new quarters.

The materials included some small pieces of wood, along with string and thread and wax and glue, as well as tiny nails and screws and other minute metal parts.

Shortly after the arrival of my tools and materials I conferred with Theseus again, and the idea for a plan of escape began to germinate between us. I was now possessed of sharp-edged and pointed tools, with which a determined man might eventually be able to conquer a wooden door. The lock on the door of my cell was protected, as I have said, with metal plates that would make such an attack neither quick nor simple. But Theseus reported that his cell door was almost entirely of wood.

"If only I had one of those tools they've brought you, Daedalus . . ."

It was the king's idea that if he could get out of his cell, he could attack the next warder who came along—he was sure they tended to travel this corridor alone—and get a key with which to open my cell, and any other occupied ones nearby.

But how was I to pass him one of my little chisels or augers? The only conceivable way was by means of the curving and recurving speaking-tube.

Once an appropriate tool had been passed through, Theseus, given some time to work, would be able to make a hole in his wooden door. After that it would be a matter of heroism, in which he had few peers. He could grab a guard by the throat, and stun or strangle the man, get a key from him to unlock his own door and then mine.

It occurred to me that if only it were possible to pass a thread or a string through the devious passageway where our spoken words passed, then Theseus could pull through any number of small objects. I had a great deal of string.

We tried to see a way of pushing, blowing, or forcing one end of a thread or string through the twisting passage, but none was immediately apparent.

Frustrated, the young king, standing on his own table, tried with his great strength to break away the stonework at the narrow opening of the communication passage, but the massive ashlars there refused to budge.

Only the idea of the string seemed to offer any hope. But how to force a thread through a Labyrinth, even such a comparatively simple one as this?

The first possible solution that occurred to me had to do with the fact that air and water could flow freely through even such a convoluted structure. But I could conceive of no way in which to create such a forceful flow of either fluid as to carry a long thread through the several windings.

A better idea came to me while I was watching a tribe of ants. These were very large and active creatures, who had dug their own passage up into my cell through the interstices of the stone paving. Then they had established a trail between their entry and some scraps of food that remained on the floor after my most recent meal.

After taking thought, I first induced the ants to re-form their trail over a scrap of fabric—my clothing had been restored to me—which piece of cloth I then lifted from the floor and introduced into the labyrinthine passageway.

The next step was to capture some ants. To

one of these, held in a fine tweezers on my improvised workbench, I cemented one end of the finest gauzy thread I had available in my model-building kit.

Seldom have I attempted any job requiring greater patience. Several ants were spoiled in the process, before one with an end of thread firmly affixed to its small back could be placed in the entrance of the miniature Labyrinth, where it joined its fellows who had gone up there with the cloth. And then the thread came loose, and yet another attempt was necessary.

On the second trial, the burdened insect, after some minutes of frenzied indecision as to what route to take, pulled the fine thread through the passage. Theseus seized it at once, and soon, at my direction, was able to pull through a stronger thread, and after that a piece of string. My supply of string was practically unlimited, and once an end was through any small object that could be tied to string securely could be passed from one cell to the other.

It would certainly have been more practical to use some larger creature, say a beetle of substantial size, instead of an ant. But as always it was necessary to work with the tools available.

Given a day in which to work with the small bronze bit or chisel, the King of Athens had no difficulty in boring several holes almost through his cell's door. A weakened panel was thus created, through which Theseus meant to put his fist at the proper moment.

Meanwhile both of us had noticed, though neither of us had paid much attention to, some sounds like distant thunder, which seemed to me unnaturally steady and prolonged. And while Theseus exulted at the strange behavior of our guards—they were leaving us to ourselves for long hours together—I wondered if this might be an ominous sign. It was as if both queen and Bull, and perhaps their soldiers also, were occupied with other matters and had no time for us.

Eventually one of the jailers did come around to bring us food and water, which were customarily passed in through a slit at the bottom of each door. As soon as the man had come into a properly vulnerable position, a huge fist came smashing through the solid-looking though greatly weakened wood of the cell's door. I could see nothing of the ensuing struggle, but I could hear the victim's yelp of surprise, and with a little imagination I was able to visualize the succeeding struggle.

Our plan worked. Moments later the young king was opening my cell door with a key he had just taken from the guard. When I saw Theseus again he was already carrying a sword much needed as a weapon.

Theseus was still suffering the psychological pressure of confinement, and we moved quickly as we made our way out of the dungeon portion of the Labyrinth. The continued scarcity of guards at first puzzled us almost as much as it delighted us. But we had not gone far before distant shouts and other sounds, running feet and the rattle of arms, gave us to understand that some kind of revolt against the power of queen and Bull was already under way or at least imminent, and the men were needed elsewhere.

My secret exit was far distant from this portion of the Labyrinth, and thus no use to us at all. The nearest way out lay just beyond the chamber in which we had been questioned by both queen and Bull, and after a hurried consultation with Theseus I led the way in that direction.

The chamber was deserted now, the cabinet in which my wings had been placed locked but unguarded. In a moment Theseus had forced it open. The wings were a part of his plan—as soon as we were able to get outdoors, he intended to have me use them to scout.

The windows in this meeting-chamber were not quite big enough for us to crawl through, but through them we had our first look at the sky for several days. What we saw gave us pause. The plume of smoke from distant Thera's volcano, that for many years had hung intermittently upon the northern horizon, had now greatly increased above its ordinary volume. Again now, even as we watched, that sound as of continual distant thunder came ominously to our ears. While struggling to escape our cells both of us had been much too concerned with other matters to pay much attention to these distant phenomena. But now I studied them and I liked them not.

"Hark! What was that?" Theseus paused, listening to a new and different sound, even as we were on our way out into the next corridor.

"It might be real fighting."

When we listened attentively we could hear shouts of alarm, much closer now, in the open portions of the Labyrinth. There was an even louder uproar, farther off in the streets of the town and courtyards of the House.

And then in the next moment the northern sky was lighted, briefly, as if by some unnatural dawn. The light grew in the space of a breath to equal that of the sun itself, behind distant clouds. The decline began at once, but it was much more gradual.

"What was that?"

This time neither of us could guess an answer to the question.

Only a few minutes after the strange light came the first shock of the tormented earth; the ground swayed like taut sailcloth beneath our feet, so that both of us cried out in surprise. In several places the walls of the Labyrinth broke down, fine masonry of a Daedalian bond crumbling and shattering like mud walls. Stone fragments rained about our heads. The water that ran perpetually beneath some of the floors splashed up through drain-holes, making perfect little fountains that lasted for no more than two heartbeats.

In a moment the little fountains had vanished again, but the grumbling and the shifting of the earth went on.

"Look! There!"

I looked, up in the sky. It was the flying machine of Dionysus once again, glittering away from Crete through distant air, presumably headed for some quieter island.

And yet again the ground lurched and quivered under our feet. Some of the walls around us were collapsing entirely, and we bolted through the newly created apertures for the open air.

Tremors tormenting the subterranean foundations of Crete were nothing new—just Poseidon Earth-Shaker flexing his muscles again—but shocks of such violence were certainly extraordinary. And today the initial shock was followed in three or four minutes by a horrendous noise, of a kind that I have never heard at any other time, before or since, that which I pray all the gods of earth and sea and sky I may never hear again. All I can say in the way of description is that it resembled a whole battery of distant thunderstorms raging at once, and with an ominously different quality in the thunder.

Theseus and I, climbing our way out of the half-ruined Labyrinth over one after another of its broken walls, found that no one was paying any attention to our escape, though we were in sight of several of the queen's guards and soldiers.

Nor, in fact, did we pay these potential enemies much attention either. I saw Theseus staring into the sky, a look on his face that I had never seen there before. I raised my own gaze to the heavens.

A dark cloud, racing toward us over the sea from the north as swiftly as the magic vehicle of Dionysus had fled away, was overspreading the whole lower third of the sky in that direction, in the process blotting out the northern horizon entirely.

Theseus was murmuring the names of gods, as if he were appealing to them for help, one of the few times that I have ever heard him do so.

The roar of human voices that went up from

the streets of the town grew stronger gradually, but still it was tiny by comparison with the world-sounds that had preceded it.

As we made our way from palace and Labyrinth, and through the town, we were met by numbers of people, civilians of both sexes, of all classes and ages, all of them running in blind panic.

Some at least of these distraught citizens were headed for the Temple of Poseidon, and I saw one group of them vanish into the broad, dark doorway, two blocks away. Only moments later, another earth-shock brought the great lintels and roof-beams of the temple crashing down, and I am sure that all inside it perished.

Theseus stopped to harangue the people remaining in the street, grabbing them by the arms and forcing them to listen when he could. He even made some headway among those not totally blinded by panic, convincing a dozen men or so at least to take up such arms as they could find and follow him. It was their duty as Cretans, he told them, to rid this, their beautiful island, of the queen and monster whose unnatural union had provoked the gods almost to the destruction of the entire world.

Before an hour had passed, my friend the king and hero had placed himself once more in command of an army, albeit only a small and rudimentary one.

CONTINUING EDUCATION

Initially our small army looked as if it might achieve some success. This profitable skirmishing lasted until the following day, when my heroic friend led his hastily organized force against the palace and it ran into some disciplined resistance from the queen's guard. Then, like other inspired mobs, it melted away like mountain snow brought down into summer's heat.

Despite the best leadership that Theseus could exert, most of the poorly-armed rabble that were his followers turned and fled at the first volley of arrows. Shortly afterward the King of Athens and I, with a mere handful of adherents, found ourselves in an alley of the city, trying to reorganize. Even the omens in the sky had turned against us for the time being; the great cloud in the northern sky had slowed its advance, the sun was shining brightly, and for the moment the earth beneath our feet was quiet.

Following our rout, a company of soldiers had pursued us from the palace, and now they pressed an attack. Just as we were on the verge of being overrun completely, panic began and spread swiftly in the enemy ranks, and I was sure that they were being attacked somehow from the rear.

In a few moments I had my explanation. Our long-sought comrade Heracles burst into view, riding a wild bull that he had somehow tamed into carrying him. He steered the beast by twisting on its horns. His mighty left hand sufficed to manage this, while with his right he swung his huge log-club, and thrust with it. Bronze armor dented in and crumbled under his blows, and human flesh was mangled. As in the fight at sea, his own body seemed almost impervious to weapons.

In what seemed no time at all, the company of guards who had been on the verge of defeating us were killed or scattered. Now the hard core of revolutionaries, a dozen men or so, who had remained with us were much heartened, as well as being better armed with weapons picked up from the fallen soldiers.

Now a different cloud, higher up the northern sky and composed of slower-moving darkness, appeared to be threatening to engulf the entire heavens eventually.

During that first period of active fighting I had made no effort to put on my wings. At first Theseus had wanted to keep his winged man as a surprise weapon, in reserve; and then when things began to go badly, danger had been so close and immediate on every hand that I had feared to put down my weapons long enough to fasten straps. But now, on the orders of Theseus, I put on my wings again at last, and soared into the smoky air to reconnoiter.

A couple of slung stones passed my way before I had attained very great altitude, but the arm of Talus was not behind them, and they represented only a minor threat. When I had climbed through the air for the better part of an hour, I was able to see a great deal.

The whole island of Crete, or at least a very large portion of it, was now in a state of general revolt. Flying close to the ground, I exchanged shouts with two of the rebellious leaders, informing them of the presence of Theseus near the palace, and urging them to press on in that direction. Nine out of ten who saw me flying only stared at me, but a few were still capable of rational thought and communication, and I had hopes of these, which I reported to my lord when I rejoined him shortly before sunset.

By morning our small army had again grown considerably, and it was greatly augmented by more fearful citizens after the dawn had come up frighteningly red and dim. Throughout the morning the sun struggled behind a thickening veil of darkness that had now come to dominate almost the entire sky.

Still the elite troops guarding the Labyrinth remained loyal to the queen, and were too strong for us to engage successfully in a direct attack; even Heracles, who led our initial charge, was stunned by a hurled rock in the first minutes of the fight. His bronze helmet was bashed in, and

his head suffered a blow that would have crushed
any ordinary human skull.

We had to drag our strong man away to save
his life, and the morale of our irregular forces
suffered greatly as a consequence. Heracles, to
our great relief, soon regained consciousness,
but for some hours he remained almost helpless. Out of necessity we retreated again, and
sought hiding places in the buildings of the
ruined city. That ruin was proceeding rapidly;
what the earthquake had so far failed to destroy,
fire and war were quickly starting to devour.

Whenever I climbed to a high place, or took
wing on another scouting expedition, I could
see that most of the palace and the Labyrinth
still survived.

Fortunately by the next morning Heracles
appeared almost as good as new, save for the
gash on his head. Theseus, wisely as I thought,
decided to hold him in reserve, until our army
as a whole should appear to have a chance of
standing up to the regular troops in a pitched
battle.

During the subsequent hours and days, as
long as the unnatural darkness continued to dominate the skies of Crete, Heracles kept our spirits up by refusing to be overawed by any of the
outrageous behavior of the sea or earth or sky.

He also regaled us with many a wild tale of
the adventures he had experienced in getting
ashore despite the Bronze Man, and in traveling
overland during the following days to reach the
point of rendezvous. Talus, we gathered, had
pursued him a good part of the way. Nor had
anything discouraged the Bronze Man in his

pursuit until Heracles from the top of the cliff had pried loose one boulder after another and thus launched a landslide onto him. Whether the metal man had actually been destroyed or not Heracles could not say. But at least his arrival in the vicinity of the palace had been considerably delayed.

Several times, also, while trying to reach the point of rendezvous, Heracles had grown angry at somewhat less threatening delays, and had lashed out at those Cretans he considered responsible. Each of these episodes had been followed by a period of remorse, in which he had tried, not always successfully, to make amends for some damage that he had caused. If he had been days overdue in reaching the point of rendezvous, he was sorry, but really there had been no help for it.

Theseus assured his best fighter that he was forgiven, and asked him questions. What else had Heracles observed on his trip overland? Were the people really rising everywhere against the queen and Bull?

Yes, just about everywhere, Heracles responded confidently. Once he had realized that a civil war was breaking out, he had quickly become convinced of the justice of the rebels' cause, and had openly taken part in some of the fighting, even before he had reached us.

"Good!" And Theseus clapped him heartily on the shoulder. I noticed that the impact even had a different sound than it would have done on ordinary flesh.

The cause of the rebellion in the vicinity of the palace was now immeasurably strengthened.

With Heracles now recovered from his injury and fighting at full strength beside us, the two heroes provided a nucleus of strength around which the local resistance was able to gather with increasing confidence.

At last, for the first time since the dawn had come without the sun's appearing at all, Theseus ordered me to slip on my wings and scout. It needed courage for me to soar up into that unnatural haze. The cloud was very low over the city and Labyrinth, and the inside of it was unexpectedly warm. The atmosphere there choked me in a way that no normal cloud ever did. I was breathing dust and noxious gases, not watery fog. Yet I determined to press on, and was at last rewarded by a thinning of the shadow above me.

When at last I broke out, I was perhaps higher in the air than I had ever flown before, though it was hard to be sure, as the ground was almost nowhere visible. The higher cloud was still above me, but it was thinner than before. With tears in my eyes I gave thanks to all the gods of creation that the sun and sky still existed, that all the powers of the greatest curse the Bull could devise were unable to destroy them. The cloudscape around me and below me had a magnificence beyond anything I had ever seen, even in the educational visions induced by the Bull.

At last I descended, finally regaining the territory held by my friends. Happily I was able to report to them that above the unnatural blackness, sun and sky existed just as before.

Some of the men whined fearfully: "But what

good is that to us if we are never more to see them?"

I tried to be reassuring; what I had seen of the sky had convinced me that eventually, this cloud, like any other cloud, would pass.

Meanwhile we heard that the students of the upper school, chronically rebellious, had turned against their teachers and administrators, and tried to seize control of the school. They had had at least some limited success.

I was worried anew about Thorhild, who had survived the collapse of the Labyrinth dungeons and had managed to rejoin us a day later. Since the fighting had started she had been never far from my side, and indeed she had become my constant companion by day and night. Now, almost the only times we were separated were when I put on my wings and soared into the sky.

For days the panic, the strange smoky darkness in the sky, and the rebellion raged together, each phenomenon seeming to draw strength from the others. Then the darkness weakened. There were no longer periods in which it was absolute, for which we thanked the gods. Yet the unnatural gloom persisted, with only occasional tantalizing periods when the cloud lightened enough for the sun to seem on the verge of breaking through. Meanwhile the after-shocks of the great earthquake continued, though on a diminishing scale. Everywhere in Crete, people going abroad at midday had to grope their way, muttering fearful incantations against the divine wrath. Sometimes armied clashes began, only to break off in mutual terror when the combatants felt some renewed trembling of the earth beneath their feet.

Within a few days, all across the island, or so we heard from harried refugees and other travelers, most of the palaces that had been built by Minos over a period of decades lay in ruins.

And wherever music and wine could be found, the worship of Dionysus raged—there is no other word for the license and the savagery, as they were reported, and as I was able to see with my own eyes on one or two occasions. Comely young men and women alike were kidnapped, and I feared for Thorhild, who was an attractive girl. Also the god himself was reported to have returned to Crete, and to have been seen in several places on the island. It was not impossible, though I believed that Dionysus would not risk the situation as it now stood, and would be conducting his parties elsewhere.

So fragmentary and contradictory were the reports that Theseus had reluctantly come to the same conclusion. He accepted that his plans for a confrontation with Dionysus must be indefinitely postponed. The young king resolved to find glory in the fighting and the danger of the revolt, and when the two of us were alone he once or twice whispered to me his dreams of adding Crete to an Athenian empire. For the moment even his revenge for humiliation at the hands of Dionysus could be forgotten or at least delayed.

And another event took place that caused me to rejoice. Sometimes in the midday darkness it seemed likely that the whole world more than a mile from our shores might have been destroyed, but it was not so. My friend Kena'ani still lived, and with his shipful of shaken men, came sailing into port at Heraklion a few days after the explosion. Fortunately he and his men, on coming ashore, immediately fell in with a rebel patrol and were brought to us.

For once Kena'ani was unnerved, and had no thought of making a profit out of his situation. His ship had been much closer to Thera than to Crete when the smaller island literally exploded.

We believed the testimony of the captain and his crew when they reported that the island of Thera was no more—only a mere fringe of rock was left of it, they said. Eventually we were to learn that they were exaggerating the degree of destruction, but not by very much. Most of the island was indeed gone, totally destroyed in the great explosion. The sea had rushed in, over what had once been solid land, and for months thereafter renewed explosions under water sent geysers of steam up into the clouds, as the gods of sea and earth contended.

But at the time of the great darkness, the people of Crete knew nothing of all this, and they cared less regarding events beyond the shores of their own island. The monumental disaster, as Theseus and others told them again and again, had to be considered as a punishment visited upon the land and people of Crete for their toleration of the unnatural union of their late queen with a beast—no one seemed to think it mattered that the beast had some claim to being some kind of a god.

It was only later, when the great darkness was gone at last, that those disposed to be irreverent wondered aloud why the people who had lived on Thera should have been so punished.

In the time of the greatest darkness and the repeated earthquakes, as I have said, the great majority of the people of Crete turned against the faction of the queen and the Bull.

But the Bronze Man, that we had dared to hope had been destroyed in the avalanche sent down on him by Heracles, returned intact two days later. Heracles speculated that it might have taken Talus that long to dig himself out from the mass of rock that had been precipitated upon him.

Once back in the vicinity of the Labyrinth, Talus once more fought on the side of the White Bull, and Talus was as invincible as ever.

The first squadrons of spearmen and pikemen sent against him by Theseus were slaughtered to a man. No human force survived once it was placed in direct opposition to the metal man. Arrows and slung stones rebounded harmlessly from his bronze skin. As a pursuer he was impossible to shake, even temporarily—unless one could hurl avalanches, or happened to have wings—and he cared no more for kings and heroes than he did for peasants who marched against him only to die with their useless spears in hand.

I was with Theseus when the king surveyed the battlefield a short time after the slaughter. The march and countermarch of our contending armies had moved away, and there was a chance

for the commander to try to determine just
what had happened here.

A battlefield is never a pretty sight, but this
one had a mystery about it that made it especially horrible. Some of the men appeared to
have been burned to death, while still an arrow-
shot away from Talus.

Theseus had some grim comments to make,
and warned me to say nothing of the special
horror of the burning. But of course word of the
horror got out somehow. Whole units of the
military who had deserted the established government and joined our cause, or had wavered
in their loyalty, now swung their allegiance back
to Bull and queen.

During the next few days we were driven into
an ever more constricted territory. Theseus
feinted swift attacks upon the Bull and the queen
themselves, and caused them to hold Talus in
reserve as their personal bodyguard, and only
this saved our remaining forces from swift
destruction.

Still the time came when the remaining rebel
forces in the region of the palace, Theseus and
myself with them, were outnumbered and surrounded, bottled up in a small valley not far
from the harbor.

The White Bull had himself carried on his old
uncomfortable litter to a high place from which
his voice, still powerful, could reach us. He spoke
to us sadly, saying that we were doomed to
defeat by the science and engineering of a vastly
more advanced society. To those of our army
who surrendered, he promised that their lives

would be spared, and that eventually they would
be set free again, after a period of re-education.

It was at this moment, while the Bull was still
speaking, that the sun came out in perfect clear-
ness for the first time since the great unnatural
darkness had descended. Its rays gleamed im-
personally on the bronze-colored and undamaged metal of Talus, who stood by the White
Bull's side. This was taken by everyone as a
significant omen, and a cheer went up from the
loyalist army.

On our side, Heracles still grumbled, and
uttered low-voiced challenges to the metal man.
Still the two had never yet come into direct
personal confrontation, and it seemed unlikely
that they ever would before the very end. The
orders given by Theseus still stood, and I thought
that only they had saved his soldier Heracles
from certain destruction in combat against the
man of metal.

When the White Bull had finished his speech
the fighting resumed, the men on our side now
fighting mainly for survival. Few had surrendered, because they were suspicious of the Bull's
idea of education, and some of them feared it
more than death. Still it was becoming plainer
and plainer to everyone that the revolt was a
hopeless cause, doomed now to an early collapse.

The fighting, as I say, resumed. Heracles and
the Bronze Man once more dueled with missiles, Heracles holding the high ground atop a
cliff that was all but impossible for even Talus to
scale quickly.

Unfortunately there was not enough loose rock
on the height to afford the material for another

avalanche. And at last Heracles was stunned, by the flying fragment of a hurled rock that exploded because it hit the cliffside near him with such force.

Looking down from my position of aerial advantage, I saw to my dismay that the loyalist infantry were closing in, and that Theseus too had somehow been knocked out of the fight, at least temporarily. He was down on the ground, and his helmet had been knocked off.

With a sinking heart I realized that in terms of leadership, the main burden of what remained of the resistance had now fallen upon me. Not that I was, or had ever been, a military leader; but my possession of wings gave me a status in the eyes of friend and foe alike, far beyond what the mere possession of a brain had ever done.

I resolved to do my best. I thought that at least, perhaps, I could distract the enemy long enough to give Theseus some kind of a chance to recover.

As I circled nearer over the chief combatants on the ground, dodging arrows and slung stones as best I could, I caught a glimpse of Thorhild watching. From the stillness of the pose I realized that she must be preparing herself for my death as well as for her own.

Talus, methodical and untiring as always, was now climbing upon a minor crag to get himself that much closer to me. I realized at once that he meant to bring his throwing arm and his deadly heat-ray within easy killing distance of his chief remaining enemy. Fear whispered in my heart that winged escape was still easily possible for me, and there was nothing more for

me to do. Anger and weariness replied that I
might indeed get away for a moment; but hardly
more than that. Nowhere on Crete would now
be safe for me to land. And I was too weary, too
much weakened with the minor wounds I had
sustained in recent fighting, to be able to fly far.

Soon, quite soon, I would have to come down
out of the sky somewhere, and Talus would be
waiting for me when I did. Then, if not sooner,
he would kill me as he had killed my son.

Something, a great shadow of some kind, came
across the face of the sun, and I turned in the
air to look up and behind me, even now alarmed
to think the mass of atmospheric dust and ashes
might be returning. But this was only an ordinary, or almost ordinary, summer cloud, pre-
saging and carrying rain. No help there in omens
for the lost cause.

I thought I heard the voice of Icarus, crying
his fear and pain to me, crying out of the fresh
wind that blew in advance of the approaching
thunderstorm.

The wet mists came closer and I rose into
them. Dodging flying in and out of the lowering
cloud, I maneuvered as if to reach a position
from which I could handily dive and attack the
litter of the Bull— and that of the queen—as
they were being carried away from their victory.

As I came marginally closer, Talus aimed his
heat-ray and fired it at me. There was a violet
burning of the air around me, and a violet afterimage in my eyes. Sudden, blasting heat seemed
to make the vaporous cloud boil around me as I
dodged through it as best I could.

Thunder crashed again. I remembered the

Bull, talking to me in a friendly way long months ago, telling me that his people came from some world where for some reason there were no thunderstorms or lightning.

I prayed to Gaea, the goddess of Earth, and what I can only describe as divine guidance came to me— perhaps some special education from the Bull, received earlier, helped me to the essential insight. The voice of my dead son spoke to me again, out of the steaming whirl-wind that the cloud around me had become. This time I was assured that the gods of earth had heard my prayers.

I saw blue fire, such as will sometimes visit the mast of a ship at sea, dance along my own limbs, radiating vibrantly from each of my mov-ing wingtips.

Talus fired his beams at me again.

But at that very moment the blessed Gaea entered the combat on my side. Her great spear flashed in the air, blinding and deafening me, but striking down my enemy. Unable to see clearly, still I sensed the dazzling pathway of that spear-thrust, I felt and understood the force that followed the electrified track made in the air by the much smaller searing beam of Talus, the overwhelming force that traced that track down from the cloud straight to its grounded source, and blasted it, almost into nothingness.

My eyes were blinded and my ears rang with the thunderclap, yet somehow I managed to keep myself aloft. Then when I could see again I landed, and rejoined my comrades.

Everyone in both armies had had a clear view of what happened to the Bronze Man on his crag. Within minutes afterward, nine-tenths of the enemy troops were scattering in blind panic, at this final evidence that the divine powers were not arrayed against them. The remaining tenth soon thought it wise to follow them, or to surrender where they stood.

Theseus, given a brief breathing space, had already somewhat recovered. Walking with Heracles and myself, he climbed to the place where Talus had been struck down, and looked in awe upon the smoldering wreckage that was all that remained of him. There were only bits of bronze and other, stranger materials, all far too hot to touch, and none of them bigger than my hand.

Shortly the irregular troops of our victorious army were thronging around Heracles and Theseus, congratulating them upon the favor of the Fates who had allowed them to escape, and had even at last given them the victory.

Great victories are not for artisans, but for kings and heroes, and I prudently and gradually retreated into the background, letting those have the glory who were much better equipped to deal with it. Until now I have kept quiet about the truth of the matter; but now, as I say, I seek to glorify the truth.

With the passing of the line of thunderstorms, the last of the gloom that had lain upon the land for days was gone, though for many days to come the sunsets and sunrises were spectacularly beautiful.

Of course much human confusion, political, religious, and military, still lingered in the aftermath of the volcanic eruption. But Theseus and those who followed him could for the time being do what they wished.

Last-minute turncoats, eager to bring good news to the winners, informed us that the queen, seeing Talus destroyed by lightning, and herself deserted by her entire army, had committed suicide.

Someone, an hour later, brought Theseus her head upon a pole. Methodically, acting as de facto chief of staff, I made sure that it was properly identified.

But Pasiphaë had never been our chief concern anyway. Now I, along with the hero who had been confined in the dungeon with me and escaped its various dangers, at last entered it again in pursuit of the White Bull.

As I was guiding the pursuers, our foe could neither hide from us nor get away. We at last found him in his innermost lair, where he lay defenseless, deserted now even by his litter-bearers.

Yet our enemy still possessed impressive dignity. Ignoring the others, even the King of Athens, the White Bull said to me: "Dae-dal-us, I have sought to bring your world the bless-ings of ed-u-ca-tion. In mak-ing your-self my en-emy, you have caused all of your peo-ple in-cal-cul-a-ble loss."

I said to him, where he lay almost helpless in his clumsy litter: "You have killed my woman and our baby. And then, using your bronze tool that walked on two legs, you killed my only living son. And you tried to kill me too. And then, through Minos who once was a great king you tried again to destroy me. And wantonly to

slaughter many who did not even know you.
Know that the curse you meant for Sicily and
for me has fallen upon Thera instead."

I have no doubt that the Bull knew that already, having lived through the darkness and
the earthquakes with the rest of us. He was
grieved by the failure of his plan, but I think
only because his revenge had failed of its object,
and not at all because of the wanton destruction
that failure had visited upon others.

Then he was philosophical about it. "Why do
you hate me, Dae-dal-us? Why?"

I had already told him one or two of the
reasons. But now I admitted that even before
the death of Icarus I thought I had had cause.

He could not or would not understand. "I am
not to blame for your wo-man's death, Dae-
dal-us. That was a mat-ter of sci-ence."

"Science!" Thorhild, standing now by my side,
savored the strange word and did not like its
taste. She took me gently by the arm, as if to
remind me that our battle had been won.

"Kal-lis-te was cho-sen by lot to be a member of the con-trol group in the test."

"The test?"

"One of the man-y tests sci-ence re-quires.
To con-vince my med-i-cal stu-dents, by dem-
on-stra-tion, that the meth-ods I had been teach-
ing them were wor-thy. Mem-bers of one group
re-ceived the aid of an ed-u-ca-ted phys-i-cian.
Mem-bers of the o-ther group did not. The
re-sults were, I think, con-clu-sive. I am sor-ry
that she died, but her life was sac-ri-ficed for
sci-ence. Few peo-ple can die deaths of such
mean-ing, if that is com-fort to you."

"Your death too will be meaningful, White Bull."

He looked at me, waiting for the stroke to fall.

I was not sure that the Bull was listening to my words, but waiting for me to draw a weapon. Instead I told him what the king had told me. "Dionysus has somehow escaped. But Theseus, with the consent of what remains of Crete, means to transport you to Athens, and there offer you as sacrifice upon the altar of Athena."

And so it came to pass.

Here is a preview of the latest Miles Naismith novel, **BROTHERS IN ARMS,** *by Lois McMaster Bujold, coming from Baen Books in January 1989.*

BROTHERS IN ARMS
Lois McMaster Bujold

The battered Dendarii Free Mercenary Fleet arrived in Earth orbit for rest and refit. Equipment failures that had cost lives on the last operation were tops on Admiral Miles Naismith's mind. A close second was, how were they going to pay for it all?

Lieutenant Lord Miles Vorkosigan reported to the Earthside Barrayaran embassy's military attache, Captain Duv Galeni, hoping to solve this problem.

"Just what is the relationship between the Dendarii and Barrayaran Imperial Security?" the captain asked plaintively.

"Fairly simple," Miles reassured him. "The Dendarii are kept on retainer for covert operations which are either out of Imperial Security's range, or for which any direct, political connection with Barrayar would be politically embarrassing. I'm the go-between. I leave Imperial HQ as Lieutenant Vorkosigan and pop up—wherever—as Admiral Naismith, waving a new contract."

The captain glanced dryly down at Miles's dossier, displayed on his desk console. "Twenty-four years old—aren't you a little young for your rank, ah, 'Admiral?'"

Miles's age was not the only source of Galeni's doubts. Miles was always conscious of the peculiarities of his body—oversized head exaggerated by short neck set on a twisted spine, brittle bones, all squashed down to a height of four-foot-nine, legacy of a congenital accident; hardly what one would expect of the son of the exemplar of Barrayar's soldier-castle, Prime Minister Count Aral Vorkosigan. "The mutant's only here because his father got him in," Miles fancied he could hear Galeni thinking.

"I will add you to my staff, while we await clarification," said Captain Galeni.

"Very well. If you can advance me the Dendarii's immediate expenses I could wrap up this mission."

"How much?"

"Roughly eighteen million marks, sir."

"Lieutenant—that is ten times the budget of this embassy for a year! Sector Security HQ on Tau Ceti will have to handle this one."

A ten-day wait. The Dendarii could handle a ten-day wait, while the request went through. Miles sighed and yielded.

But Galeni also ordered Miles strictly confined to the embassy. The captain was mildly panicked at having the Prime Minister's son on his hands, especially when he learned that "Admiral Naismith" had suffered several assassination attempts from the Dendarii's recent enemy, the Cetagandans. Miles's involuntary incarceration was rendered even more chafing by the surprise presence of his handsome cousin, Lieutenant Lord Ivan Vorpatril, on Galeni's staff.

The return orders ten days later from HQ

were a shock—Miles found himself officially assigned to the embassy as Galeni's subordinate. Even more appalling, the Dendarii's eighteen-million marks were not included. Miles persuaded Galeni to send again, resigning himself to another ten-day wait. But Miles was bored out of his mind with the routine data analysis and social duties of the peacetime embassy. Escorting a dowager about at an embassy party, his thoughts wandered, as he broke off bits of roil for the goldfish in the fountain.

How interesting, one fish refused to eat. Perhaps the stubborn one was a fiendish Cetagandan construct, whose cold scales glittered like gold because they were. He might pluck it out with a feline pounce, stamping it underfoot with an electic sizzle— "Ah! Through my quick wits I have discovered the spy among you!"

But if he were wrong, ah. The *squish* under his boot, the dowager's recoil, and he would have acquired an instant reputation as a young man with serious emotional difficulties— "Ah ha!" he pictured himself cackling to the horrified woman as the fish guts slithered underfoot, "You should see what I do to *kittens!*"

Fortunately, Miles was saved from his imagined social embarrassment by a very real emergency, reported to him by comm link by his trusted Dendarii officer and sometimes-bodyguard the beautiful Commander Elli Quinn. Some drunken Dendarii soldiers on downside leave in London had barricaded themselves in a wineshop after an altercation with the shop's clerk, holding the poor woman hostage. Miles went AWOL from the embassy, changing back to his forbidden identity as "Admiral Naismith," and was on the scene in minutes.

Miles breathed easier when he had all the soldiers' weapons in his possession. "Quickly, because the police are getting nervous out there—exactly what happened here?" he asked his men.

"The bitch wouldn't take our credit! Good Denarii credit!"

"Why wouldn't she take your credit cards? You weren't trying to use the ones left over from the last planet, were you?"

"Actually, it was the machine that spat them up, sir."

"It shouldn't have done that," Miles began, "unless—" *Unless there's something wrong with the central account*, his thought finished coldly. "Meanwhile, let's get you out of here before you're fried by the local constables."

He marched his men out to be arrested. A soft foomp! broke from the door of the wineshop. Blue flames licked out over the sidewalk.

Miles hurtled back through the wineshop doors, into darkness shot with twisting heat. The alcohol-soaked carpeting was growing flames. Fire was advancing on the bound woman on the floor; in a moment her hair would be a terrible halo—

Miles dove for her, wriggled his shoulder under her, staggered for the door, bright like the gate of life. The room behind them brightened, roaring. Miles and his burden fell to the sidewalk, rolling, flames lapping over their clothing. Miles choked on a faceful of foam, sprayed by the fireman who had rushed forward. Miles climbed to his feet, staring at a person pointing a piece of equipment at him resembling, for a dizzy instant, a microwave cannon. He blinked it into more sensible focus as a holovid camera.

"Miles!" his bodyguard Elli Quinn's voice over his shoulder made him jump. "Do you have everything under control?"

Miles, worried, extended his AWOL beyond hope of concealment for the sake of a visit to his Dendarii fleet accountant, in orbit on his flag-ship, the *Triumph*. She only confirmed how precarious the mercenary force's financial status had become. Miles, treated for his wineshop injuries and tanked on powerful painkillers, re-turned downside with Elli Quinn, unwilling to return to his prisoner-like state at the embassy. Instead they went window-shopping in night-time London.

Elli paused in real intrigue before a shop labelled, "Cultured Furs." Miles eased her inside.

"Cultured Furs are guaranteed not to shed, fade, or discolor," the salesman assured them.

An enormous width of silky black fur poured through Elli's arms. "What is this? Not a coat . . . it purrs!"

"The very latest in biomechanical feedback systems," said the salesman. "Most of our stock is ordinary tanned leathers—but this is a live fur."

"A live fur?" Elli's eyebrows rose enchantingly.

"A live fur," the salesman nodded, "blended from the very finest assortment of *felis domesticus* genes. But with none of the defects of a live animal. It neither sheds nor eats nor," he coughed discreetly, "requires a litter box. An electro-magnetic net on the cellular level gathers energy from the environment. And if it seems to be running down, you can give it a boost by placing it in your microwave for a few minutes on the lowest setting. Cultured Furs cannot be responsible, however, for the results if the owner accidentally sets it on 'high.' "

"They did *that* to a cat?" Miles choked.

They exited the shop carting the unwieldy bundle in its elegant silver plastic wrappings. The package, the salesman had finally convinced them, did not require air-holes. Well, the fur had delighted Elli. And Miles longed to delight Elli.

In a public lift tube returning to the embassy, Miles suddenly realized his and Elli's height difference was voided. They hung face to face, his boots dangling above her ankles—impulsively, his lips dove onto hers. Her arm clamped around his neck in eager response—surely the first time his being pinned to the mat meant *he'd* won. But as they staggered onto a bubble-car platform they stared at each other, shaken. In one lunatic moment, Miles realized, he'd up-ended their carefully-balanced working relation-ship—it could be a fatal error. . . .

As Elli went to credit their tokens, Miles looked up to see his own dim reflection staring back at him from the mirrored wall, face suf-fused by frustration and terror. Miles squeezed his eyes shut and looked again, moving in front of the pillar and staring—most unpleasant. For a second he had seen himself wearing his green Barrayaran uniform, not his Dendarii greys.

Damn the pain pills. Was his subconscious trying to tell him something? Well, he wasn't in real trouble till a brain scan taken of him in his two different uniforms produced two different patterns.

Upon reflection, the idea was suddenly not funny.

Captain Galeni was most irate at Miles's unauthorized excursion, proof of which he now had before him in the form of the news coverage of the wineshop fire. Galeni's nerves were justified when Miles ran into the same reporter at an embassy function, who promptly tried to identify him as "Admiral Naismith." Inspired, Miles passed Naismith off to her as Lord Vorkosigan's clone.

Then the impossible occurred—the courier returned for the second time from Sector HQ without the Dendarii's money, nor any explanation. Miles's paranoid suspicions leaped to new heights—could Captain Galeni have embezzled the money? As a Komarran, one of the first of that conquered planet's citizens to be permitted to enter the Imperial service, Galeni's loyalty was suspect—might he be a thief, as well as a traitor? Miles begged a day with the Dendarii, ostensibly to attend to Admiral Naismith's duties, actually to dispatch a loyal officer directly to Sector HQ to check up on Galeni.

Miles was attacked while crossing the shuttleport tarmac toward the waiting Dendarii shuttle—a float truck hurtled upon him, blotting out the bright morning sky. It was to be death by squashing. Miles squeaked and spun and scrambled. The truck fell like a monstrous brick. He dove, rolled—the float truck lurched sideways and flopped again, obliterating the spot where he'd just been lying. He clutched his useless stunner convulsively, his knuckles scraped and bleeding. With a deep vile whine the truck clawed its way into the air behind him.

A violent blast blew Miles onto his face. He tried to melt a hole down into the pavement by heat of fear alone; his ears hammered with a roaring white noise. He jerked up, glared around for the falling truck. There was no more falling truck.

Elli Quinn cantered up, winging a rocket launcher one-handed. She must have fired from the hip. Her face was terrorized.

"Wasn't that a little close?" snarled Miles's embassy bodyguard. Jealous, Miles realized, because he hadn't had a rocket launcher. Miles hurriedly got rid of the embassy personnel before the local police arrived.

The police arrested Elli, for the murder of the two men driving the float truck. Miles perforce went on up to the *Triumph*. The need to check up on Captain Galeni had become even more urgent, particularly when Elli, released again by the police, reported back with the news that the would-be assassins were local hit men. Anyone—including Captain Galeni, covering his tracks—could have hired them.

But Miles had other business with Elli.

"Um, duties . . ." Miles fumbled. "Just as Lieutenant Vorkosigan contains all of Admiral Naismith's duties, plus some of his own, so Lord Vorkosigan contains all of Lieutenant Vorkosigan's, plus others of his own. Political duties overarching the military duties. And, ah . . . family duties."

"You make yourself sound like a Venn diagram," said Elli, amused. "What contains Lord Vorkosigan?"

"Miles. Just Miles."

"And what contains Miles?"

"This skin."

"Gods. I've fallen in love with a man who thinks he's an onion."

"Let me rephrase that," he said at last. "Will you marry me?"

The silence this time was much longer. "You don't want much, do you? Just to completely rearrange the rest of my life. Oh, love. You aren't thinking."

"I think the world of you."

"And so you want to maroon me for the rest of my life on a—sorry—backwater dirtball that's just barely climbed out of feudalism, that treats women like chattel, that would deny me the use of every military skill I've learned in the past twelve years. . . . I'm sorry. I'm not an anthropologist, I'm not a saint, and I'm not crazy."

"You don't have to say no right away," said Miles in a small voice.

"Oh, yes I do. Before looking at you makes me any weaker in the knees. Or the head."

"I see it now. You are in love with Admiral Naismith. Not Lord Vorkosigan."

"I am *annoyed* with Lord Vorkosigan. He sells you short, love." She drew back a moment. "Can I still jump your bones? Carefully, of course. You'll not go away mad, for turning you down?

Turning Barrayar down, that is. Not you, never you . . ."

I'm getting used to it. Almost numb . . . If Naismith was all she wanted, she could surely have him. Half a loaf for half a man. They tilted bedward, hungry-mouthed.

Miles sent the Dendarii out looking for work on a piecemeal, individual basis—security guard contracts, tech work, anything to help the cash flow—and returned reluctantly to the Barrayaran embassy. Ivan Vorpatril was waiting for him, shifting from foot to foot with a strained smile. Oh, God, now what?

"Captain Galeni left the embassy about half an hour after you did yesterday," Ivan reported. "He hasn't been seen since."

In an effort to solve the mystery, Miles and Ivan broke into Galeni's sealed personnel file. Indeed, their missing captain did have connections with Komarran revolutionaries—his aunt had been murdered by Barrayaran security forces during Barrayar's conquest of Komarr, and his father had figured in the Komarr Revolt several years later, dying in an attack on a Barrayaran installation. But the high command knew all about Galeni's family history. In Miles's father's own words, ". . . if we can capture this one's true allegiance, it will be something like what I'd had in mind for Komarr in the first place. A generation late, and after a long and bloody detour, but—a sort of redemption. Let him run, and prove himself."

The secret file raised suspicions, but proved nothing. Miles, frustrated, dumped the problem of finding Galeni on the Dendarii intelligence department. On the third day Elli Quinn called in.

"Captain Thorne was just contacted with a *fascinating* contract offer for the Dendarii—how does a kidnapping grab you?"

"Absolutely not!"

"You're going to make an exception in this case," she predicted with verve. "Our mysterious and wealthy strangers want to hire Admiral Naismith to kidnap Lord Vorkosigan from the Barrayaran embassy!"

Fascinated indeed, Miles, Ivan, and Elli went to the rendezvous planning to capture the would-be kidnappers. But their mysterious opponents turned the tables. They snatched Miles, and replaced him with an exact physical duplicate who ordered the Dendarii back to base, and himself back to the Barrayaran embassy. Miles found himself locked in a windowless room in an unknown location—but not alone. With him was Captain Galeni, rather the worse for wear.

To Miles's dismay, Galeni confirmed that the alter-Miles was indeed a clone, produced by the Komarran underground. They planned the clone to return to Barrayar in Miles's place, there to attempt to take the Barrayaran Imperial throne in a bloody coup. During the uproar, Komarr was to revolt again. The mastermind behind this plan was Galeni's father, Ser Galen, still alive.

But Galeni refused to fall in with his father's plans. The two were now locked on a deadly see-saw. If Captain Galeni would not forswear his new loyalty to Barrayar, Galen's death must inevitably result unless he killed his son first. Ser Galen was putting off this resolution as long as possible, holding Galeni captive while draining him, under drugs, of Barrayaran security procedures. Miles too was questioned under drugs.

Miles resolved to sabotage the clone, if he could, by feeding him false information and clues to trip him up. But when they came face-to-face at last, in an interview unauthorized by Galen, Miles found himself speaking truth without drugs.

"Do you realize you have a name?" Miles demanded. "Second son—that's you, my twin-six-years-delayed— gets the second names of his maternal and paternal grandfathers. You are Lord Mark Pierre Vorkosigan, in your own right, on Barrayar. What have you ever dreamed of being? Any education you want, Mother will see that you get. The galaxy at your fingertips. Choice—freedom—ask, and it's yours."

On Jackson's Whole, where the clone had been made, clones were raised for illegal brain transplant operations, the old rich brain into the new young body, the young brain thus murdered. The clone's face was white. "Barrayaran Security will never let me live. I know the score. Just this once, a Jackson's Whole clone is turning it around. Instead of you cannibalizing my life, I shall have yours."

"Then where will your life be?" asked Miles desperately. "Buried in an imitation of Miles, where will Mark be then? Are you sure it will be only me, lying in my grave?"

The clone flinched.

Miles—he could hear his mother's voice in his head—*what have you done with your baby brother?* But Galen, infuriated, broke in on the interview before Miles could drive it to a conclusion. And the next time Miles and Galeni were taken from their cell, it was for their execution.

The guards raised their weapons to fire.

"Wait!" squeaked Miles.

"What for?"

Miles was still groping for a reply when the garage doors slid open. "Me!" yelled Elli Quinn. "Freeze!"

A Dendarii patrol streamed past her. As she strolled up to Miles and Galeni, an expression of extreme disquiet stole over her face. "Gods, Miles, how did you get here?"

"Elli, you genius! I should have known the clone couldn't fool you!"

"What clone?"

"He blew it—and you came to rescue me— didn't you?"

"Rescue you from what? Miles, you ordered me a week ago to find Captain Galeni, remember? So we did."

Even though his rescue was inadvertent, Miles was profoundly grateful for it. But Galen had escaped. They returned to the embassy to capture the clone, who was presumably still playing the part of Lord Vorkosigan.

Ivan Vorpatril met Miles at the embassy entrance. "Ah, they let you out, then." He looked more closely, then stared. "Miles . . ."

The clone, it turned out, had been detained by the local police—for conspiracy to commit murder. Through a trail of misinterpreted but perfectly real clues, some dropped by Miles himself, they suspected Lord Vorkosigan had hired the local hit men to assassinate Admiral Naismith at the shuttleport the previous week.

But when Miles arrived at police HQ in hot pursuit, the clone was already gone—picked up by Galen. Miles set Dendarii intelligence to look for them, parallel to the embassy's own efforts, and dropped gratefully into bed.

Miles and Elli were rudely awakened all too soon by Ivan. The Sector Security commander himself, Commodore Destang, had arrived post-haste from Tau Ceti in response to Miles's Dendarii-delivered inquiry. Not only had the Dendarii's eighteen-million marks never been sent from HQ, word of Miles's arrival on Earth had never been received there—the courier officer had been under the control of the Komarrans.

"Then I was never actually assigned to the embassy!" said Miles.

A very small noise, as of deep and muffled pain, escaped the otherwise deadpan Captain Galeni.

Destang said, "Only by the Komarrans. Apparently it was a ploy to keep you immobilized until they could attempt their switch."

Destang ordered Miles to return to his identity as Admiral Naismith, while his own Sector Security team took over the hunt for Galen and Mark, with deadly intent. Miles made plans to return to the *Triumph*, but not to withdraw from the affair.

Ivan's voice grew stern. "Just what are you

hatching in the back of your twisty little mind, coz?"

Miles paused seriously. "I may yet see a chance to save . . . something, from this mess."

Elli remarked, "I thought we had saved something. We uncovered a traitor, plugged a security leak, foiled a kidnapping, and broke up a major plot against the Barrayaran Imperium. What more do you want?"

Miles's frown deepened. "Something. A second chance. A . . . possibility."

"It's the clone, isn't it?" said Ivan, his mouth hardening. "You've gone and let yourself get obsessed with that goddamn clone."

"Flesh of my flesh, Ivan."

"What about Galen?"

"Galen is a problem I . . . have not solved."

Miles's words proved prophetic. Back aboard the *Triumph*, he received a call.

"I will not repeat myself." Galen spoke low and fast. "You will come to the Thames Tidal Barrier, halfway between Towers Six and Seven. You will walk out on the seaward side to the lower lookout. Alone. Then we'll talk. If any condition is not met, we will not be there when you arrive. And Ivan Vorpatril will die at 0207."

Galen had snatched Ivan as a handle on Miles, in hopes of still making the switch—not with Lord Vorkosigan, but with Admiral Naismith. The Dendarii were to give him a ride out of Earth—and a new power base.

But Miles brought Captain Galeni and a fat bribe with him to the rendezvous, in hopes of diverting these awkward relatives he and Galeni had acquired for their lethal purposes. Ser

Galen, still reluctant to kill his son, handed the nerve disruptor to the clone. "You must learn to kill if you expect to survive. Begin!"

"But—" said the clone, agitated.

"As of this moment, you're a free man," Miles spoke low and fast. "Galen bought you and paid for you, but he doesn't own you. If you kill for him, he'll own you forever."

"Now, dammit!" yelled Galen, and made to grab back the nerve disruptor.

Captain Galeni stepped in front of Miles as Miles scrabbled in his jacket for his stunner. The disruptor crackled—Galeni gasped—face harrowed, Miles sprang from behind Galeni and raised his stunner—

To see Galen crumple, convulsing—and slump in death.

"Kill your enemies," breathed Mark. "Ah!" he added as Miles started forward, "stop right there!"

The soft whirr of a rappel spool unwinding was barely audible over the hiss of the sea foam underfoot. Quinn was flying down in one long swoop, like a falcon stooping.

Mark kicked open the hatch and fled into the Tidal Barrier. Miles sent Galeni to look for another entrance. Miles and Quinn split up at a cross-corridor.

Miles found a lift tube, and rose. At an exit, a total stranger whirled at the sound of his footstep, dropped to one knee, cried, "There he is!" and fired a nerve disruptor. Miles had found Commodore Destang's death squad, pursuing Mark.

Miles found Mark shortly after. "Where's Ivan?"

"Get me out of this, and I'll tell you."

They descended the now-switched-off lift tube by rappel, back down into the Tidal Barrier, evading Destang's men. Mark led Miles to a pumping chamber. Sealed, it would become a death chamber at high tide—0207—as the water rushed through it.

"Ivan?"

"Ah!" The cry from within was nearly voice-less. Miles helped Ivan slither through the hatch. Ivan stood, boots planted apart, hands on knees, breathing heavily. His green dress uniform was crumpled and beslimed. His hands looked like dog meat. He must have pounded and scratched in the dark, muffled and unheard . . .

Miles turned. Mark was nowhere in sight. And Miles had lost touch by wrist comm with Elli Quinn.

Miles and Ivan headed down the corridor in the direction Quinn had taken earlier, away from the tower containing the Barrayaran security team. Miles was getting extremely worried about Quinn. Moments later, Mark rounded the curve and skidded to a halt before them with a hope-less cry. The right side of his face was burned. "There's some painted lunatic back there with a plasma gun!" The Cetagandans had caught up with Admiral Naismith at last.

"Miles," said Ivan, "aren't we trapped in the center of a pincers movement?"

"Not while we own a cloak of invisibility. Come on!" Miles led his little troop back to the pumping chamber, inviting as a coffin, where they went to ground.

His ploy worked better than he'd dared dream. The two hit squads, Cetagandan chasing Admiral Naismith, Barrayaran chasing the clone, converged on each other, and were in turn trapped and removed by the local police. "My God," said Ivan, entranced to the point of wholly forgetting his hermetic enclosure, "it's just like the proton annihilating the anti-proton. Poof!"

Mark shook his head, watching the chaos in the corridor through the monitor Miles had planted. "Whose side are you on, anyway?"

"Haven't you been paying attention? This is all for you. If you were free . . ."

Mark's lips rippled. "Me? Free? What chance?"

"Suppose you were. Free of Barrayar and Komarr, free of me too. Free of Galen and the police. Free of obsession. Who are you? Or will you never know, as long as I'm standing over you?"

Mark spat the dregs of his hatred. "You're the free one!"

"Me! I'll never be as free as you are right now. Waking or sleeping, near or far, makes no difference. Yet—Barrayar can be an interesting place, seen through eyes other than Galen's."

"I will never go to Barrayar. You can have it. It's a wonder you're not trying to switch identities with me."

Miles laughed, painfully. What a temptation. Ditch his uniform, walk into the nearest tubeway and disappear with a credit chit for half a million marks in his pocket. To be a free man . . . His eye fell on Ivan's grimy Imperial dress greens, symbol of their service. No. Barrayar's ugliest child would choose to be her champion still.

They had a break in the police cordon at last, and fled to the next tower, where Denarii scanners had located a signal from Quinn's wrist comm. They found her stunned, only stunned. Miles looked up at a blurred Ivan hovering anxiously, swallowed, and steadied his ragged breathing. It had, after all, been the most logical possibility.

Outside the tower at last, sneaking through the park strip carrying Quinn, they encountered Captain Galeni.

"I'll be damned. You're still alive," whispered Galeni.

"I'd sort of been wondering about you, too," Miles admitted.

Galeni looked bizarre. Gone was the blank witnessing stillness that had absorbed Ser Galen's death without comment. His grin was alarming, all those long teeth gleaming in the darkness; electric with an off-center exhilaration, breathing heavily. His face was bruised, mouth bloody. Last seen weaponless, he was now carrying a Cetagandan plasma-arc.

"Have you, ah, run into a guy wearing blue face paint yet?" Miles inquired.

"Oh yes," said Galeni in a tone of satisfaction. Galeni had found the Cetagandan outer-perimeter backup.

He now led them to the Cetagandan's ground-car. Miles whistled silently at the fresh dents in the side, about the size of a man's head. Two shapes huddled in the back seat, hitched up with their own equipment, the remaining Cetagandan officers. And while Miles played Admiral Naismith, Mark played Lord Vorkosigan for their benefit.

"Think that charade'll work?" asked Ivan after they let the Cetagandans off.

"There go two loyal officers who will swear under chemohypnotics that Admiral Naismith and Lord Vorkosigan are without question, two separate men," said Miles. "That's going to be worth a great deal to us."

"But will Destang think so?" asked Ivan.

"I do not believe," said Galeni distantly, staring out of the canopy, "that I give a good goddamn what Destang thinks."

"Where do you want to be dropped off, Mark?" Miles asked.

"A tube station. Any tube station."

He got out with Mark as the car settled to the pavement in the drop-off zone, and drew a coded card out of his jacket. Mark turned it over in wonder and suspicion.

"There you go," said Miles. "If you, with your background and this bankroll, can't disappear on Earth, it can't be done. Good luck."

"What do you want of me?" Mark demanded, half-panicked. "What do you expect me to do?"

"Whatever you please. I'm not your owner. I'm not your mentor. I'm not your parents. I have no expectations. I have no desires." *Rebel against that—little brother—if you can figure out how. . . .*

Mark swung into the lift tube. "Why not?" he yelled, baffled and furious.

Miles threw his head back and laughed. "You figure it out!"

As they drove slowly back to the embassy in the London dawn, Miles said to Galeni, "You know I didn't mean it to work out that way. The confrontation last night." And a damned sorry weak apology that sounded, for getting the man's father blown away.

"Did you imagine you controlled it? Omniscient and omnipotent? Nobody appointed you God, Vorkosigan." Ghostly faint, one corner of Galeni's mouth turned up. "I'm sure it was an oversight."

"At least our new assignment should be simpler than our late vacation on Earth," said Miles hopefully to Elli, once they were back aboard the *Triumph*. "A purely military operation, no relatives, no politics, no high finance. Straight up good guys and bad guys."

"Great," said Quinn. "Which are we?"

Miles was still thinking about the answer to that one when the fleet broke orbit.

FRED SABERHAGEN

Fred Saberhagen needs very little introduction these days. His most famous creations—the awesome Berserkers—are known to SF readers around the world. He's reached the bestseller lists several times, most recently with his "Book of Swords" series, and his novels span the territory from hard science fiction to high fantasy. Quite understandably, Saberhagen's been labeled one of the best writers in the business.

These fine novels by Saberhagen are available from Baen Books:

PYRAMIDS

A fascinating new twist on the time-travel novel, introducing a great new series hero: Pilgrim, the Flying Dutchman of Time, whose only hope for returning home lies in subtly altering the history of our own timeline to more closely reflect his own. Fortunately for us, Pilgrim's timeline is a rather more pleasant one than ours, and so the changes are—or at least are supposed to be—for the better. Learn why the curse of the Pharaoh Khufu (builder of the Great Pyramid) had a special reality, in *Pyramids*. "Saberhagen's light, imaginative and enjoyable adventures speed along twisting paths to a climax that is even more surprising than the rest of the book." —*Publishers Weekly*

AFTER THE FACT

This is the second novel featuring the great new series hero, Pilgrim—the Lost Traveller adrift in time and dimensionality. His current project: to rescue Abraham Lincoln from assassination, AFTER THE FACT!

THE FRANKENSTEIN PAPERS

At last—the truth about the sinister Dr. Frankenstein and his monster with a heart of gold, based on a history written by the monster himself! Find out what happened when the mad Doctor brought his creation to life, and why the monster has no scars.

THE "EMPIRE OF THE EAST" SERIES

THE BROKEN LANDS, Book I

A masterful blend of high technology and high sorcery; a unique adventure in a world on the brink of ultimate change; a world were magic rules—and science struggles to live again! *"Empire of the East* is one of the best science fiction fantasy epics—Saberhagen can be justly proud. Highly recommended."—*Science Fiction Review*. "A fine mix of fantasy and science fiction, action and speculation."—Roger Zelazny

THE BLACK MOUNTAINS, Book II

East meets West in bloody conflict on a world where magic rules, but technology is revolting! *"Empire of the East* is the work of a master!"—*Magazine of Fantasy and Science Fiction*

ARDNEH'S WORLD, Book III

The gripping climax of the "Empire of the East" series. "Ranks favorably with Tolkien. Exceptional in sheer unbridled zest and imaginative sweep."—*School Library Journal*

* * *

THE GOLDEN PEOPLE

Genetically perfect, super-human children are created by a dedicated scientist for the betterment of Mankind. As the children mature, however, they begin to wonder if Man *should* survive . . .

LOVE CONQUERS ALL

In a future where childbirth is outlawed and promiscuity required, one woman dares fight the system for the right to bear children.

MY BEST
Saberhagen presents his personal best, in *My Best*.
One sure to please lovers of "hard" science fiction
as well as high fantasy.

OCTAGON
Players scattered across the continent are engaged in
a game called "Starweb." Each player has certain
attributes, and can ally with or attack any of the
others. But one player seems to have confused the
reality of the world: a player with the attributes of
machinelike precision and mechanical ruthlessness.
His name is Octagon, and he's out for blood.

*You can order all of Fred Saberhagen's books with this
order form. Check your choices and send the combined
cover price/s to: Baen Books, Dept. BA, 260 Fifth Avenue,
New York, New York 10001.*